7-12-12

THE HOLLY TREE

THE HOLLY TREE

Nicola Thorne

This first world edition published 2010
in Great Britain and in the USA by
SEVERN HOUSE PUBLISHERS LTD of
9–15 High Street, Sutton, Surrey, England, SM1 1DF.
Trade paperback edition first published
in Great Britain and the USA 2011 by
SEVERN HOUSE PUBLISHERS LTD.

British Library Cataloguing in Publication Data

Thorne, Nicola.
    The holly tree.
    1. Women art teachers–Fiction. 2. Evening and
    continuation school students–Fiction. 3. Friendship–
    Fiction.
    I. Title
    823.9'14–dc22

ISBN-13: 978-0-7278-6933-3   (cased)
ISBN-13: 978-1-84751-270-3   (trade paper)

Except where actual historical events and characters are being
described for the storyline of this novel, all situations in this
publication are fictitious and any resemblance to living persons
is purely coincidental.

All Severn House titles are printed on acid-free paper.

Severn House Publishers support The Forest Stewardship Council [FSC],
the leading international forest certification organisation. All our titles that
are printed on Greenpeace-approved FSC-certified paper carry the FSC logo.

Mixed Sources
Product group from well-managed
forests and other controlled sources
www.fsc.org Cert no. SA-COC-1565
© 1996 Forest Stewardship Council

Typeset by Palimpsest Book Production Ltd.,
Falkirk, Stirlingshire, Scotland.
Printed and bound in Great Britain by
MPG Books Ltd., Bodmin, Cornwall.

Dedicated to the memory of
Cynthia Hayes
the inspiration for Alice in this novel,
whose long life was informed by courage,
fortitude and the gift of friendship
and, incidentally, who painted very well.
1902–1999

Love and Friendship

Love is like the wild rose-briar,
Friendship like the holly-tree.
The holly is dark when the rose-briar blooms
But which will bloom most constantly?

The wild-rose briar is sweet in the spring,
Its summer blossoms scent the air;
Yet wait till winter comes again,
And who will call the wild-briar fair?

Then, scorn the silly rose-wreath now,
And deck thee with the holly's sheen,
That when December blights thy brow
He may still leave thy garland green.

Emily Brontë

One

Sasha stood at the back of the room watching as members of the class trickled in, checking those she knew and those she didn't. Some arrived early in order to get the best seats, putting their paper, paints and brushes on the tables spread around the room. They would be the new ones, understandably nervous, not knowing what to expect, and they spent a lot of time moving their things about the table, fiddling with their pencils or brushes, looking around. The older hands were more at ease, stopping for a word with Sasha, greeting one another as they took their places.

One had taken possession of one of the easels in the room and had already started sketching the objects arranged on a table in the centre: a bowl of fruit, a vase of flowers, some leaves and twigs scattered loosely around to indicate it was autumn. This was Caroline Baxter, one of the members of the class who had been there longest but whose attendance was constantly being interrupted by a busy, complicated domestic life as the wife of a soldier with three children including a toddler. She seldom was able to complete a thing she started. Her home must have been full of unfinished pictures.

The room was nearly full and Sasha returned to her own table where she had her notes and the register, which she consulted. They were as usual a disparate group. Some would be talented, others less so, but most of them would have no talent at all. None would aspire to be great artists and some of them would just be filling in time to relieve boredom. Several would drop out in the course of the year. There should have been fifteen people and there were twelve. She looked up and smiled around at her attentive audience.

'Hi there,' she said, 'I'm Sasha Markova. I teach art and art history at the college and I am your tutor for the year. Welcome to all; some of you I know and some I don't. About half of you are new and the rest have been before. When I call your name could you raise your hand so that I know who you are?'

The register finished, there was a palpable air of people beginning to relax. She perched on the edge of her table. 'I know some of you have varying degrees of experience and expertise, and some are absolute beginners. In a minute I'm going to go round and talk to each of you.' She pointed to the objects on the table in the middle of the room. 'I'd like the more experienced students to have a go at this still life while I talk to the newcomers. At first, however, I want to emphasize that, no matter what your level of experience, almost anybody can learn to paint. It is useful to have a few basic guidelines.'

She stepped across to the blackboard on which she had scribbled a few lines. 'I'm going to deal, in this first session, with materials you need before you can start work – and incidentally saving you money – the sizes and weights of paper for example. The size of brushes and what they are used for; a range of colours in paints and the different forms they take; and next, for those of you with no experience, starting to paint on your way to becoming an artist!' She looked around. 'A few of you who are a bit rusty might benefit from putting an ear to this.'

In a mixed class, it wasn't always easy to keep both beginners and more experienced people entertained. It was a bit like teaching children of mixed ability in state schools, but usually after the preliminary session things tended to settle down.

Sasha went slowly round the room talking first to one student, asking what sort of experience they had and reassuring them if they were absolute beginners. One of them surprised her. She had noticed her coming in using a stick, easily the oldest person in the room. She was a tall, smartly dressed woman, her white hair stylishly coiffured, still good looking and with a gently lined face which seemed to echo years of experience.

'I hope I'm not too old for your class,' she said with a diffident smile as Sasha leaned over her table.

'Of course you're not,' Sasha reassured her.

'I used to paint a long time ago, but am out of practice, I'm afraid. I've always loved art and decided it was time that I had a refresher course.'

'Excellent. I'm sure you'll do very well. Come and have a

coffee afterwards and tell me more about yourself; we usually meet in the canteen.'

'I'd like that.'

Sasha moved to the adjacent table of another newcomer, one who had seemed especially shy and nervous as she came in.

'It's Pauline, isn't it?' Sasha asked.

The woman nodded. 'I don't have much experience,' she said. 'I did once go to some drawing classes . . .' Sasha looked with approval at the outline of the still life she had already drawn on her pad.

'Have a coffee afterwards,' she said, 'and we can get to know each other.'

Having stood briefly with each newcomer, Sasha turned to the easel on which Caroline was busy working.

'Very good,' she said, 'you've improved.'

'I don't know how,' Caroline laughed. 'I haven't done any all summer.'

'Tell me about it. Come and have coffee and . . .'

Sasha turned towards the door, which had surreptitiously opened, and a tall man entered and crept apologetically into the room.

'I'm very sorry,' he murmured. 'I'm late. Didn't think I'd be able to make it.'

'That's OK, Martin.' Sasha smiled at him. 'Glad to see you.'

Then, with a glance at her watch, she returned to her table, looked at her notes, and began taking her attentive class through the various basics of becoming painters in watercolours.

The Institute for Adult Education was a rather dreary building in one of the less salubrious parts of Redbury on the south coast. On a wet September evening it seemed drearier than ever, yet the interior was lit by lights shining from the various classrooms where a variety of courses were offered to a public eager for self-improvement. It was both amazing and gratifying to note how many there were.

At the end of classes the canteen was packed but Sasha had managed to secure a corner table which now had six people, apart from her, sitting round it. To one side of Sasha was the elderly woman whose name was Alice. Sasha had helped carry her coffee to the table and was eager to know why she had decided to take up watercolour painting again.

'I recently gave up my home,' she said, 'with great reluctance. But I had a hip replacement operation last year and realized how difficult it is to manage when one is incapacitated. Up to then I'd enjoyed very good health. I walked, even played tennis, into my late seventies. I'm eighty-three now.' She looked rather challengingly at Sasha as if thinking it might shock her.

'You don't look it,' Sasha said truthfully. 'Have you no family?'

Alice shook her head.

'My only sister died a few years ago. I have a distant cousin or two, a goddaughter I'm very fond of, but who lives in Scotland. I used to be a teacher, though I've been retired a good number of years, but I had my garden and beloved pets and, until four years ago, my sister. She and I shared the house. I now live in a very nice retirement apartment with communal facilities. But it is a bit lonely.' She sat back and gave a wan smile. 'Hence the painting.'

Next to her was another new student who had hardly said a word all evening and, all the time she was lecturing, he went on drawing the still-life assembly as if he was hardly listening to what she said. Consequently she had been quite surprised when he slipped into the seat next to her and had been listening intently to her conversation with Alice.

'Roger,' she said as she turned to him, 'I have rather neglected you. You are new, but so is Alice. I could see you were quite experienced. Had you been to classes before?'

'I've been on painting holidays, but nothing formal.'

She could sense his reserve, that he was a man of few words, and deduced that conversation conducted against a babble of background noise was going to be difficult. She was wondering what he did for a living, when Pauline intervened.

'What did you do during the vacation, Sasha?'

'I went to Italy,' Sasha replied, 'to Florence. I wanted to spend time in the Uffizi as it's been ages since I was there. In my art history class we are doing the Quattrocentro and I wanted to refresh myself. Oh, it was wonderful.' As the memory of the holiday came flooding back her eyes shone.

From across the table Caroline was stirring her coffee, her

expression thoughtful. She had been listening, but not taking part in any of the discussions around her.

'Did *you* manage to get a holiday?' Sasha asked her. Caroline suddenly came back from her reverie and nodded.

'Greg may be going to Afghanistan soon so we managed a few days in the Lakes alone. My mother had the children. I should have taken my paints, but Greg likes walking so we did a lot of that, and eating.' There was silence round the table as they all looked at her, finally broken by Alice.

'Is he a soldier?' she asked quietly.

Caroline nodded.

'Unfortunately, yes. It will be his second tour in Afghanistan. Before that it was Iraq, and every time the absence seems worse. I've been a soldier's wife for fifteen years but with this war in Afghanistan I'm beginning to worry much more than before. You don't ever become used to it, dreading the one call, the knock on the door. The return is sometimes just as bad because they take such a long time to settle down to an ordinary humdrum home life. He's promised me that for the sake of me and the kids he is going to leave the army. He's a trained engineer so he should have no difficulty getting a job even in this economic climate.'

'I hope so for your sake,' Sasha murmured. 'I know how you hate it.'

Pauline, sitting on the other side of Alice, interrupted rather sharply.

'Perhaps you should not have married a soldier. I often wonder why people get so hung up and start whingeing about this sort of thing when they must have known what to expect . . .'

'Oh, Pauline.' Sasha looked at her with alarm. 'That is not a very . . .'

Caroline's face was crimson as she leaned across the table towards Pauline.

'Have you ever been in love?' she demanded sharply. 'Because if you have you might know that you marry for love, not because of who a person is or what he does.'

Sasha looked at this new member of the class with some dismay. She was a dark-haired woman, of medium height, whose age was difficult to guess but maybe about her own – early thirties, or a little younger. She was not unattractive, wore little make-up, but had a rather set, dissatisfied look about her; something to do with the expression in her eyes and the firm set of her mouth.

'I don't think we should have any controversy today,' she said before Pauline had time to answer, and rose from her seat consulting her watch as she noticed that the room was emptying. 'I think we'd better make tracks before they throw us out.'

Chairs were scraped back as the rest of the table followed her example. 'Next week again, everybody?' And then to Alice, 'Can I give you a lift anywhere?'

'That's very good of you,' Alice replied. 'But I don't want to take you out of your way. I can get a cab.' She produced a mobile phone from her bag.

'Tell me where you live and I'll take you. Night, everyone.'

'What an interesting lot of people,' Alice said as Sasha drew away from the kerb. 'I'm glad I came.'

'A mixed bunch, I'd say,' Sasha replied. 'It always takes time to get to know people. I was a bit annoyed with Pauline though,' she said crossly. 'Caroline is actually quite terrified that her husband will be killed in Afghanistan. She says the absences get worse. She has been trying to get him to leave the army for ages.'

'And the older man? He didn't join us for coffee.'

'Oh, Martin. He is a bit of a mystery. I don't know what he does or where he comes from. He came last year as a beginner and has made a lot of progress. He really has a gift and should move on to a more advanced group. He never comes for coffee, doesn't socialize or speak to anyone very much, so we don't know him at all.'

'I thought he seemed rather nice.' Alice settled back in her seat, then looked askance at her companion. 'And you? Do you live alone, or shouldn't I ask?'

Sasha was taken aback by this directness.

'I have a partner called Ben. He is an artist, a professional one, and rather good. We were students together. Now,' she said, peering ahead, 'do I take this turning to your road?'

'Yes, and I am that block over on the right. Would you like to come in?'

'Not tonight, thank you.' Sasha smiled at her. 'I'd love to another time.'

'I expect Ben will be waiting for you?' Alice said as the car stopped and she started to get out. 'Thank you so much, Sasha. The evening has made a lot of difference to me, and next time I shall have all the stuff I need.'

Sasha helped her out and escorted her to the door where Alice inserted her key in the lock. 'Will you be OK now?'

'I'll be fine,' Alice said. 'You're very sweet.' Impulsively she kissed her on the cheek.

Sasha let herself into a darkened house with a sense of relief that Ben was out. These days, sometimes, as she came in, the tension rose if he was there. It hadn't always been like that. She went into the kitchen to make herself a cup of tea, changed her mind and poured a glass of wine from a bottle on the kitchen bench. Then she sat down and thought sadly about the deteriorating relationship, wondering how on earth it had come about.

They were the same age, thirty-five, and had known each other since they were students at the Slade. Initially she had not been attracted to him. His features were rather nondescript, pleasant looking but the sort that would not stand out in a crowd. Even in his youth he had gone bald, leaving a crown of fine blond wispy hair, a little tuft in the middle of his head. It was quite engaging. He was of medium height but taller than Sasha, who was rather diminutive. But what he lacked in appearance he made up in talent as an artist and sweetness of character as a person. He was also an amusing and knowledgeable conversationalist. People had courted Ben's company, liked to be seen with him. He was one of the stars of his year and went off with all the major prizes. A great future was forecast for him.

Sasha had been rather dazzled by Ben in those days. He was one of the great personalities and she admired him enormously as an artist. She was talented too, and gradually she became an accepted member of the shining circle that revolved around him.

Slowly he became a confidant and she came to depend on him to rescue her from unsuitable love affairs. Ben was a stalwart, always there, reliable and full of good advice. A moment of carelessness with a passing fancy led to an abortion. Ben was the man to go to. He forgave her foolishness, did not reproach her, arranged it for her, stood by while she had it, and comforted her and nursed her afterwards because she was sore, humiliated and miserable. In time she could not do without Ben, realized she loved him, and finally he had his reward, achieved the longed-for goal and they became lovers.

Sasha was a woman of character, attractive rather than conventionally pretty, with streaked blonde hair in a pony tail which she still wore, although sometimes when she was feeling romantic or there was a social occasion she let it hang loose. From Russian forbears (her grandfather had been an exile from Russia) she had inherited high cheekbones, deeply recessed cornflower-blue eyes, a pert nose, and a simply bewitching smile that could have melted glaciers. People found her enchanting. Above all there was vibrancy, a quality of sexuality about Sasha that drew men round her like bees round a honey pot.

After the Slade, Sasha took a teaching diploma as she realized she would never make it big as an artist, whereas Ben was tipped for greatness.

They didn't set up home together until she got her job at the Redbury College of Art, scraped together enough to buy a house and Ben, struggling to make his name in the big city, lacking a gallery to take him on and skint, joined her.

After that it was upwards for Sasha and stagnation for Ben. He despised commercial work, didn't want to teach, but couldn't find patrons. Having confidence in his genius, but not seeing it reciprocated or appreciated, was galling. He was utterly dependent on Sasha and it eventually made him bitter, boring and ultimately petty, eroding their relationship. He turned into a nag, convinced she was having a good time without him, and questioning her every time she came home late. Perhaps she was having too good a time and being unfaithful?

Hence the heavy heart, reaching for the bottle instead of the teabag.

There was a movement behind her and she turned to see Ben standing there in his dressing gown, rubbing his eyes as though he was dazzled by the light.

'Good heavens, I thought you were out,' she said. 'Are you not well?'

Ben was a night owl and never went to bed early.

'I had a headache,' he said, getting a glass and pouring himself a drink from the bottle on the table.

'Well that won't do you any good,' she said, and from the look he gave her, she immediately felt the tension rising – partly, she knew, because of her. 'Red wine is the worst thing you can take for a headache.'

'I wish you'd mind your own business,' he said, taking a large mouthful and refilling his glass. 'And anyway, where have you been?' He looked at the clock on the kitchen wall.

'I could ask you to mind your own business, too,' Sasha said. 'It is the first night of my adult education class.'

'It's still very late to come back,' he said peevishly. 'What time does it finish?'

'Really.' Sasha in exasperation grabbed the bottle of wine and refilled her glass. 'I can't stand all this interrogation. But if you really want to know it finishes at nine and then we had coffee to get to know some of the new people, and afterwards I drove home an old lady who has just joined the class. Does that satisfy you, Ben?'

'Sorry,' Ben said, unexpectedly contrite. 'I've had a rough day.'

When *didn't* Ben have a rough day? Sasha thought, but having said too much already she didn't reply.

'I thought I had a commission to paint the mayor for the town council. But they changed their minds because of the recession. Even the modest amount I ask is too much. They telephoned me today. "Very sorry, perhaps later." What the hell is the use of that?'

Sasha got up and rinsed her empty glass in the sink, turning towards him as she was drying it.

'I'm really sorry,' she said. 'But, Ben, I do think you are going to have to think more positively about the future. It is not good for you to live like this.'

'You mean it's not good for *you*,' he retorted, refilling his glass.

'No, I didn't mean that. I am OK, but the fact that I have to support you is putting a strain on our relationship. I'm sure it affects you. Surely you realize that?'

'You don't have to support me completely,' he said defensively.

'I pay the mortgage, all the household bills and most of the food. It means I can't save a penny. In fact I have no savings worth speaking of at all. And all the time we're waiting for you to make it.'

'I didn't realize you were so mercenary, Sasha,' Ben sneered at her. 'Throughout history artists have always had their patrons.'

'Yes, but they have been wealthy people. I am not an Italian duke or a French nobleman with vast estates. It's hardly the same, is it?'

'Are you trying to say you're tired of me, Sasha?'

For a moment, she didn't reply, realizing this could be a watershed in their relationship which had once been so important: two people who knew each other intimately, had shared so much love, a passion for art, companionability. At one time they had seemed so ideally suited. They had lived for years on this. Now Sasha was a senior lecturer earning a good salary and Ben was where he had been ten years before. He did deserve to be a successful artist. She believed in him. The trouble was there were so many of them around.

'Of course I'm not,' she said, feeling suddenly weary. 'I'm just stating facts.' Placatingly she put out a hand and began dragging him from the chair. 'Come on, let's go to bed.'

Bed was always where they sorted things out until the next time. It was a very fragile, uneasy truce.

Reaching home and taking off her things, Pauline rather wished she had not stayed for coffee after the art class. She realized the remark she'd made about not marrying a soldier was foolish almost as soon as the words were out, and this was confirmed from the expressions on the faces of those sitting round the table, mouths set in firm lines of disapproval. Trying to be clever meant she invariably said something which showed her up in a bad light and which she instantly regretted. It seemed to her quite obvious that soldiers were meant to fight in battle, and illogical that their spouses were upset when they did. But actually to say as she did *why marry a soldier?* had another meaning to a class where Caroline was known, was among friends, and she was a stranger. It was bitchy.

Pauline switched on the lights in the sitting room, turned on the TV, and slumped in front of it to watch the news. As if to rub in the stupidity of what she'd done there was another item about casualties in Afghanistan.

She had not been long in the provincial city of Redbury and had joined things mainly to try and make new friends and above all, if possible, to meet men. She was thirty-one and although she considered herself a modern, liberated, forward-thinking woman, secretly she was terrified she would never marry and settle down to a normal life like other people. It was true she had never really been in love. She had had relationships, several affairs, and was sexually experienced, but she had never found anyone good enough, and that meant mainly of sufficient intelligence to meet her high standards. Anyway, no one had ever asked her. She knew without any doubt that if she ever did it would never be a soldier, whatever his rank.

She had recently bought an attractive house in a nice part of the town with the help of her parents who were proud of her. So far she had been successful in life. She had taken a good degree, which she'd followed by a secretarial course, a course in business administration, a year in Spain to learn Spanish, and had come home with great expectations.

After a few badly paid jobs in London, she currently worked as PA to the managing director of a large, prestigious international engineering firm. It would be another stepping stone, but at a difficult economic time she didn't want to be jobless. She had been there two years and enjoyed the authority she had. People respected her and looked up to her and she liked her boss. Hence the decision, for a while at least, to settle. Anyway it was important to get on to the housing ladder. Property was always safe. Pauline switched off the TV and the lights in the sitting room and went upstairs to bed.

Slowly she undressed and, because she was still wide awake, decided to have a good long soak in the bath. Afterwards, as she was drying herself, she went into her bedroom and had a good look at herself in the mirror.

She was above average height, slim – she had always looked after her figure and took a lot of exercise – and she thought not bad looking. She had brown eyes, straight rather fine mouse-blonde hair, which she had occasionally permed, with streaks put in and styled medium length and back from her forehead. She was short sighted and wore contact lenses. It was her mouth that she knew could be her downfall. It was not a wide, generous mouth like a lot of people had, but was a thin line which she often caught between her teeth as though she was conscious of it. She dressed well, and carefully; had to for her job.

She finished drying herself, put on her nightie, cleansed her face, brushed her springy hair and lay down on the bed, arms under her head, staring at the ceiling.

She rather thought she had wasted her time joining the painting class. There was absolutely no one there to interest her.

The first thing Caroline heard as she opened the door was one of the children crying. She hurriedly put her bag and painting materials on a table in the hall, but before she got to the top of the stairs the crying had stopped and she heard the comforting sound of Greg's voice soothing the crying child. She went into the children's room and found him with the youngest, Adam, in his arms. The two other children remained undisturbed, which was mysterious as Adam's was usually a lusty bellow. She perched on the bed next to Greg and kissed him on the cheek before stroking the child's brow.

'Is he OK?' she whispered.

'Bad dreams,' Greg whispered back and gently laid him back on his bunk, the lower one of a bunk bed in which Christopher, the middle child, occupied the top. The third and eldest child, Jenny, had a bed of her own.

Later, they crept out of the room and descended the stairs to the kitchen where Greg had obviously been sitting with the paper and a bottle of beer in front of him.

'Do you want something to eat?' he asked.

Caroline shook her head. They had eaten together with the children before she left for her class. 'But I'll join you in a beer.'

'You sit down,' Greg said pointing to a chair. She watched him as he went back to the fridge ferreting about for another bottle. She adored him. He was a tall, big, tough, not strictly handsome but rugged-looking man, his face pocked and scarred by various encounters both in the course of his military duties and away from them. He had been a keen boxer but stopped it at Caroline's insistence. She knew he was reluctant to give up his life in the army, but he had to acknowledge that he had had enough of war, especially as it had now got so much more dangerous, and, as he was nearing forty, he valued the charms and comforts of domesticity.

Taking a bottle from the fridge he took the stopper off and handed it to her. Smiling her thanks she put it to her lips, suddenly feeling very tired. Greg sat down again and lit the cigarette he'd been rolling. 'Nice to be back?'

'In the class? OK. I am a bit late because we had a coffee afterwards. Sorry.'

'That's absolutely OK.' He smiled at her in his warm re-assuring way.

'There were a few new people, one of whom is a sour-looking and rather bitchy woman who told me I should not have married a soldier if I didn't want you to go overseas.'

Greg relit his roll-up, which had gone out.

'What did you say to that?'

'I asked her if she had ever been in love, which was perhaps a bit unkind, but Sasha put a stop to the conversation which might have turned into a brawl.' She looked searchingly at him. 'I did tell them you've promised to give it up. Am I right?'

Greg seemed unusually restless – he was normally such a controlled man. He got up and fetched another beer from the fridge, this time for himself, taking a long swig before he replied.

'I do want to give it up, but just for you. Something inside me makes me reluctant to give up a career that has given me the best times of my life – apart from being with you, that is.'

'Then when?' Caroline knew she had to be careful. Greg clammed up if she nagged, but sometimes there was a feeling of desperation. She felt he was like so many people who were always promising to do something yet failed to deliver, offering one excuse after another. She just longed for him to leave the army. If it hadn't been for the war she would have been content for him to remain in the army as she knew how much he enjoyed it. He had been a professional soldier since his teens. For herself, she would have been quite happy living in their own comfort-able house in her home town with her mother not far away to help out with the kids, and the occasional companionship of fellow service wives when he was away. But this war was another matter. Daily soldiers were being killed and sent home in coffins.

Greg had not resumed his seat but remained leaning against

the fridge, beer bottle in his hand, which now he was contemplating as though it could tell him something.

'Caro, sweetie,' he said at last. 'I didn't know how to tell you this. I've been a coward putting it off, but we have orders to leave for Afghanistan next week, sooner than I thought, than anyone expected, but they have to increase the number of troops out there. But I promise you, I make a solemn promise now that after that . . .'

He stopped and looked at her crestfallen face.

'How long have you known?' she asked.

'Not long. I knew how you felt . . .'

'You should have told me sooner.'

'Would it have made it any better?' he asked her gently.

'It would have prepared me more, and the kids. It's so sudden. I've got used to having you around.'

Caroline was an army wife used to concealing her emotions, or at least trying to. She didn't cry, or protest, when in fact she wanted to howl. However, for his sake, to keep him strong, she remained staring down at the table biting back tears and visualizing the long, lonely, anxiety-ridden days ahead – all the women clustering together for comfort but putting a brave face on it. Remaining strong for the sake of their men, as she was trying to be now. Greg gently put his hand on her shoulder. She reached up and took it, squeezing it tight and then brought it to her lips.

'I promise you,' he said, bending to kiss her head, 'this will be the last tour abroad. Solemn promise. It will soon be over, you'll see.'

When he got home Roger Hamilton put on the television to watch the ten o'clock news. He couldn't decide whether he wanted more coffee or not and, deciding he didn't, turned up the sound and slumped into a chair. He was very tired.

He didn't know why he'd joined the painting class except that it was something to do, somewhere to go. He wanted to extend his horizons and he had always been keen on art. Roger was someone who wanted to change his life, make a fresh start. He had recently got divorced, moved to a new place, a new job, and wanted to meet new people. So much of his life in the last ten years had been mired in domesticity and an increasingly unhappy marriage.

Roger was a tall, lean man with smooth fair hair neatly parted at the side, pale complexioned, clean shaven with greyish-green eyes. Not bad looking, but not handsome either, with no distinguishing features that would set him apart in a crowd. He dressed well, conventionally, and with care to suit his profession. In addition he was locked into a rather awkward personality. Basically he was shy, but people thought him uppish and aloof. He was interested in art and music, but culturally Redbury was a bit of a desert. He felt he had to do something every evening as he was easily bored with his own company. He did keep-fit one night, music appreciation another, he might go to a film once or twice a week, now he had his art class and every other week he had his two children, who remained with his ex-wife in the country about twenty-five miles away. He had taken the job in Redbury to be near, but not too near them. He loved his children, two boys, now seven and nine. It was his wife who had wanted the divorce as she had met another man, but they had been drifting apart for years. He and his ex-wife had agreed to be civilized about it in the interests of the children. And he also agreed that she should have custody, but that he should have full visitation rights. In a way, at thirty-three it was rather nice to be a single man again, fancy free and open to adventure and maybe another, more hopeful relationship.

However, he did not think the women in the painting class would provide that opportunity, except maybe the teacher. He liked her. He thought she was attractive with an elusive sexual quality. Difficult to guess her age. He wondered if she was married. There was no ring on her finger, but these days it didn't necessarily follow. However, he thought she was too attractive, too sexy to be single. But he felt she might be a little bit out of his range. He might be attracted to her, but doubted if she would be attracted to him. His wife had always told him he was boring, laboured the point – 'a boring old accountant' she'd said often enough to give him a complex. And he certainly had clammed up when Sasha, whom he had angled to sit next to, had tried to engage him in conversation. That had been a chance and he had blown it. Well he wouldn't let it happen again. Besides, she had praised his effort at painting that evening.

There was fighting on the screen. Afghanistan. There was always something in the news about Afghanistan. He thought of the woman who had made the nasty remark to the woman married to a soldier. What a bitch she was. Hard. He would certainly be careful to avoid her.

After the news he watched another programme and nearly fell asleep, so rousing himself, he switched off the light and went to bed.

Two

October

A week later on a cold, very wet, wintry morning Caroline stood, her children huddled beside her, outside the barracks, part of a small, desolate but desperately trying to be cheerful group of army wives seeing their men off. But now it would be the last time. He had promised. It never occurred to her that he might not come back at all. Or if it did she kept it well out of her thoughts, never let it surface. They all had to or life would be impossible.

Some of the women were smoking; one or two had brought flasks of tea. She had only just arrived hoping she would be on time. They had made their farewells the day before. Greg had asked her not to come, but she wanted to be there as she always had, seeing him off, fearful, but trying to hide it from him, waiting for his return. But every time going away seemed just that bit more difficult.

Suddenly there was activity. Buses arrived, drew up outside the barracks and, as dawn was breaking over the dark skyline, the doors of the barracks swung open and the battalion of uniformed soldiers marched smartly out towards the waiting buses. Few if any of them looked, or appeared to look, towards the little crowd on the other side. But Caroline knew that Greg would and she waved in the hope he would see her. The men appeared stern but composed, resolute as army men are. They were off to a warm climate, but most of them would undoubtedly wish they were staying at home. The younger ones without families perhaps regarded it as an adventure. This, after all, was why they had enlisted. But most of them went because they had to; they were professional soldiers obeying orders; it was a job. Undoubtedly many nursed a sense of resentment even if well hidden. After all it was not *our* war, but fought in a far-off place for people we didn't know. Half of the country doubted its wisdom. Why were we there? The argument ranged back and forth but no one really knew the answer. Most people blamed the government for landing us in a situation to which there seemed no end, adding to the mounting distress about the economy, increasing unemployment, bankruptcies, house repossessions, even the weather. All the fault of the poor Prime Minister who had started his term the previous year on a high note of popularity, with such great expectations. Almost immediately, some thought prophetically, there were widespread floods and his popularity began to wane.

If the men were solemn the women showed various signs of suppressed distress. Difficult to smile when you saw your loved one taking off for a region from which some of them might not return.

Just as Greg began to climb into the bus, Caroline saw him look directly at her and raise a hand in greeting, and she blew him a kiss as he disappeared out of sight.

The children were cold; she was freezing. She exchanged a few words with some of the women and went to where she had parked her car to take them back to home and warmth. Just as they left, the first bus rolled away and she gazed after it for a long time wondering if Greg was in it. It was no time to sit and think or to have long periods without something to do. One had to keep busy, free the mind from worry and doubt. After taking the elder children to school, putting Adam down for a rest, she vigorously cleaned the house, changed beds, did some washing and telephoned her mother to ask if she could look after the kids while she went to her art class in the evening. It was very convenient to have her mother so near and always willing to help out. It was also very convenient to have the art class that night to occupy her mind. She knew she was good and she enjoyed it. As a woman who, despite a good education, had sacrificed any career for her marriage and children it made her feel fulfilled, even important, as though she had a life of her own to lead, more important than ever now that Greg was away again.

As she was about to enter the classroom Pauline, who had been waiting outside the door, stepped up to her, face flushed.

'I wondered if I could have a word, Caroline?'

Surprised and taken aback, Caroline nodded and they stepped to one side to let others pass.

'I just wanted to say how sorry I am about what I said last week. It was very unkind and uncalled for, and was wrong of me.'

To her embarrassment Caroline felt tears spring to her eyes, which she rapidly brushed away.

'That's OK,' she murmured in a strangulated voice and, unable to say anything else for fear the tears would surface, she hurried into the class. Putting her materials on her table she went to a free easel and, arranging her painting, began furiously to apply the finishing touches.

By now everyone had more or less settled down. Sasha had divided them into two groups – the beginners who were still learning the fundamentals of painting in watercolour, and the more experienced who were at work on the latest still-life arrangement. Some were working on the painting on their tables; others had transferred their work to an easel.

The beginners were learning the techniques of applying flat washes to their paper, some more successfully than others. There was a newcomer, a pleasant looking woman of middle age called Moira who had apologized for the late start, but she had been on holiday when the session started and had registered late. She told Sasha she had some experience and arrived with paint box, paper and brushes. Sasha had put her among the beginners and saw her listening intently as preliminary instructions had been given.

The studio was quite large, untidy, with an assortment of tables and easels. It was a typical artists' work place, used by many people and a bit grubby and untidy, with a large sink in one corner and a variety of jars and pots of various shapes on a bench beside it. Discarded paint boxes, stiff brushes, dirty used palettes were littered about. The floor was stained with paint. The place looked as though it was seldom, if ever, visited by a cleaner. Nevertheless there was a cheerful atmosphere in the studio and Sasha thought that the group had settled well. She wandered around supervising each one, stopping to offer advice, praise or make a point, as gently as she could, that something wasn't quite right. One had to be careful not to offend beginners by being too critical or, losing confidence, they would soon drop out. Some people were just not meant to be painters and that was that.

The lights were full on in the studio and she turned to the curtainless window and stared into the darkness outside. Thick drops of rain splattered against the windowpane. The rain never seemed to stop, the climate somehow reflecting the prevailing gloom in the country about the deepening recession, dissatisfaction with the government who were given all the blame for the decline in the economy, although in fact it was worldwide, one of the worst of the century.

Sasha turned back into the room and stopped by the side of Caroline who was peering anxiously at the painting on her easel taking a step back in a critical examination of her work. She looked up at Sasha.

'I can't seem to get that jug right,' she said. 'It's not exactly that colour, is it?'

'Try a bit of raw sienna,' Sasha advised. 'It will tone the colour and also lift it a bit. Know what I mean?'

'I think so,' Caroline said dubiously and, turning to her paintbox, dipped her brush in clean water before mixing the darker colour. Wearily she passed a hand across her brow. 'I need to concentrate. So many things going on.' Lowering her voice to just above a whisper she leaned closer to Sasha. 'Greg left today.'

'So soon?' Sasha looked surprised.

'He only told me at the last minute. He knew I didn't want him to go. I feel ashamed of myself that it matters so much, that I wasn't brave for him. I should have been used to it by now.' Aware that the tears, never far below the surface, were beginning to well up she vigorously blew her nose. 'The good news is,' she continued, struggling to control herself, 'he has promised me that it will be the last trip abroad. This time I think he means it.'

Sasha, not knowing how to respond, felt inadequate. 'I'm sorry . . .' she began but it didn't seem quite right. After all, it wasn't a bereavement but his job, as Pauline had rather nastily pointed out. It was always worse for the women left behind.

Noticing one or two faces turned curiously towards them Sasha gave her a comforting pat on the arm. 'We'll talk about it later,' she whispered and went across to Moira, the newcomer, who was showing no difficulty producing excellent washes, not only flat but graduated and variegated, well in advance of the rest.

'I think I should have put you into the advanced group,' she said after studying her work. 'You seem to know quite a lot. Your washes are very good.'

'Oh, I'm very rusty,' Moira said. 'I haven't done any for a long time. I am quite happy to stay here for the moment.'

'Come and have coffee in the canteen afterwards,' Sasha said encouragingly 'and meet some of the others.'

Reluctantly she moved on to Pauline who she had noticed trying to listen to the conversation she'd conducted in muted tones with Caroline. As a putative artist she was struggling, one of the beginners showing least promise. She seemed to have little instinctive feeling for painting either and Sasha wondered what had made her take it up. Pauline had failed to endear herself to her so far, neither by her rather sulky attitude to criticism, nor the standard of her work, and Sasha rather hoped she would soon throw it in.

As expected, Pauline, with the air of one struggling to make a great effort, leaned back and stared up at her.

'I can't see the point of the wash,' she said despairingly, gazing at the sheet of paper in front of her as Sasha stooped to inspect her work, what little there was of it, a dullish blue wodge of colour unevenly and clumsily applied.

'It is basic to watercolour painting,' Sasha explained patiently. 'A wash is necessary in any area too large to be covered by a brush stroke.'

Pauline had already mastered the technique of stretching the paper, though she ruined several sheets of paper in the process.

'Have another go.' Sasha tried to sound encouraging and moved over to Martin who, by contrast, was one of the best students in the class and who had almost completed his painting, which Sasha studied critically. It really stood out compared to all the work surrounding him in various stages of completion. He was the most accomplished student, yet the one she knew least about. She knew his name but that was it. He had never in two years stayed for coffee and, while not unfriendly, he didn't socialize and was seldom seen talking to anyone other than herself, and that was only occasionally when he needed advice or she felt she had to give it.

'I think you've almost finished,' she said. 'I shall have to find you a more difficult subject. You are too advanced for this class,

you know, Martin. You should move on. I've told you this before.'
She looked searchingly at him.

'I like it here,' he said stubbornly. 'Do you mind?' His rather
piercing gaze made her uncomfortable. 'I feel at home. Does it
bother you?'

'Not in the least,' she said. 'It's just that I feel if you have talent
you should develop it. It's up to you.' And she moved away feeling
offended by the brusqueness of his manner. He was a difficult
man to connect with.

But that night he stayed for coffee. As she sat down, with Moira
in tow, she was surprised when he slipped into the chair beside her.

'I think I offended you,' he said at once. 'I was rude. I do
apologize.'

She gazed at him for a moment, rather doubting his sincerity.
Somehow he didn't fit into the class, too independent, self-
confidant, too defiant with his dark steely eyes and thrusting jaw
line. She decided that she really didn't like him at all and said
coldly, 'I was only thinking of you. You could be more stretched
in another class. But it is up to you, Martin, and if you wish to
stay here I'm pleased to help in any way I can.'

She then turned pointedly to Moira. 'Where did you go for
your holiday?'

'India, have you been?'

'No.'

'It's a wonderful place, but also distressing in the poverty, the
beggars in the streets. I don't think I would go again. I went with
my son who knows his way around, but even he was put off –
although there are some marvellous things to see. The colours
and the countryside are a feast for an artist. We travelled right
round and did all the touristy things – the Taj Mahal, the Agra
Fort, the fabulous Palace of the Winds in Jaipur and so on – and
it was a shock to come back to England and the gloom and the
rain. Nothing seems to worry them much in India although their
problems are much worse than ours.'

'I used to work in India,' Martin interrupted them. 'I must say
I didn't miss it.'

'Oh, when . . .?' Moira turned to him with interest, leaning
across Sasha so that as he and Moira began to chat, Sasha, sensing
an opportunity to escape from Martin, offered to change places.

'I see you've got a lot in common,' she said. 'I'm in the way. I just want a word with Pauline.' And she went across to the next table where she had observed Pauline by herself, which had caused her some concern. She sat down beside her. 'I hope I wasn't too discouraging today.'

'I really am the worst in the class,' Pauline replied. 'I feel I might hold people back.'

'Don't worry about that. If you want to stay on I am happy to help all I can.'

'I do want to stay on,' Pauline said.

'Then stay. No problem.' The voice was Roger's who, late with his coffee, came in on the tail-end of the conversation and, espying Sasha, sat next to her but addressed himself to Pauline. 'Sasha is very patient, or haven't you noticed?'

'I think she's fantastic,' Pauline said sincerely, keen to make amends and ingratiate herself with her tutor.

'I'm not much good either. That gives us something in common. If only we were all like Martin.'

'There's plenty of time,' Sasha said and, sensing that the canteen staff wanted to go home, rose, taking her empty cup with her to join Caroline who had just come in and was queuing for her coffee. 'Another cup?' she asked as Sasha joined her.

'OK, it's a cold night, but I think they want to shut soon . . . Well, just a quick one. You're a bit late.' She groped in her pocket for change but Caroline waved her away.

'Have it on me. I think you were right about the raw sienna. It does lift it.'

'Is it finished?'

'Not quite. I think I'll take it home and work on it. Now that Greg's gone there is plenty of time.'

Together they moved to a table and sat down.

'Sorry, I was a bit of an ass just now. Pauline came up to me just before the class and I nearly blubbed then.'

'It is perfectly understandable.' Sasha sipped her coffee.

'I think I'm losing my grip, all these tears. I didn't know what to say to her or how to respond, so I just murmured something and walked away. She wanted to say she was sorry for last week. You know, about marrying a soldier. Now I'll have to go and apologize to *her*.'

'I did think it was unkind and unnecessary. But I feel guilty about Pauline. I sense she is an unhappy woman, but somehow she doesn't quite fit in.'

'How doesn't she fit it?' Caroline looked at her curiously.

'I don't really know why she's here. She seems to have no feeling for art. She says she's the worst, and she is.' She sighed. 'However, she assures me she wants to stay.'

Sasha had a rapport with Caroline, who had been with her from the beginning and had made enormous progress. She was someone who really threw herself into her work, but was nearly ready to go a higher class and when she did Sasha would miss her. She only hoped she might take Martin with her. The two women were about the same age and, Sasha thought, pretty much the same temperament. She found her very simpatico. As if guessing her thoughts Caroline said, 'Would you like to come and have supper one evening? I don't know if it's in order to ask a tutor . . .'

'There's nothing I'd like better,' Sasha replied enthusiastically. 'I was just thinking that you really should move on then and how much I'd miss you; your enthusiasm is infectious and you work hard.'

'When Greg's away I am rather thrown into the company of army wives and all we do is talk about our blokes and how worried we are about them, even more so now that the pace of the war is hotting up. You know for the first time today as I was watching them go off I found myself wondering how many of them might not come back and if Greg would be among them. It's unusual for me to have such morbid thoughts.'

The lights flickered on and off once, a signal that the canteen was closing. Tables began to empty, students rising with their books, cases and rucksacks, shrugging on jackets and coats, muffling themselves in scarves against the cold. Sasha's little group began to make their way in similar fashion to the door and she noticed that Roger and Pauline were still deep in conversation, that Martin had disappeared and that Moira was walking slowly beside Alice.

Sasha, accompanied by Caroline, caught up with them.

'Do you want a lift, Alice?'

'My dear, this kind of you, but Moira has just offered. She lives in the next road.'

'It will be a pleasure,' Moira said and, turning to Sasha, 'I have found the evening most interesting. Really I'm so glad I came.'

Sasha watched them go and turned to Caroline. 'You OK for a lift?'

'I've got my car,' Caroline replied. 'How about supper on Tuesday?'

'Can I ring you? I'll have to look at my diary when I get home. I've got your number.'

Together they walked towards the car park watched by Pauline who had waited for Roger to get his coat. She was gratified that he had gone out of his way to be nice to her, waited for her as she came out of the canteen. Everyone else seemed keen to avoid her, which was why she had gone to sit on her own in the canteen. She wished she'd been able to speak to Caroline again, but no opportunity had presented itself. She turned as Roger came over shrugging on his coat and wrapping his scarf tightly around his neck.

'I wanted to speak to Caroline. I really said the wrong thing the other evening, about marrying a soldier. Did you hear it?'

'Yes I did.'

'Did you think it was very rude?'

'I knew what you meant and in a way I agree with you. Shall we just say that in the present fraught circumstances it was unfortunate?'

'I always seem to put my foot in it. Say the wrong thing. I did try and speak to her before the class but she went off. I wanted to try again, but she seems to be avoiding me.'

'Maybe next time. Do you have your car?' As if impatient Roger cupped his mouth in his hand, blowing into it against the cold.

'No, I walked. I don't live so far away.'

'Let me give you a lift. It's not a very good night to walk back alone in the dark.'

'That's very kind of you.'

Pauline got in beside him and sank back against the seat.

'You've been awfully nice to me,' she said as he engaged the gears. 'I mean about encouraging me to stay on. I really am the worst in the class. I seem to lack any talent at all.'

Roger smiled as he turned into the road. 'You give me directions.'

When they stopped outside the door she said, 'Do you fancy another coffee?'

'Well . . .' Roger doubtfully looked at his watch. 'Just a quickie. But I mustn't be too late. I have an early meeting tomorrow.'

Rather surprised by this unexpected turn of events Pauline put the key in the front door, switched on the hall lights and led him into the sitting room, putting on more lights as she went.

'What a nice place,' Roger said, divesting himself of his coat which he threw on a chair.

'I haven't been in this house for very long. I didn't really think I was going to settle here, but I rather like my job and in this climate one has to hang on to what one has. I'll just get the coffee or would you prefer a proper drink?'

'Just coffee would be nice.'

While she was gone he sat down and looked around the room, nicely and quite expensively furnished, good paintings on the wall, a tall bookcase full of books. Family photos. He got up as Pauline entered and took the tray from her, placing it on a side table.

'This is all very nice. Do you live here by yourself?'

Pauline paused in the act of pouring the coffee and stared at him.

'I mean,' he said, faltering as he saw her expression. 'None of my business really.'

'I don't share it if that's what you mean, and yes I do live alone.'

She continued to pour the coffee from a pot thinking she was not alone in making clumsy remarks.

She passed him his cup. 'Milk and sugar?'

'No sugar thanks,' Roger seemed to sense her feelings. 'I hope you didn't think I was being nosey.'

'Not at all. I haven't been here very long. I thought it was time I got settled and on the housing ladder while the going was good.' She sat opposite him and sipped her coffee. Maybe asking him in had not been such a good idea, a bit premature as if she was making overtures and, strictly speaking, she didn't fancy him so she hadn't asked him in for any reason other than politeness.

'I haven't been here very long either. I rent my place. I'm not quite sure whether or not I'm going to stay but, as you say, with the economic situation as it is, and all the signs are that it will get worse, I might decide to stay where I am.'

'What is it you do?'

'I'm what my wife called a boring accountant.'

A married man. It had been a very real mistake to ask him in. Maybe he was the one with ideas, being invited into a strange woman's house late at night. She'd have to keep an eye on the clock. Getting rid of him might be a problem. He'd looked harmless enough, too harmless to be interesting.

'I don't suppose they are all boring or take classes in painting.' She gave a polite yawn, putting her hand to her mouth.

'Oh, some of them are, but we do have that reputation.'

'I'm sure your wife doesn't find you boring.' Pauline glanced meaningfully at the clock on the mantelpiece.

'Yes she does, or did. Her attitude never changed. We're divorced; that's why I came to live in Redbury. I have two kids so I want to be near enough to see them and take them out, but not too near, if you know what I mean.'

Sensing her restlessness, and having seen her glance at the clock, he swallowed the rest of his coffee and got up.

'I think you're tired and, as I said, I must be up early. Thanks very much for the coffee, Pauline. And don't be discouraged. I'm sure you'll make it in the class if you want to.' He reached over for his coat and scarf. 'Sasha is very good.'

Watched by her he shrugged on his coat, wrapped his scarf securely about his neck and said offhandedly, 'I wonder if she's married or has a partner. Would you happen to know?'

'I don't know the least thing about her. How could I?' Pauline exclaimed, taken aback.

'I just wondered, maybe you discussed girlie things when you registered – you know women sometimes do – because she is so attractive. Don't you think? I quite fancy her.'

Too surprised to speak, wordlessly Pauline shrugged her shoulders, led him to the door and after the briefest of goodbyes watched him as he walked to his car and drove off without glancing back.

Slowly, thoughtfully, Pauline strolled back into the sitting room. 'Girlie things' indeed. So he was sexist as well as being boring.

She wondered who had got rid of whom in the break-up of his marriage. She picked up the cups and took them back into the kitchen thinking, as she went, at the strange turn of events and emotions in the course of a single evening. It certainly wasn't her he was interested in. It was Sasha.

In fact Moira Cunningham was quite an accomplished artist. It had been her hobby for a long time but, until the death of her husband, Bob, she had little chance to practise it as she had nursed him during his last prolonged illness. After settling all the tiresome details of Bob's estate, the disorientation and grieving that follows the death of a beloved companion, she had had an extended tour of India and Asia with her son Toby. When he returned to university, from which he had taken a year off, the house suddenly seemed very empty and she thought, once again, of returning to her painting. She had seen the class advertised in the adult education brochure that came with the local paper.

The Cunningham house was a large, attractive 1930s building in what was considered the better end of the town. In fact it was almost the country and since her daughter Vanessa had left home Moira had turned her room into not exactly a studio, but the place where she painted, as it was a quiet pleasant room at the back of the house and had an attractive view over the large garden to the fields and hills beyond.

It had occurred to her to sell the six-bedroom house and get something smaller, but she had lived there since her marriage and it had been a very happy home.

In every sense Moira had lived a good life and, except for the relatively early death of Bob, had much to be grateful for. So her sense of loneliness, which merged at times into depression, puzzled her. She found the days long. Although she had lived in the town since her marriage she had few outside interests. Bob, who had been a successful businessman, had belonged to the usual men's clubs and the chamber of commerce and while he was still active they had been out a great deal. But she was always with Bob, seldom on her own. She was of the generation when her family had absorbed her completely, and Bob's long illness had done the rest to heighten her current sense of isolation. It was amazing the way friends, even those one considered good friends, seemed to drop off when misfortune struck, and after Bob died the invitations stopped altogether. No one wanted a woman of a certain age on her own; the numbers simply didn't add up and the circle closed in.

Moira glanced at her watch and put down her brush. She was painting a scene familiar from the bedroom window yet done countless times from different perspectives, rather like Cezanne's various depictions of Mont Sainte-Victoire. The garden was dominated by a large holly tree full of berries in the winter which Moira used to capture in her paintings before all the birds had got to them.

Vanessa was due for lunch. She was already late. Unlike her, Vanessa had a busy life, but, due to the affection between the two women, frequently came to see her mother and when Ian was away, which was frequently, often came to stay with the children.

Just at that moment the doorbell rang and Moira hurried down and greeted Vanessa, slightly breathless and carrying a large bunch of flowers, with a hug. After their embrace Moira took the flowers, thanked her daughter and led the way inside to the kitchen.

'Lovely to see you,' she said, looking for a vase for the flowers. 'I'm trying to get back to my painting.'

'How are you getting on?' Vanessa perched on the edge of the table while Moira produced a vase and began to arrange the flowers with the skill of an artist's eye.

'Well I only began a couple of weeks ago. I was late registering. It's a nice class with some quite interesting people. It has beginners and more advanced students and I have put myself among the beginners because I've a lot to catch up on. There, how's that?' She stood back and surveyed her arrangement. 'Let's go into the dining room. The lunch is ready, all cold. I guessed you'd be in a hurry, as usual.'

Vanessa was a popular young woman, always busy. She had a lot to do with the children's school and was into voluntary works, particularly among handicapped children.

Moira put the vase on a sideboard on which there was a selection of cold cuts, salad and a cheese board. Each of the women took a plate, helped themselves and sat down at the table.

It was a pleasant day, chilly outside, but the autumn sun streamed in through the window and Moira looked across at her daughter who she thought was looking particularly attractive and vivacious. There was a special bloom to her she had not seen before – or maybe she had but not for a long time – and she wondered what had brought it about or what she was doing that had excited her. Doubtless she would hear about it in due course.

By any standards Vanessa was beautiful. She had short curly hair that was naturally blonde but helped a little by the skilful addition of one or two highlights. She had an oval, almost sculptured, delicately contoured face and the deepest of cerulean blue eyes. She was an ex air hostess who had given up her career reluctantly to start a family and hoped one day to return to it, so she took care of her figure which was slim and supple. She wore jeans with an attractive knee length tunic top, a chiffon scarf casually tucked in at the neck. She always exuded vitality, glamour and health. And today was no exception.

'Do you want a glass of wine?'

Vanessa shook her head. 'Just water. I've a lot to do this afternoon. I can't stay long, Mum. Sorry I was so late.'

'What are you up to? Anything special?'

'Just meeting a pal. Tell me about the class.'

'The tutor is particularly nice, a woman maybe a bit older than you, very simpatico and obviously popular with the class. She's got a Russian name and looks vaguely Slavic with high cheekbones and deep-set eyes, very attractive. There is also a very nice older woman I gave a lift to. She lives in sheltered accommodation not far from here, that rather nice new posh block of flats you pass just before our turning. She is in her eighties, but very alert and young looking. I'm going to ask her for tea. I think she is a bit lonely like me.'

'Careful you don't get too involved, Mum. I know it's rather a nasty thing to say, but otherwise you'll find yourself being called on for all sorts of little tasks if she doesn't drive.'

'Oh, I don't think she is a bit like that. Struck me as a very independent woman and she was about to call a taxi on her mobile when I offered her a lift. Now, darling, tell me what you've been up to. When does Ian come home?'

Vanessa shrugged. 'Who knows? He's in Kenya and comes

home via Europe. Ages I think. He's been away such a lot this year. The children miss him.'

'I'm sure you miss him too.' Moira looked anxiously at her daughter who gave a dismissive shrug.

'Of course I do, but it is the kind of thing you get used to.'

As she pointedly bent her head over her plate Moira surreptitiously studied her, trying to fathom that rather mysterious expression, almost of indifference. Due to her extreme good looks, Vanessa had never been short of men who were interested in her, and Moira knew she had played around a bit. However it was Ian, a frequent traveller and a man also endowed both with looks and charisma, who finally captured her heart, and they were married a very short time after they met. Moira knew that one of the reasons for it was that Bob was showing the signs of the cancer that would eventually kill him, but as it turned out, happily, it was not until five years later, something which no one expected as, at first, the prognosis was poor.

She realized then that Vanessa, having finished what was on her plate, was gazing at her. 'Penny for them, Mum?'

'Oh just thinking, about Dad actually, and how much he adored you. You look really lovely today, darling. I was thinking back to your wedding and what a lucky man Ian is.'

Vanessa glanced at her watch and with an exclamation moved away from the table. 'Just seen the time. Really I must fly. Sorry but . . .' At that minute her mobile rang and with an apologetic glance at her mother she put it to her ear. After a moment she got up and, looking again at her mother, went to the door and shut it after her, leaving Moira wondering what was so secret she couldn't hear it. She went to the sideboard and cut herself a piece of cheese, took a stick of celery from a jug and idly chewed on it as her train of thought continued.

Vanessa was Bob's darling, his golden girl, and she had wanted a big wedding for Daddy and for him to take her down the aisle. Moira had often wondered if, but for that immediacy, Vanessa and Ian would have married before they had really the chance to get to know each other. There was no doubt however that at the time they were passionately in love. Moira remembered how special her daughter had looked that day, what gasps her radiance had drawn from the congregation as she walked up the aisle with her new husband. And as far as she knew the marriage had been a happy one with two lovely children. The only snag as far as Moira was aware was Ian's long absences abroad on business as overseas director of a large pharmaceutical company.

Vanessa was away quite a long time and when she returned the beauty seemed to have drained from her face and Moira looked alarmed. 'Nothing wrong I hope. Was it Ian?'

'No.' Vanessa slumped in her chair. 'It was the pal I was going to meet, cancelling. So I've plenty of time.' She also went to the sideboard and put some cheese on a plate. 'Maybe I will have that glass of wine after all.'

'There is an open bottle in the kitchen. Red if that's OK. I only opened it last night.'

'Do you want one, Mum?'

'Why not?' Moira said with a nervous smile. 'Nice with cheese.' A glass of wine would bolster her up, calm those nerves. A curious tension and unease seemed suddenly to have pervaded the atmosphere following the phone call. The radiance had disappeared completely, as if all the life had gone out of her daughter.

Vanessa returned with the bottle and two glasses, poured her mother one and another for herself. She slumped on her chair again and moodily moved her cheese around her plate.

'Is there anything you want to talk about, darling?' Moira said quietly.

'No, why should there be?'

'You seem very upset by that phone call.'

'Yes I am upset. Well . . .' Vanessa leaned back in her chair and looked rather defiantly across the table. 'Well, it was a bloke.'

'The pal you were going to meet was a *bloke?*' Moira made a great effort to restrain her incredulity.

'It might shock you Mum, but yes.'

'Is it something serious, Vanessa?'

'No, it's just an affair.'

'An affair can be serious, darling.'

'This isn't. At least I don't think it is.'

'How long has it been going on?'

'A few weeks.' Vanessa got up and paced restlessly around the room looking at last out of the window. As if to fit in with her mood the sun had also been replaced by the usual clutch of heavy, grey, rain-bearing clouds. 'The whole thing is ridiculous. That's what I tell myself. He is deeply unsuitable. It is all absurd, but somehow it means a lot to me.'

She turned from the window and took her seat at the table again.

'Can I know who he is, what he does?'

'He is a lifeguard at the pool where we swim and he is nineteen. You can see why it is deeply unsuitable and why it won't last. The thing is, I don't even know how I let myself get into such a ridiculous situation. Excitement I guess.' She looked on the verge of tears.

'Does he know you are still married?'

'Of course. I think that's what excites him. He knows there is no danger. I actually got to know him because of the children. He gave Freddie extra coaching and we started talking one day. There was a real mutual attraction. He is very good looking and also very mature. He looks older than he is. He has had a very difficult life, unloved as a child, that sort of thing, father drank, mother couldn't cope, and is making his way in the world. Doesn't want to be a lifeguard forever; he got it through one of those youth opportunity schemes. He would like to go to university and study law, but is relatively uneducated. Doesn't even have GCSEs . . .' Her voice trailed off.

'So I suppose you thought you could help him and advise him?' Moira knew how much Vanessa enjoyed helping the disadvantaged, and how good she was because she really cared.

'Exactly. You know me so well, Mum. And it did only start like that. He confided one day his ambitions to improve his education and I knew I could help him. There are all sorts of government schemes for helping young people get into higher education and I said I had contacts and would look into it, with no ulterior motive, I promise you. So I made some enquiries and . . . well, one thing led to another. We became closer, took to meeting away from the pool and . . . you know how it is.'

Moira, having been a faithful wife, didn't know but could imagine how it might be.

'And where does all this happen?'

'You mean the sex bit?'

'Naturally.'

'In his time off, usually at my house when the kids are at school. Sometimes his. He rents a room and the owners work.'

'That would have happened today?'

'Yes. At my place. I was picking him up, which was why I was in a hurry and was cross with myself for being late, but I was getting some information for him actually. Turns out one of the other guards is sick and he has to work.'

Which was why Vanessa had looked so beautiful, as radiant as she had been on her wedding day.

'I really don't know why I'm telling you all this, Mum.'

Moira got up and stood behind her daughter's chair encircling her with her arms and hugging her.

'Because we're close,' she whispered. 'You can tell me anything.'

'That's true.' Vanessa reached up and touched her mother's arm. 'Don't think I'm at all happy about this. I'm not, nor proud of myself. But it is very exciting. It's like a drug. And he is very nice. You'd like him, Mum, I'm sure you would. I would in fact very much like to help him succeed.'

'What if Ian finds out?'

'Ian will never find out. I'm too careful. I don't want to ruin my marriage, which suits me as it is, upset the apple cart for him and his career and of course hurt Ian, who would be devastated. His name is Tim. Not that I think the pool could or would sack him but anyway we don't even consider it. I'm quite happy with things as they are. Tim of course, besides his age, has no money. Anything more permanent is quite out of the question.'

Moira went back to her place, leaned her arms on the table and looked across at her daughter.

'Vanessa, when I asked you if you missed Ian you were rather offhand. I would never have asked you this, but now that all this has come out do you mind if I do ask exactly how you feel about him?'

Vanessa shifted her cutlery around the table and poured another glass of wine.

'I don't really know how I feel is the honest truth. I mean there is nothing wrong with Ian. I like him, love him I expect, in a married kind of way – after all it is eight years. I'm used to him. But he is very involved in his work and he does spend a lot of time abroad. It's hard to get all excited when he comes back. I am almost like a single parent.'

'And how does he feel about you?'

'Always pleased to be home. Brings us presents. Makes a fuss of the kids. Life resumes as it had before. But he is a very controlled, single-minded man and I think his job comes first – he has ambitions to be managing director one day and always gets good results – then the kids, with me a poor third. That's the way I feel anyway. I don't suppose he even thinks about it.'

'Have you ever discussed it with him?'

'Never, no point. Why risk rocking the boat now that I have a lover and sex is a bit more exciting? It has never been very exciting with Ian and that is the truth. Also there is not much of it. When we are home he is busy catching up with things, seeing people; we are out a lot and entertain mostly business friends. I think I'm a good and dutiful wife and that's how it's going to stay.'

'So the affair with Tim could go on?'

'On and on – for a bit anyway as far as I can see, or until I suppose he finds someone better, maybe younger and more exciting, as he undoubtedly will once he is a successful lawyer.'

But as far as Moira could see, that time was a long way off.

Three

Sasha had one last lingering look round the gallery and, making her way through the crowd, was about to go out when she recognized a familiar figure, his back to her, studying the Arnolfini portrait. At least she thought it was familiar, but didn't want to confirm her suspicion in case she was right. It was the last person she wanted to see, so she began to sneak past, hoping to avoid a meeting. As luck would have it, at that precise moment he turned round and looked straight at her, first in surprise and then a smile of recognition gradually dawned on his face. She could hardly continue her exit; it would look like flight, which would be undignified.

'Sasha, what a coincidence seeing you,' he said, advancing towards her. 'Have you just arrived?'

'I was on my way out,' she said rather coldly. 'Nice to see you, Martin. Don't let me disturb you. The Arnolfini is beautiful.' And she prepared to continue on her way.

'I was just about to go too. Having a last lingering look.' He paused. 'Fancy a quick coffee?'

'Actually . . .' Sasha didn't know how to decline without sounding rude. After all he was one of her students. 'Well . . .' She looked at her watch. 'I do want to do quite a few things. I'm only in London for the day . . . Oh, alright,' she concluded lamely.

'Did you come up especially for the exhibition?' Martin asked, as they made their way up the stairs.

'Yes, did you?'

'I'm here on business for a few days. Look.' He glanced at his watch as they reached the top. 'It's lunch time. Let me offer you lunch. There's a nice Italian restaurant in St Martin's Lane.'

'Well . . .' Sasha in fact was starving, having had no breakfast. The thought of an Italian meal was very tempting, even in the company of Martin. She really hadn't got anything to do, but was just going to mooch round the shops until it was time for her train. Also there was nothing she particularly wanted to buy.

'Well, why not?' she said, and managed a smile.

He gazed at her quizzically before leading the way out through the crowd gathered outside the National Gallery and across the street to St Martin's Lane.

The restaurant was crowded but a table was found for them and Sasha began to relax. This might not have been what she intended, but at least it was different. Besides, she could always have said no, so why hadn't she?

'Drink?' he asked as the waiter handed them the menus. 'I was going to order a bottle of wine, but maybe you'd prefer something else?'

'Wine would be great,' she said, putting the menu back on the table. 'This is very nice of you, Martin, quite unexpected.' She felt herself beginning to thaw. 'I'll just have the spaghetti Bolognese. It's a long time since I had genuine Italian spaghetti.'

'Nothing to start?'

'Spaghetti is fine.'

Martin ordered spaghetti for Sasha and a steak for himself.

'So, just up for the day?'

'I got the early train. I'm teaching tomorrow.'

'It's my second visit to the exhibition and I'll go again before I leave.'

'It is quite special. Van Eyck is a great favourite of mine.'

'Not so much Titian?'

'It depends what it is.' They were talking about the exhibition of Renaissance artists on view at the National Gallery. 'But I especially like Van Eyck.'

'I love his self-portrait.'

'If it is a self-portrait. We're not quite sure.'

'Do you think it is of him?'

'I don't know. In fact, there is a lot we don't know about Van Eyck. He died in 1441 but we are not sure when he was born. I saw you studying the Arnolfini. Is it a particular favourite of yours?'

'I suppose it is.' He broke off as the waiter produced a bottle of Verdicchio and poured two glasses. 'Hope you like this wine. It is one of my favourites.' He held up his glass, 'To you, Sasha, a fortunate chance encounter. Very nice for me anyway as it breaks up my day. Cheers.'

'Cheers,' Sasha replied, 'and thanks for the invitation. I was a bit slow in accepting but . . .'

'You don't like me very much, do you, Sasha?'

Taken aback by his directness she tried to hide a blush by taking another sip of wine and saying, 'In fact this is very good.' Then defensively, 'Why shouldn't I like you? I don't know anything about you.'

'It shows. I can sense it. I guess you were about to creep past me when you saw me in the gallery.'

'Are you a psychologist?' she asked with a derisive smile.

'No, but I know when people don't like me. Don't you? Or I imagine not many people wouldn't like you.'

'Oh, I suppose I have my enemies or detractors. The teaching profession can be very bitchy. We have our little fights, struggles for promotion, but on the whole I am happy at the college and like what I do.'

'Everyone in the class loves you.'

'I like my class.'

'But not me?'

'Oh, Martin,' she said in a tone of exasperation, 'please don't go on about it. I assure you I do not actively *dislike* you. But you are someone who likes to keep himself to himself. Also you don't seem to want to socialize. You never come for coffee afterwards. I respect that. It is your choice and I don't question it. Some others don't either and I don't know them very well.'

'I did the other day, and you pointedly moved away.'

Sasha realized that her first instinct was right, that she should not have accepted the invitation, which now seemed to be leading to a bruising encounter with someone with whom she had to work. At that point their food arrived and she picked up her fork and tucked into her spaghetti with relief. 'Very good,' she said after a few mouthfuls then, managing a smile with some effort because she did now in fact feel very annoyed with him, 'Tell me what is it you do?'

'I am a structural engineer. Not very romantic, I'm afraid.'

'Was that why you were in India?'

'Yes, for several years. I work for Warrington's. I don't know if you've heard of them but they are quite a large firm of builders in Southampton.'

'And you commute there every day?'

'Yes, that's why I'm sometimes late – also tired as it is an hour's drive so I like to go home early.'

He too was eating his steak with relish but now put down his knife and fork. 'I am truly sorry about this contretemps, Sasha. It's not what I meant at all and I can see I've annoyed you, which I certainly didn't mean. It's just that no one likes to be disliked and I wondered why . . .' Seeing her expression he held up his hand in a placatory gesture. 'No honestly, I won't say any more. I'm sorry I even brought it up. Let's talk about art instead, something on which I'm sure we agree.'

They couldn't even agree on that, Sasha thought to herself, sitting in the train on the way home, much later than she had intended. In fact they spent most of the time disagreeing, however in an amiable, half-joking kind of way. He was indeed deeply knowledgeable about art, had travelled widely, and explained at some length and in some detail why he was fascinated with Titian. But all in all she discovered little about him and probably revealed too much about herself, especially about Ben. She went to some length to explain that he should have been here, but at the last minute had decided not to come. She'd enjoyed herself. Not having Ben had given her an unexpected sense of freedom. She felt now she had said too much and he must have realized what a deeply unsatisfying relationship she was in. She had not wanted to expose herself to such a degree and put it down to the drink, the shared bottle of wine.

Also he was a very good listener. He could easily have been a psychologist because she felt oddly at ease with him and found herself too easily confiding in him. And this was someone she had thought she disliked and wanted to avoid.

Instead she was intrigued by him and also, loath as she was to admit it, increasingly attracted to him as they sat facing each other in the restaurant. A totally unexpected intimacy had developed through eye contact, shared proximity, an entirely different environment from the art class. The fact that it was a chance encounter in London made it seem even exotic.

Martin was a heavily built man, powerful, not especially good looking, with a receding hairline and a crooked nose. His features however were strong and his penetrating deep brown eyes seemed not only to take in a lot, but also to have been witness to a lifetime of experience. How old? Maybe early forties. He'd told her practically nothing about himself; it had all been about her and their favourite artists.

She felt stimulated and happy in his company, but also guilty, although why she wasn't quite sure.

The lunch hadn't finished until after three and she had wanted to get an earlier train. He offered to take her to the station but she refused, saying she wanted to do a bit of shopping, which wasn't quite true but seemed the right thing to say, so they parted outside the restaurant while he went towards Trafalgar Square and, feeling strangely elated, she drifted through Soho exiting halfway up Regent Street and then sauntering along Oxford Street gazing at the shops. She didn't in fact want to buy anything but couldn't resist wandering round Selfridges, which had changed since she was last there as she seldom went into town.

Finally she got a bus to the station and waited half an hour for the next train, which was a stopping one so she was later home than she expected. Even then she dawdled, expecting the usual encounter with Ben about why she was late and where she'd been, which was exactly what she got. There was the smell of cooking and he emerged from the kitchen as she entered, wiping his hands on a cloth.

'I expected you to be in for supper. You said you would be. I told you it was special, casserole. I went to a lot of trouble.'

'Sorry,' she said, stripping off her coat. 'I meant to but I got detained. I daresay it can be heated up and eaten tomorrow.'

'Who were you detained by?' he asked suspiciously.

'I met someone I knew.'

'Who was that?'

'No one you know, one of my students. He was also in the gallery and invited me to lunch.'

'And you never thought to phone me and say you'd be late?'

'Frankly I never did.' She smiled at him. 'I'm not very hungry anyway.'

'And who was this student?'

'A man called Martin. One of the best in the class. I met him in the gallery.'

'By arrangement?'

'No, and in case you don't remember, you and I were originally going together. But you pulled out with a sulk.'

'It wasn't a *sulk*. I just didn't feel like it.'

'Anyway it was fairly last minute and I would hardly have made an assignation, would I?' Her tone grew heated. 'Look, Ben, this wasn't an assignation but a chance encounter with a student who has been in my class for two years, whom I didn't know very well and with whom I would never have made an assignation anyway.'

'I suppose he's about nineteen,' Ben said scathingly. 'I suspect you always hanker after younger men, Sasha. I think you dread getting old, losing your looks.'

The good humour, the sense of well-being engendered by lunch with someone who quite obviously admired and valued her, had well and truly left her and she snapped: 'Don't be so silly, Ben. I'm getting sick of this petty jealousy. It is childish and absurd. Anyway,' she said, suddenly feeling very tired, 'I don't want to continue this ridiculous conversation. I truly forgot you were making supper and I'm sorry, but I have an early class for which I am ill prepared, so I'm off to bed.'

It was a very long time before Ben joined her. In fact she didn't even know about it because she was fast asleep.

Caroline woke with a start, her heart hammering. There had been a loud knock on the door and she knew immediately what that meant. She got out of bed, drew the curtain and looked down to the front door but could see nothing in the pitch dark. She turned on the light, sat on the edge of the bed shaking with fright. She glanced at the clock. It was only just after six. Surely they wouldn't come at *that* hour – or would they? In case it was on TV? She listened for the knock again and then, still shaking, put on her dressing gown and, clasping it around her for warmth, slowly descended the stairs quietly so as not to disturb the children. Her heart still racing she stood by the front door and switched on the outside light, putting an ear to the door, listening for the sound of voices. Silence.

'Is there anyone there?' she called timorously. No answer. Then she drew back the bolt, fastened the chain and opened it a fraction. No one there. She took a step outside and gingerly peered round, then over to the gate; no sign of a car. Could it possibly have been her imagination? It had been so realistic that it didn't seem possible. Her heart still beating she tottered into the kitchen where she made herself a mug of tea and crept slowly upstairs. Then she put the tea on the bedside table and lay down, trying to quieten her rapid heartbeat.

A dream, but such a realistic one. Rationally, she wondered, who would have knocked on the door when there was a bell? But she wasn't feeling rational.

It had not been like this during Greg's other tours abroad. She had worried, sure, but it had not become a real obsession that was destroying her peace of mind, tearing at her life, possibly unsettling the children. For them she tried to keep cheerful and for herself too, endeavouring to occupy herself all the time with tasks, painting, wishing she had a job, anything that would stop her turning on the bulletins to watch the latest from Afghanistan.

Caroline was a tall, fresh faced, pleasant looking woman of thirty-seven, rather buxom, with a tendency to be overweight, which was mitigated by her above-average height. She seldom wore make-up unless she was going out to some function with Greg, when she made an effort. These days she made no effort at all.

She didn't allow herself to doze off again having been well and truly startled because it would soon be time to get the children up and off to school, and in the evening she had Sasha coming for supper, so at least she had something positive to aim for, something to do.

These days she often turned to her painting, a form of therapy as well as entertainment, only she had moved on from flowers and still-lives to imaginary depictions of war scenes. It gave her an interest and a purpose and she discovered an aptitude for painting the human figure which she didn't know she had. The scenes of brown, barren earth and bombed buildings were captured from the television. So, after she had taken the children to school and prepared the evening meal she sat down at the kitchen table and resumed her work, trying to imagine that it linked her to Greg and his life out there. It had been important to hide from him the fact that she was so worried. They e-mailed and talked as frequently as the army and circumstances allowed, so there was no problem keeping in touch and her attitude remained positive for his sake, though often it was an effort.

That evening Sasha listened sympathetically while Caroline, somewhat to her surprise and embarrassment, poured out her heart to her – her mistaken panic about the knock, her fears for Greg. The children were safely in bed and Caroline, who was a good cook, had served braised beef with potatoes and plenty of vegetables. A bottle of red wine stood on the table between them. Finally Caroline realized she had been gabbling and, face flushed, took a gulp of wine. 'I shouldn't be saying all this,' she said. 'I don't know what got into me, you'll be bored stiff.'

'On the contrary,' Sasha said, 'I'm very glad you feel you can talk about it.'

'It's so *unlike* me,' Caroline went on. 'I have been married for fifteen years and I knew when I married that I would be a soldier's wife. But I didn't know that we would be engaged in the sort of war they have in Afghanistan. Compared to this, Ireland didn't seem too bad. You were worried, but the effect on the military was nothing like this. For a while we were based in Germany and he stayed at home training the men who were sent to Iraq. That was bad enough, but he only had a brief spell there. But you'd think I would be used to it by now. Instead it seems to be getting worse.'

'Can't the company of the other army wives help?'

'I can't show my worries to *them*. Greg is in a position of authority, a sergeant, and I have to keep up appearances. I am expected to give a lead, help them. I must be strong, stiff upper lip sort of thing. In fact when I am with them it helps me. It's when I get home that the fear starts, and this time I have been very conscious of what is going on out there. I've had this awful premonition that something would happen to Greg, which I never had before and . . .' To her dismay Caroline burst into tears and for a while sat there sobbing uncontrollably. Sasha got to her feet and put her arms round her.

But she had a terrible feeling of inadequacy. What sort of comfort could she give? So she stood there, hugging her and occasionally patting her back and making soothing noises. Until at last the sobs stopped and Caroline straightened up, dried her eyes and blew her nose vigorously. 'I'm terribly sorry,' she said and reached for the bottle. 'I shouldn't have put you through all this. It's not me at all. Let's have another glass of wine and go and sit down somewhere comfortable.'

'What about the washing-up?' Sasha looked at the plates piled up by the sink.

'Don't worry about the washing-up.' She put an arm round Sasha and led her into the sitting room. 'I want to show you some of my artwork.'

Sasha was quite genuine in her praise of the war pictures. 'They really are astonishingly good,' she said. 'I mean it. For someone who has never done anything like this they are excellent. How you get the colours just right I don't know.'

'I got them from the telly. I record programmes and study them. Pause them while I sketch. I don't know what Greg will say when he comes back.' She stopped abruptly and Sasha felt she was going to cry again.

'He will come back,' she said, 'I promise you.' She marvelled at her boldness and foolhardiness in making such a promise, but it seemed of some comfort to Caroline.

'Do you really think so?'

'I do,' Sasha said firmly, 'and you must be quite sure that *when* he comes back he keeps his promise to leave the army. Tell him that it will really compromise your health, and throw in your marriage for good measure!' She went back to a study of the new paintings. 'I'm afraid you really will have to leave my class. You are getting too good and should go to the advanced level.'

'I don't want to leave you.'

'That's what Martin said, too. I can't understand my popularity. I don't deserve it.'

'You're a good teacher, and kind.' Caroline studied her face. 'Not everyone is like you. Look how sweet you've been to me tonight.'

Sasha put an arm round her waist. 'By the way, I bumped into Martin in London at the National Gallery a couple of weeks ago. He took me to lunch. In a way it was a revelation, quite exciting. He's not so bad. I never really got to know him despite the fact he has been in the class for two years. I want him to move on, but he said he wants to stay.'

'Perhaps he fancies you.'

'Oh, I don't think it's that. I don't know what it is. Anyway he hasn't been to the class for two weeks, so perhaps he's changed his mind and getting to know me better put him off! I think I told him too much about myself. Wine at lunchtime always does things to me. But there was something about him that invites confidences. I said I thought he was a psychologist.'

'And what does he do?'

'He's an engineer. But he does know a lot about art. He's been to most of the main galleries in the UK and abroad. I stupidly told him a lot about my relationship with Ben and I kind of regretted it. Maybe it was too confiding and it embarrassed him.'

'What about Ben?'

'Ah, there you're asking,' Sasha slumped into a chair. 'I'm beginning to feel we're all washed up. It's getting stale. We've been together for eight years. It hasn't gone well for some time. It's deteriorating. The trouble is he depends on me. He doesn't sell any of his paintings, or a few at low prices, and I virtually keep him. He is actually very good, but unlucky so far. It is difficult to know what to do. I don't want to be disloyal to him, and desertion would probably kill him. I don't know how he would handle it, or even if it is really what I want.' There was an unhappy tortured expression on her face.

'Do you talk about it?'

'We row constantly, if you call that talking. I can't throw him out. My mother warned me it would come to nothing if it went on too long, and she likes Ben, and she was right. You see, we were students at the Slade and . . . well. He was one of the personalities. Everyone admired him. It was flattering and exciting for me. I'd had some unsatisfactory relationships and he was very simpatico. He was also a good lover and we had good sex. We enjoyed the same things – art, music, travelling during the holidays. We had some very good times.' For a moment she appeared rather nostalgic for the good times, the really good times they had once enjoyed and when she had really been wholeheartedly in love.

'For a long time we got on very well but about a year or two ago it started to go sour. He is disappointed he hasn't been more commercially successful with his painting. He resents being so dependent on me. But above all he has become very petty and jealous, always asking me where I've been and who with. I have never ever been out with anyone else other than Ben. I told him, almost deliberately I suppose if I'm honest, to make him jealous, about bumping into Martin and he made a thing about it, insinuating I had made an assignation. Since then we've hardly spoken.'

'And I thought I had problems,' Caroline said. 'At least I have a good marriage. Did you ever think of marriage?'

'I never did, and he never suggested it, though he did ask me once if I wanted a baby.'

'And do you?'

'Not with Ben. Not now. But I'm getting on and maybe that is something I think about.'

'I wonder if Martin is married?' Caroline mused.

'Don't be silly,' Sasha laughed and glanced at her watch. 'Golly, did you see the time? I must go.'

In the taxi on the way home Sasha reflected on her evening with Caroline, who thought that the fact she had a good marriage made her problems seem less important than Sasha's. But wondering if your husband was going to get wounded or killed, living in dread of the knock on the door, was a much more serious situation than her relationship with Ben. Neither of their lives were threatened. It was just a miserable existence. Even now she quite dreaded the reception she would get when she got home as she had left no note saying where she was going. In fact she had gone to Caroline straight from the college and hadn't been home all day.

The taxi stopped and she got out, paid and went up the garden noting the fact that none of the house lights were on. It was after eleven and maybe Ben was in bed or sitting in the kitchen ready with his reprimands. She felt that little knot tightening in her chest.

Sasha let herself in and turned on the hall light, went into the kitchen. It all looked very tidy – no unwashed dishes as there usually were because Ben could seldom be bothered to put them in the dishwasher.

She went upstairs, switched on the light in the upstairs hall and entered the bedroom, but she could already see from the hall light that the bed was empty. It all felt kind of strange. She switched on the light and sat on the bed taking off her shoes, partly undressing, and went into the bathroom for her gown. The first thing she noticed was that none of Ben's things were there. Everything looked strangely tidy, nothing out of place, as if someone had gone through the house giving it a good clean; even the bedroom had seemed unusually neat. None of his clothes were flung over the chair. Even the things she usually left around – she wasn't the soul of tidiness either – had been hidden away. A suspicion began to form in her mind and re-entering the bedroom she opened the wardrobe to find that Ben's two, rarely worn, good suits had gone.

It seemed an indisputable fact, now, that Ben had left.

Her first feeling was one of alarm, almost fear. It was not as she had expected to feel, but then she had never seriously entertained the idea.

She looked around wondering if she'd missed a note of some sort. Nothing. Then back downstairs to the kitchen and living room and, finally, in a place they hardly ever used, she saw the envelope on the mantelpiece just as one saw countless times in a film or book.

She realized her heart rate was increasing as she sat down and slowly slit open the envelope.

Dear Sasha,

As you are reading this letter by now you might have realized I have gone. I hope it is a relief, though it might also be a shock. Maybe it was sneaky of me to do it this way, but I couldn't face you, and I didn't relish the prospect of a confrontation with all the recriminations that would follow. Or I might have stayed on and we would have gone through all this again. As the do-gooders say, our relationship seems to have broken down.

I have known for some time that you were getting tired of me. Maybe you also despised me for living off you and not realizing the hopes we had for my career as an artist. I decided I would rather do it this way than suffer the indignity of being pushed out. I also think we had begun to be cruel to each other and I am sorry I made the remark the other night about younger men. It had no truth at all in reality and I think you are a terrific looking woman and it was a nasty and unnecessary thing for me to say.

This way I think it is best and it is permanent. I will be staying with my parents, for now, but I would ask you not to call me or contact me in any way for the time being and I promise not to pester you, though I shall miss you.

It is quite a wrench for me to leave the place which has been my home for so many years. Maybe I should learn to stand on my own feet, get a 'proper' job, be independent? Please Sasha, darling, don't think I am ungrateful for all you have done for me. I still love you and hope that after all we have been to each other you may retain some affection for me. I hope one day we meet again as friends.

Then it was just signed with his name.

Sasha didn't know how long she sat there, brooding, thoughts jumbled, but she began to feel very cold and finally, aware how emotionally exhausted she was, she slowly made her way upstairs to bed. As she pulled the duvet over herself she realized how long it was since she had slept alone.

Relief or shock?

She couldn't yet be sure, or even, now that it had happened, if it was really what she wanted.

Four

Moira and Alice sat in the car drinking tea out of a thermos and eating slices of rich fruit-cake that Moira had baked. The car faced the sea, which shimmered enticingly in the wintry sun, and on the horizon was the blurry outline of a ship passing on its way to Southampton or Portsmouth. They had decided to watch the last rays of the sun setting over the bay before going to the painting class.

The companionable silence was finally broken by Alice, who turned to Moira.

'What a lovely scene it is, on a perfect winter's day. It is so mild you can't believe it's so near Christmas. I can't tell you how grateful I am for bringing me.'

'It's a pleasure,' Moira replied, dusting the crumbs from her lap. 'It's a treat for me too. I realize that I seldom make the time to stand and stare, as the poet has it. Too beset with worries and problems at the moment I guess.'

'Oh?' Alice looked at her in surprise. 'That bad?' Her expression changed to one of sympathy. 'I expect you have not got over the death of your husband.'

'That and . . .'

Moira felt a sudden urge to confide in this kind, sympathetic and obviously wise woman who she hardly knew. They had only met a couple of times outside the class and yet already she felt a bond with her.

'Well, I have recently discovered something about my daughter Vanessa which has upset me a lot. There is no one I can talk to about it.'

'Do you want to talk to me about it?' Alice enquired gently. 'Is that what you're saying?'

'If you can bear it. It's pretty shocking.'

'Try me.'

'Well, she has by any standards a very good life, has everything she wants. There is no shortage of money. She is married with two beautiful young children, a lovely home and a good and loving husband – in short a happy and affluent lifestyle you would have thought would be enough for anybody. However . . .' Moira paused and took a deep breath as if reliving the pain of the moment that Vanessa broke the news. 'She recently told me she is having an affair. Her husband is away a lot, half the year if not more. He is the overseas director of a big pharmaceutical company; but I still don't consider that any excuse for Vanessa's behaviour.

'The man in question is also much younger than my daughter. In fact he is a swimming guard at the local pool and she also thinks she can help him to get a better job. She said this is how it started. He has had little education, comes from a dysfunctional family, the usual story. The sort of thing that appeals to Vanessa. She is always into good works and helping people. This time she has in my opinion gone too far, jeopardized her whole life and that of a normal happy family. I am terrified of the effect on her marriage, especially if Ian, her husband, finds out. He is a very nice man and I like him, but I don't think he would be at all understanding about it. There. I hope it hasn't shocked you. I was afraid it might.' She looked anxiously at Alice who impulsively put a reassuring hand on her arm.

'It hasn't shocked me at all. I was the headmistress of a big inner city comprehensive and I think nothing now does or ever will shock me. I am just so sorry for *you*, my dear.'

Moira had found little out about her new friend apart from the fact that she had been a teacher and had never married. She supposed that, because Alice was such a gentle person, in her mind she had formed the idea of a charming little country school cut off from anywhere, giving her few chances to meet anyone. She had invited Alice to tea and in that time had talked mostly about herself and losing Bob. So much for misconceptions.

'However,' Alice went on when Moira didn't answer, 'what can you really do about it? I imagine she is a headstrong young woman?'

'Oh yes. She was an air hostess. She is considered very beautiful and always had men swarming round her. I was quite surprised she married Ian so quickly after meeting him, or rather after dating him. As he travels a lot she saw him quite often on the plane before he asked her out. But he too is very attractive, charming and somehow settled and solid, which appealed to her, a rock not unlike her adored father, who was already ill. Their marriage was rather hurried because of this. She wanted her father to take her down the aisle. But I think they were in love and really happy, so why she should find it necessary to rush into bed with a teenager I do not know, and it makes me very cross.'

'Oh, he is as young as that?'

'Nineteen and she is twenty-eight. Isn't it absurd?'

Alice didn't answer but reached for Moira's hand and squeezed it.

Moira seemed to come to with a start as if recovering from a reverie. 'There,' she said briskly with an air of false jollity. 'I feel better already. Now we must get a move on or we will be late for our class. By the way,' she said, 'I wonder if you would like to have Christmas lunch with us? We take it in turns, Vanessa and I, and this year it is my turn. Just the family. No fuss. I'd love you to be there.'

Alice was too moved for a moment to speak.

'Well,' she said at last. 'If you're sure, there is nothing I'd like better.'

'That's settled then,' Moira said and, after stowing the picnic things in the boot, she drove off towards the town, the pair remaining silent as if both were lost in their respective thoughts.

Sasha walked slowly round, inspecting the work of her students who were busy with their tasks. It was the last class before Christmas, and time for assessments. Some had progressed well during the term. Some, notably Pauline and another woman called Jess, had made no progress at all. Yet she thought Pauline was at least trying, even though she had no real feeling for painting, and would probably want to continue.

Of Martin there had been no sign since they had met in London. This was the third week he had not shown up. Out of sight out of mind? Not quite. She wondered if he would ever come back. But she certainly didn't care – or told herself she didn't – as, except for that brief frisson in the restaurant, he meant nothing to her on a personal level. However, it left a funny little question mark in her mind as if wondering if there was, or just might be, a connection with their meeting. It was like unfinished business. Once again, she was sorry she had confided so much in him, revealed so much of herself. Perhaps it was not a good idea to become involved with one's students, and yet she and Caroline had a definite friendship going. Maybe she should also be careful about that, not become too close. It was a dilemma one faced as a teacher with adult students.

Caroline had made most progress of all. She had become quite ambitious and had begun to give extra dimensions to the picture by adding a wash and sharpening the image. Sasha stood by her side studying her work. 'You could heighten the colour and texture of the fruit by using a stipple effect, with cadmium yellow and maybe viridian. Just a suggestion.'

Caroline put her head on one side. 'I'll think about it,' she said, sounding apathetic.

Caroline looked tired and Sasha leaned closer and whispered: 'Everything OK?'

'OK.' Caroline replied and something about her fixed expression and the way she bent her head immediately back to her work made Sasha feel she didn't want to talk about it. Maybe she regretted confiding in her too.

So she returned to her table and began looking through some of the work that had been handed in. There were also some cards, for which she had thanked individuals, and a little, as yet unwrapped, gift from Alice which moved her a lot. She felt warmed, perhaps even loved, by her class and it did a little to improve her mood, which these days was largely one of dejection and depression. She felt tired all the time. Tired and somehow disconnected. Ben's abrupt departure had radically changed her life; left her feeling vulnerable and insecure in a way she could never have anticipated. Also angry, so she was beset by a strange mixture of conflicting emotions and, yes, she wasn't sleeping well and had difficulty concentrating on her work.

All the bad things that had happened before, the reproaches, the rows, seemed of minor significance compared to this desertion. After all they had lived together for nearly ten years, but as students they had known each other for a lot longer. It was almost as though they'd grown up together. So when did it begin, this inability to communicate? Slowly and subtly it had somehow slipped into their relationship, them growing more apart without ever even noticing it, until it was too late. She supposed she would never have guessed how much she would miss Ben until he'd gone. Christmas being round the corner didn't help. They usually went away for a few days and this year had thought they might go to Paris. She wondered if he had even considered this.

The bell rang for the end of classes and people began the usual routine for packing up. Some remained at their tables or easels rapidly finishing something off.

'I'd like to wish you all a Happy Christmas,' she said. 'See you in the new year.' There were responsive murmurs all round.

Caroline was the first to join her as they left the room. 'Sorry if I seemed offhand,' she told her.

'Don't worry about it. I think you have lot on your mind.'

'I shouldn't have burdened you with it.'

'Oh, you didn't at all. If anything I reciprocated.' She realized that she didn't want to tell Caroline about Ben. That would really make her feel foolish.

'That's what friends are for, isn't it?' Caroline asked as they entered the brightly lit canteen and queued for coffee.

Moira and Alice were already sitting down as Caroline and Sasha joined them, Roger slipping nimbly into the seat beside her, something she thought he made a habit of doing, though he never seemed to find much to say. Roger however was making quite a lot of progress in his work and she didn't want to discourage him.

'What's happened to Martin?' Roger asked. 'We haven't seen him in class recently.'

'Honestly I have no idea.' Sasha sipped her coffee.

'Has he given up?'

'I really don't know.' Irritated by his question, which seemed rather pointed, she turned to Alice.

'The work you handed in tonight was really charming. Is it a scene you know?'

'I painted it from memory.' Alice smiled with pleasure.

'It's very good. I think you have had a lot of experience and it shows.'

'Thank you.'

'What are you doing for Christmas?' Moira asked.

'Oh nothing much, and you?'

'Spending it with the family. I always do.'

'I expect I shall too.'

'Happily, Alice is joining us this year.'

'That's really nice.' Sasha looked pleased and was.

'I'm really lucky to be asked,' Alice said. 'My art class has been a blessing in more ways than one.'

It was accepted by now that Moira drove Alice home and, after a while and a little more desultory conversation, Sasha got up. 'I hope everyone will excuse me, but I need an early night. To everyone again, Happy Christmas.'

As she shrugged on her coat Alice got up and kissed her.

'Thank you so much for all you've done. I have thoroughly enjoyed the term.' She stepped back and regarded her critically. 'You look very tired tonight, my dear, are you all right?'

'I'm absolutely fine, but have a heavy load at the moment at college and with Christmas coming there is a lot to do, so I'll be glad of the break.'

With a wave of her hand she left the room and, buttoning up her coat, wrapping her scarf more securely round her, as it was a cold, blustery night, she made her way across the Institute grounds to her car. Suddenly she was aware of footsteps hurrying behind her. It was a very dark, moonless night and the car park was some distance away from the Institute. Feeling a moment of apprehension she stopped as she put the key in the lock and looked behind and saw Roger approaching.

'Oh,' she said, partly relieved and partly irritated, 'I thought I was being followed. It's you.'

'Sorry if I startled you.' Roger paused and even in the dark she could sense his apprehension.

'Is there something you want?' She was unable to keep the ice from her voice.

'It's just that, Sasha, well I wondered if you would like to have a meal one night. You know . . .' He faltered. 'In a restaurant.'

'Well . . .' Completely taken aback, now it was Sasha who was floundering. 'It is very nice of you, Roger, but . . .'

'I'd like to discuss my work with you, know what you really think of it. In a relaxed, more informal atmosphere. They say Luigi's in the High Street is good. It hasn't been opened long.'

'We could certainly discuss your work, Roger, but I would prefer to do it in class or after class. Please don't misunderstand me, and I don't misunderstand you, but I have a partner and he might get the wrong impression if I went out with a bloke. It may sound feeble, but that's the way it is. Now if you don't mind I must get home as it's late. Maybe we can talk about your work next term in class? If you remind me again I'll make time for it.'

In the light of a headlamp of one of the cars reversing out of the bay next to them she saw the chagrin and disappointment registered on his face, so she added in a kindly voice: 'I hope you understand. Have a good Christmas.'

By now freezing, she then jumped into her car not listening to his reply, if there was one, because he turned his back on her and walked quickly away.

She drove home furious with herself and him. It was an obvious attempt at a date, explained now by the way he always sidled up next to her in the canteen. In such a place and at such a time this encounter had been totally out of place. But the way she had dealt with it had, she felt, been too abrupt, even ruthless. The truth was Roger irritated her and always had. There are people who for no reason seem to rub one up the wrong way and for her Roger was such a person. Why should he have asked her where Martin was? It was almost as if he knew of their London meeting, which was impossible, but there was something about the way he asked it. Something knowing, even suggestive, which annoyed her even more.

Caroline couldn't get to sleep. This followed a similar pattern since Greg had gone. She either couldn't get to sleep or was awakened by a bad dream, trembling and sweating, imagining once again she had heard a knock on the door. She knew her nerves were frayed and this bothered her even more. She had been rather terse with Sasha and thought that Sasha had been odd with her, offhand and remote. As it was, she was beginning to lose friends because she didn't want her unease to show, particularly to the army wives. She was meant to be so strong: a leader, tough and resolute, focused like Greg.

She didn't want to go to the doctor because that would be a sign of weakness too. Anyway, she thought these army doctors noticed things like that and might even report them to the authorities, were perhaps expected to – crack-ups, warning signals, that kind of thing, which inevitably would reach Greg. There might be no end of trouble. So she didn't want anyone to know of her fragile state, and that included Sasha to whom she had shown her weakness all too clearly. Her only tower of strength was her mother in whom she had often confided, but then she didn't want to upset her either, at a critical time so near Christmas, by revealing the depth of her depression. So far she had done her best, she thought successfully, to hide it from the children and in a way it helped her to maintain some normality, but essentiality she was in a terrible spiral of fear and despair and didn't know what to do about it, how to overcome it. The fact that Christmas was coming made it worse except that they would go to her mother's for the day. Her sister, who was a single parent, would come from Manchester with her kids and everyone would do their best to have a good time and she, and perhaps also her sister, would drink a bit too much to try and blot out their worries, and perhaps for a moment, just a moment, she would overcome her sense of a bottomless pit opening beneath her feet.

It was dawn before she drifted into an uneasy sleep from which she was almost immediately woken by the alarm clock and time to get the children up for school.

Roger's children were of an age, seven and nine, when they were relatively independent and easy to entertain. They were surprisingly normal, well-balanced boys considering the trauma of their parents' separation and subsequent divorce. This was largely due to the efforts made by both, but especially their mother Kay, being careful not to burden their children with their own discord, and they had also been careful never to row in front of them. In fact, there had been very few rows. They had just grown apart in a chilly, silent kind of way. Kay was a teacher and had developed interests of her own and a social circle of busy, like-minded people that excluded Roger.

Roger had always been a rather quiet, introverted kind of man and consequently was attracted to women who were his opposite: Kay was outgoing, friendly. In time they came to lead separate lives and in the end even had separate holidays, though there was the regulation summer break at the seaside with the boys.

There was a game of football going on in the park which the boys had joined and Roger stood on the sidelines watching them, hands deep in his pockets, scarf wound tightly round his neck. After the game he would take them to McDonald's and then maybe a film. They were spending the night with him and the next day would be similar, a walk or game in the park or maybe drive to the sea if the weather was in any way decent.

Roger missed his kids, but he didn't miss family life as it had been with Kay. As their marriage grew stale she spent a lot of time putting him down, making him feel inadequate, 'boring' becoming a word she used often. She would even joke about it in public, showing him up, when on rare occasions they were out together.

However, since the divorce his life had been almost as aimless and pointless as it was before and he found it difficult to be interested in anything except his painting, which he would like to have taken more seriously. He would also have liked an affair and in Sasha he had decided there was a woman who combined femininity and sexual attraction with expertise in something that interested him: art. She had a lot in common with Kay in her extrovert personality and sexuality, but he didn't think she would have Kay's unkindness and acid tongue.

He felt he had handled asking Sasha out very stupidly, on a cold night, in the dark when she had already said she was tired. He had also frightened her by following her into the car park, which in retrospect was also a stupid thing to have done. He should have asked her to step aside indoors, in the light and warmth but away from other people. In short he had made a disaster of the whole thing and he could imagine Kay saying, in her nasty, sneering way, that it was typical of him.

But any thoughts of reviving the opportunity on a more propitious occasion were dashed when she said she had a partner who would object to her going out with another man. Of course a woman like her would have a partner. She was far too attractive to be single.

This had been a bitter blow. He had been encouraged by her in what he thought was her interest in him in class when she frequently stopped by his table to make encouraging remarks. He even imagined she glanced at him provocatively because he knew he wasn't a bad-looking guy. He thought that, though clever and attractive and bit of a flirt, like Kay, she was innately a kind woman, which Kay wasn't, and this was the sort of thing he was looking for. He was wrong. Sasha's reception of him had been unnerving and rather unkind in a way he hadn't expected.

The game was still going on and the boys were obviously enjoying it, but he was getting colder standing still on the spot so he decided to take a walk and try to warm himself up.

He set off at a brisk pace along the path that led to a pond. It was a large pretty park and he felt that on a good day like today he should make more of it. There were tennis courts, a children's playground and a large pond teeming with birdlife. In many ways he lived too much the life of solitude which, despite his solitary nature, he didn't particularly enjoy. He stood by the side of the pond watching a woman throwing a stick into the water for a large golden retriever, which kept on fetching it and running back to her, shaking itself as it lay it at her feet while she laughingly stepped back to avoid a soaking. It was at that moment that they caught sight of each other, their faces breaking into expressions of recognition and surprise.

She threw the stick far out into the pond again and, as the dog dashed after it, she walked across to Roger.

'Hello Roger,' she called.

'Why, hello Pauline. Fancy seeing you here. I didn't know you had a dog.'

'I haven't; he belongs to a friend and I occasionally walk him for her if she is busy or unwell, as she is at the moment with a migraine. What brings you to the park? The rare glimpse of sunshine?'

She cocked her head on one side, not quite sure whether she was glad to see him or not. Since he had gone to her flat they had scarcely spoken to each other except in a desultory way after class, when he always made a beeline to secure a place next to Sasha, which was so obvious it was almost embarrassing.

'My children, actually.' He pointed towards the playing field in the distance. 'They are indulging in a vigorous game of football and I was freezing.'

The dog bounded up to Pauline, shaking drops of water all over her and she stood back, grasping Roger by the arm who stood back too.

'He's a lovely dog,' Roger said.

'His name is Rusty. He is only three. I think I'll finish with the water or I'll be soaking.' And she threw the stick towards the trees at the side. 'I wouldn't mind walking too. It *is* terribly cold.'

'Come and meet my boys. They should be finished soon.'

'I'd like that, but unfortunately . . .' Pauline glanced at her watch. 'I have to take Rusty back to his owner, who also wanted me to get some stuff for her from the chemist. Maybe another time?'

'Well I have them every other weekend. You'll find me by the playing field.'

'I'll look out for you,' Pauline said. 'Nice to see you again.'

'And you. Oh, and I'll also have them for some time over Christmas,' Roger said, almost as an afterthought. 'Are you around at Christmas?'

'I'll be around some of the time,' she said. 'I'm going to my parents' for a few days, but Rusty is bound to need walking so I'll look out for you. Bye.'

She summoned Rusty, put him on a lead and gave Roger a cheery wave.

'Cheers,' he said and stood for some time watching her as she walked briskly off with the dog. Seeing her in this new setting, away from the class, made him appraise her afresh. She didn't have the allure or sensuality of Sasha, but she had a good figure, and there was a certain something about her which he seemed to have missed before: she was more alive, her cheeks pink from the cold, her eyes sparkling, a fetching woolly cap with a tassel at a jaunty angle on her head.

He turned towards the field, arriving at the touchline just as the final whistle blew on the game.

Alice had just converted her small spare room into a studio and had set up her easel by the window. She was flattered by Sasha's praise of her painting done from memory, so today she had set out to try and recapture the scene of the sea when she and Moira had sat in the car drinking tea from a thermos and looking at the view.

How fortunate that she had decided to refresh herself and take up watercolour painting again, abandoned many years ago when her sister became ill, and how lucky to have met such a nice crowd of people, Moira in particular.

After retirement Alice had moved with her sister to a small village in the Blackmore Vale in Dorset where they had taken holidays in the past, mostly for the opportunity it offered for bracing country walks in beautiful countryside. This had turned out to be a mistake, a case of misplaced optimism. Despite the fact that they had bought a pretty house with a large garden, they had forgotten that they were both older than when they used to be able to walk for miles; arthritis made gardening increasingly difficult and also they knew nobody and made few friends. They had only one or two distant relatives who led their own lives and seldom made contact with them. After her sister became ill it was an especially isolating place to be. So when she died Alice had eventually decided to move to a larger town near the sea and thus she had come to Redbury, where again she knew no one, after seeing an advertisement for a newly built block of luxury retirement flats with all facilities and a live-in warden. It guaranteed independence but also security and help if needed, which at her age she had to face, reluctantly, that one day she might. This proved to be the case when her arthritis worsened and she had to have a hip replacement. All this Alice had coped with by herself, except for professional and medical personnel, and to feel that her social life might be expanding thanks wholly to the watercolour class was a boon and gave an added zest to her life.

Wholly absorbed in her task, trying in her mind's eye to recapture that day and the special way the light played on the sea, Alice heard the doorbell ring and reluctantly placed her brush in water and went to open the door.

To her surprise Moira stood on the other side, an apologetic look on her face.

'So sorry I didn't telephone, Alice, but I have been in town and left my mobile at home, so I took a chance to pop in. I hope I haven't disturbed anything?'

'Of course not.' Alice stepped back, a broad smile on her face. 'I am delighted to see you. I have been doing some painting and I needed a break. Coffee?'

'Coffee would be lovely,' Moira said and, shutting the door behind her, followed Alice into the kitchen and looked appreciatively around, as it was the first time she had been right inside. 'These flats are really very nice. I remember when they were building them.'

'I'm very happy here.' Alice put the kettle on and pointed to a seat by the kitchen table. 'It has everything I need, there is plenty of space, and yes it is all very nicely done.'

'Do you see much of the other residents?'

'Practically nothing. Like me they seem all very independent, preferring to keep themselves to themselves. There is a communal lounge that I never use. I think people mostly bring guests there. Some of the flats are smaller, but I wanted one of the larger ones. Of course we always greet one another in the hall but that is about it.'

'So no new friends?'

'No. A warden pops in every day to see we are OK, but I don't think he is overworked. He is also a janitor and we report any problems or defects to him. He was very good when I had my hip replacement – and so were social services, I must say. I was well looked after.'

The kettle having boiled, Alice spooned coffee into two cups. 'I'm afraid it's only instant.'

'It's what I use myself.'

'Milk, sugar?'

'Both, please. One spoon.'

She took the cups from Alice who led her back into the spacious sitting room which was pleasurably uncluttered, with good furniture, obviously brought from her house, one or two antiques, and paintings on the wall.

'Yours?' Moira asked.

'One or two. That and that.' She pointed to a couple of attractive rural scenes. 'I painted around where we lived in Dorset. The Blackmore Vale is very beautiful. The others are originals but not by me. I like to buy paintings at exhibitions by local artists and it is surprising how good they can be.'

'I know.' Moira sank into a comfortable chair and placed her cup on a small table on which was a plant and some books, but not coffee-table books; the sort that people actually read.

'It is very cosy,' she said, looking round. 'And what are you painting now?'

'Oh, from memory again. I so loved the day we had by the sea and I'm trying to recapture that. Not very well, I'm afraid. I don't know that Sasha would approve. I've made my tiny spare room – or box room maybe it should be called – into a studio.'

'I did the same thing with my daughter's room when she left home. But we have rather a big house so there was plenty of space.'

'And your son still lives with you?'

'Well, no. He is a research fellow at Oxford and he has a flat there. He visits quite often though.'

'How nice. I love Oxford. My sister trained at the Radcliffe. There and London.'

'Was she older or younger than you?'

'Older. She was the matron of a large hospital in the north of England, but she became disillusioned when it all changed and hospital managers stepped in, so she took early retirement. Now I think they want to return to the old idea of a matron-in-charge, which is as it should be.'

'She was matron and you were the headmistress of a large school?'

'A comprehensive in Birmingham.'

'Then you both did very well in life. You should be very proud.'

Alice sighed. 'Yes, but both missed out on marriage and children, which is something I think we both came to regret as we got older. We had no family much of our own to speak of, one or two distant cousins. But you have to make some sacrifices in life and that was how it all turned out. There are compensations. We were able to travel and enjoy holidays abroad together.'

Alice, having finished her coffee, looked at Moira's cup. 'Have you finished? I'd like to show you my studio.'

Moira got up, put the cups together, and went into the kitchen, rejoining Alice in the small hall.

'This is my bedroom.' Alice opened the door into a good-sized room also plainly but simply furnished with built-in cupboards and wardrobe, a separate dressing table and a single bed. Paintings again on the walls and some portraits in heavy silver frames on her dressing table.

'This is my sister, Sybil,' she said, and Moira looked at a handsome but rather stern-faced woman who she could imagine maintaining strict discipline in the hospital.

'These are my parents.' She lifted one of the frames which showed a handsome couple sitting side by side with a large dog between them, the man heavily moustached, the woman serene and beautiful. 'My father was a doctor, Mother a teacher and this . . .' She took up a third portrait of a good-looking, much younger man, and flicked a spec of dust off with a finger. 'This is my fiancé, Bernard.'

'Oh?' Moira's face lit up with interest. 'What happened to him?'

For a moment a shadow seemed to pass across Alice's expressive features.

'He died, I'm afraid. He was in the Colonial Service, a teacher too. He went to Nigeria with the idea that we would be married on his first leave, but he caught that horrible disease bilharzia while swimming in a river in a remote part of the country and when he eventually reached hospital it was too late to treat it.'

Moira instinctively put her hands to her face in shock. 'How awful. You must have been devastated.'

'Yes, of course I was. I had the chance to go to Africa with him. He wanted to get married before we went, but I enjoyed my teaching career and I was only twenty-seven at the time, young and carefree, so I thought a few more years would make no difference. Well I was wrong.' She faltered and gave a deep sigh as though the memory was still too vivid to be bearable and gently, almost tenderly, replaced the frame on the table.

By this time they had moved slowly into Alice's studio, which was strewn with her work in various stages. Moira picked up one of the large sheets of paper and studied the painting with admiration. 'I don't know why you joined the beginners' class. You are much too advanced.'

'It's kind of you to say so but I was very rusty. Since Sybil's death four years ago I hadn't painted at all, and only a bit during her illness. Painting is a great therapy.'

'I agree with you about that,' Moira said. 'It helped me a lot after Bob died, but I am not nearly as good as you; you should move on.'

'But I like our class and I love Sasha. She is such a kind person and . . .' She looked hesitantly across at her friend. 'I met you. I hope you don't consider me a burden?'

'On the contrary! I regard it as a very great bonus to have met you, but look, there is something I feel I must tell you. That is really why I popped in.'

'Let's go into the sitting room again.' Alice led her into the sitting room lit by the pale wintry sunshine.

'It's about . . . well . . .' Moira paused awkwardly. 'Vanessa has invited Tim the boyfriend to spend Christmas with them. She says it is purely out of pity, as he has nowhere to go. I can't tell you how cross I am. It seems such an extraordinary, really stupid and thoughtless thing to do.'

Alice could hardly hide her own surprise. 'Well . . . I don't quite know what to say. I mean, her husband will be home?'

'Of course. She says she is going to tell him that he is teaching the children to swim and has nowhere else to go and she is helping him to improve himself and she felt sorry for him, all of which is true in part. She has it all worked out.'

'Well it does seem odd . . .' Alice paused, still rather lost for words.

'The thing is they will be bringing him to our place for Christmas lunch and . . .' Moira shrugged, almost it seemed on the verge of despair.

'Would you rather I didn't come?'

'Not at all. Not for a moment. That is if *you* don't mind.'

'*I* don't mind at all. In fact I must confess I am rather intrigued, though perhaps I shouldn't say it.'

'I haven't met him myself, but at times I have felt tempted to pop into the swimming baths to see this man who has ensnared my daughter, although maybe she ensnared him. I am so upset about the situation because Ian is such a nice bloke.' She gave a deep, heartfelt sigh. 'I just wanted to tell you that Tim will be there, so that you know the situation.'

'And don't put my foot in it.' Alice smiled and reached across for Moira's hand. 'Don't worry. I shan't let you down.'

There was a lot to do before the holidays began, lectures to think about and prepare, and Sasha sat at her desk drawing up sched-ules for the new term before leaving in a few days to spend

Christmas with her parents. She enjoyed her work, was one of the senior lecturers and she knew that, on the whole, she was highly regarded by her students and colleagues. Of course, as she'd told Martin, there were the usual discords which seem inevitably part of academic life. Some people one liked more than others, and some who she knew didn't like her – maybe because they were jealous? But she had the respect and confidence of her boss, Trevor Judge, Head of Department and quite an eminent artist in his own right. He was one of the few people she had told about Ben, one of the very few whose sympathy she knew she could count on.

The College of Art was near the building that housed the adult education classes, in the same rather worn-down area of the town, which had been quite badly bombed during the war, in common with many seaside locations on the south coast. Like them too the area had been rebuilt in a rather higgledy-piggledy way and could have done with a bit of modern town planning, which had been absent in those chaotic post-war years when people just wanted somewhere to live.

Sasha shared an office with two other members of staff who had already left for their holidays. It was a welcome change to have the place to herself. Her desk in a corner was surrounded by books and papers, with a notice board festooned with memoranda, schedules and all the paraphernalia of a busy and productive life. Compared to the job of teaching future professional artists the evening class was a picnic. Few of the College of Art students would ever achieve greatness, or even a decent living in a precarious profession, like poor Ben. The evening class students were there as a hobby, and she enjoyed teaching them or helping them to improve their talents, if they had them, and even if they didn't, if they were enthusiastic enough.

There was a tap on the door and she called, 'Come in,' without turning round. Whoever it was remained silent whereupon Sasha swung round in her chair, and saw Martin standing looking at her.

'Martin!' she exclaimed and then, realizing that she had gone pink, she turned back to her desk in an endeavour to hide a moment of extreme confusion and embarrassment.

'Sorry,' he said. 'Did I disturb you?'

'Of course not.' Removing her spectacles, Sasha got to her feet. 'It's just that it was a surprise to see you. I was not expecting you.'

'Of course you weren't. I was passing the college and thought that I should pop in and explain why I have been away from the classes, wish you a happy Christmas.'

'Oh, that's quite OK.' She feigned indifference and, feeling that she had regained her composure, pointed to a chair. 'Do sit down. How are you? It's nice to see you.'

'I am very well, and you?'

'I'm fine.'

'And Ben?'

'He's fine too.'

'Good.'

There followed an awkward pause, of the kind that occurred when people knew that, although there was a lot to say, they didn't know how to say it.

'I wondered if you'd like to have dinner? Tonight, if possible. I've been exceptionally busy and I'm going away straight after Christmas. I'm not quite sure when I'll be back. That's what I wanted to explain.'

'Oh dear.' Sasha, aware of a crushing feeling of disappointment, knew it was absurd, but didn't know what to do about it. Martin had somehow achieved a place deep in her subconscious.

'I'd like talk to you. I've missed you.'

She was certainly not going to say that she had missed him too. She turned back to her desk and pretended to consult her diary, which she knew quite well was free of social engagements for that night and most others.

'Well, tonight . . .' she murmured, looking at the blank entry as if that was in doubt.

'Would Ben mind?'

'Oh, I don't expect so.'

'Did you tell him about London?'

'Of course, why should I hide it?'

'I thought it was quite special.'

'Yes, it was really nice.' Trying to sound offhand, while feeling anything but. 'Well, tonight I think will be alright,' she said eventually 'They say Luigi's is quite good, in the High Street. I could meet you there.'

'Oh, I thought of somewhere out of town. Do you know The Fortescue?'

She shook her head.

'It's a pub that does very good food. A bit more discreet, out of the way. I could pick you up here.'

'Well,' she looked at him and smiled, 'what can I say? You have a date. I do have to work a bit late, so seven?'

'Seven it is.'

As she saw him to the door she knew she was shaking, and wondered if it showed.

The Fortescue was quite a distance from the town, isolated on a narrow country lane between two villages. It was small and intimate with a dining room off the bar in which, on a cold winter's night, and in spite of the festive season, there were few drinkers. The dining room had fewer than half a dozen couples and Martin and Sasha, who had been given a choice of tables, selected one in the corner near a blazing fire.

'You wonder how places like this keep going,' Sasha said, rubbing her hands.

'Are you cold?' he enquired solicitously.

'Oh no, I don't mean that. So few people.'

'It's busy at weekends. You have to book a table on a Friday and Saturday and they do a carvery on a Sunday.'

'So you come here quite often?'

'No, not a lot, but I like it and when I have the chance I take it. What are you doing for Christmas?'

'Nothing much – and you?'

Martin shrugged. 'The same. Preparing for an important over-seas trip, I expect.'

They were interrupted by the waitress, who looked like the lady who had been behind the bar as they came in, with menus and an enquiry about drinks.

'It's only a short menu,' she said. 'The recession, you know,' she added meaningfully. 'Little evening trade during the week.'

'My friend here was commenting on it,' Martin said, pointing to Sasha. 'But I told her you were very busy at weekends.'

'It will perk up the week before Christmas,' said the waitress, who might have been the landlady. 'We're booked up at lunch time for the Christmas menu, but people are not so keen on going out in the evenings, what with the smoking ban and the police busy trying to catch drink drivers. Well, I don't need to say anything else, do I?'

'I'll just have a beer to drink,' Martin said, 'as I'm driving. You?' He looked across at Sasha.

'I'd just like a glass of wine.'

'We've a nice chardonnay, or do you prefer red?'

'Chardonnay sounds fine. I might have a glass of red later, depending on what I eat.'

They both settled for smoked salmon as a starter followed by steak, the best and most obvious of the basic choices available. Martin stuck to his single bottle of beer and Sasha added a glass of red to go with her steak. Intent on their food they had just chatted casually over dinner, mostly about the economic situation and the worldwide collapse of confidence in the banks and its effect on the country. Sasha had not thought she was hungry until the tempting, nicely served dishes were placed before her.

'Excellent meal,' she said, when they had finished. 'I see why you like it.'

'Pudding?'

'No, I'm absolutely full up. But you do . . .'

He waved a hand. 'Nothing for me. We must come again.' He looked at her searchingly and his tone of voice changed. 'I really have missed you, Sasha. I've been away a lot on business, but I thought about you a great deal. Between ourselves, Warrington's are having a very difficult time. The building business is in the doldrums, even abroad in places like Dubai where I was last week. Most of their ambitious building plans are on hold. I won't be able to come to many art classes next term or in the future.'

'That's a pity, Martin, because you are good.'

'And I like it. It gives me a break from business worries.' After a pause, he asked, 'How are things with Ben? Tell me to mind my own business if I shouldn't ask, but you did say . . .'

'I know I said too much on that day. I felt afterwards I'd given a lot of myself away, which I didn't mean to do. But there is something about you, Martin, that engenders trust. That's why I asked you if you were a psychologist.'

'I was flattered by your confidence and trust.'

'Well the truth is that Ben and I have parted. We no longer live together or see each other. I didn't completely tell the truth when I said he was fine. I don't know how he is or where he is and, frankly, now I don't much care.'

'Oh dear.' Martin looked down at his plate. 'I am sorry. I mean, the relationship had lasted for some time?'

'Years. He just left me. I came home one night and he was gone.'

'How distressing for you. Or was it?'

'It was very distressing. The way it happened was not nice. It was like a betrayal. I don't know if that makes sense? No talk, no discussion, no second chances, nothing. Do you know what I mean?'

'I think I understand,' Martin said, 'although I would not be honest if I didn't say that it was lucky for me. I hope.'

'I know absolutely nothing about you.' Sasha looked steadily at him, wanting to settle a question mark that Caroline had raised in her mind. 'Have you ever been married?'

'Once, very briefly; it didn't work out.'

'Children?'

'No children. I don't think I'm the marrying kind.'

'I don't think I am either,' Sasha said.

There was a long pregnant pause in the course of which they both looked at each other for a long time, the feeling of intimacy that had been there all evening, just lurking under the surface, deepening. Finally it was broken by Martin, who reached across and put his hand over hers.

'I think we might be together for a long time,' he said, softly. 'You know I've fancied you rotten for ages.'

'I can't say I fancied you,' Sasha said, with a teasing smile.

'In fact, you didn't like me, did you?'

'Well, not much. I though you were arrogant and opinionated.'

'And London changed that?'

She nodded. 'Yes it did.'

'I'm sorry I couldn't let you know. But I had to go abroad suddenly. It's still a very tricky situation.'

'Oh, I understand completely. After all, I still think about Ben.'

'Are you perhaps still a little in love with him?'

'No, not at all, and I don't suppose I have been for a long

time. But I was used to him, and the way he left was really hurtful.'

Martin looked at the clock on the wall and withdrew his hand. 'Shall we go? The other people have all left. I think they'll be pleased to shut up.'

They were mainly silent all the way back to Redbury, each immersed in their own thoughts.

He stopped outside her door, switched off the engine and the silence continued for seconds, if not minutes. Finally he looked at her.

'May I?'

Sasha woke at two in the morning and saw that Martin was already dressed and looking down at her as he tied his tie.

She gazed up at him, still not quite realizing what had happened to them. 'Do you have to go?' she asked.

He sat on the side of the bed and took her hand. 'I have to. I have a lot to do at the office before the holiday.' He bent over and kissed her hard and long as he had before.

Reluctantly he dragged himself away.

'I'll see you when I get back from abroad in the new year. I think it will be a good one for us. Happy Christmas.'

'Happy Christmas,' she murmured. 'Come back soon.' But she didn't think he heard her. She lay there listening to the sound of him going down the stairs, and the soft click as the front door closed, with a deep sense of loss, but also a feeling of happiness and euphoria that would last for days.

Five

Christmas

'Your father and I always thought you should have married Ben,' Sasha's mother said, looking at her reproachfully, 'before it was too late. Couples who live together do tire of each other, you know. You've wasted so much of your life.'

'It's hardly wasted, Mum. A lot of it has been very good. Besides, I am only thirty-five. It's no great age. You'd think I have completely missed out on any kind of emotional life.'

Not for the first time Sasha wished she had never said anything to her mother, but unless she told a big lie, which she didn't want to do, there was no way of avoiding it. She had to phone her parents to tell them she and Ben would not be going to Paris as planned, and when she arrived home she had to tell them why.

'I was married when I was twenty-two,' her mother went on in the same mournful tone, familiar to Sasha who had had to put up with quite a lot of criticism from her parents, who never seemed entirely to approve of anything she did. 'There is a lot of advantage in marrying young, and you and Ben always seemed so well suited.'

'We did begin to grate on each other's nerves,' Sasha said wearily.

'Maybe you'll get together again?' Her mother's tone moved up half an octave.

'I don't think that will happen. I wouldn't be surprised if Ben went back to London as he sometimes felt we shouldn't have left in the first place. He thought he would have done better there, and perhaps he would. He only moved to Redbury to be with me. Anyway I don't know that I want to start all over again. I want to move on too.'

'Where to?' her mother asked peevishly.

'Ah, that's the question.' She was certainly not going to confide in her mother, who was sure to find something critical to say about Martin.

'You don't seem to know what you do want, Sasha. That's always been your problem.'

'I don't know how you can say that, Mum,' Sasha said indignantly. 'Some people would think I've made a success of my life. I am a senior lecturer, I've written books, I can keep myself, I—'

'Not like Ben.' Her mother returned to her favourite subject again. 'Of course you kept him, which I always thought a mistake. Not that he was lazy.'

'He certainly wasn't lazy, and he was a gifted artist,' Sasha found herself saying defensively. 'He just never got the breakthrough. It will come. I feel sure it will one day. Anyway, I thought you liked Ben? You were always singing his praises.'

'Well . . .' Her mother looked doubtful, as if even this well-known fact was called into question. They were facing each other across the kitchen table where they were sitting over breakfast on Christmas Eve, her father having retired to the sitting room to read the paper and avoid the chores as he always did.

Sasha got up and started stacking the dishwasher. When she finished she looked at the kitchen clock. 'If there is nothing else I can do, Mum, I think I'll go for a walk.'

She wished in a way she could walk straight out of there and go home. It had been a mistake to come.

Her parents lived in Cornwall in a pretty house near the sea in St Ives, to which they had retired. Her father had spent all his working life with the same bank and had slowly progressed through the ranks until he became manager of a small branch in the Midlands, round about the time Sasha broke free and went to art school in London. Her mother had been a secretary to a firm of solicitors, and each in their own way was accomplished; but there was always the unstated feeling that, although it had given them security, somehow life had passed them by. Sasha was their only child and this also proved an occasion for endless reproaches because she had never been able to have any more after a difficult birth, a tragedy laid at Sasha's door as a demonstration of the fact that she had always been awkward, even before she was born.

It was a relief for Sasha eventually to get away from the stifling confines of home and escape to the big city, rather as now it was a relief to get out of the house and make her way to the cliffs overlooking the wonderful bay of St Ives. It was a cold but bracing day, so far rain-free and, well wrapped up, she walked briskly in the direction of the town towards the beach. She had been delighted when her parents moved to St Ives, a place beloved of artists, with reason, and the splendid offshoot of London's Tate Gallery with its commanding position overlooking the sea. As an artist she had always loved the special light that St Ives had, and sometimes wished she had brought her paints. Perhaps one day she would, just to help her survive the tedium of the parental home and the endless reproaches she had to endure, more so now that Ben had gone.

As a dutiful daughter Sasha loved her parents, but she had little in common with them and she felt in a way that, despite her achievements, she had disappointed them. There was always that criticism that somehow things were not quite as they should be, and being an artist hadn't been the right preparation for a 'proper' job such as her father and mother had, bringing in security and a sense of order for the rest of one's life. Being a teacher was a good thing and they had been happy about that, but there was always the unspoken fear that one day she might skim off and be tempted to do as Ben had done and try and live by her art.

Sasha walked through the town, which was crowded with people doing last-minute shopping, but she scarcely noticed them, glad to be alone. Despite the cold she was warm, hugging herself, wrapped up in delicious thoughts about Martin, the night they'd spent together, the rapport their lovemaking had established. It gave a whole new meaning to the phrase 'a happy new year'. It could be a glorious one. Yes, she was in love, no longer alone; so putting up with a few weeks without him was tolerable because she knew what was to come.

When she reached the Tate she found, to her disappointment, that it was closed, so she retraced her steps towards home. Just as she got to the front door her mobile rang and she fumbled for it in her pocket. Her instinct was to think it was Ben and for a moment she wondered whether she should answer it. But it might just as well be Martin, and as it rang she stared at it, managing at the same time to open the door to escape from the cold.

In the warmth of the hall she finally put it to her ear. 'Hello?'

It was neither Martin nor Ben but a strange female voice that said weakly, 'Sasha?'

'Yes?'

'Sasha, it's Caroline.'

'Oh, *Caroline*, I didn't recognize your voice. You sound quite strange. Are you OK?' Unbuttoning her coat she sank on to the bottom step of the staircase.

'Sasha . . .' Caroline hesitated, her voice now so faint it was scarcely audible. 'I hate to bother you, I really do, but . . . Sasha, I feel you are the only person I could think of turning to . . .' She stopped again.

'Caroline, is it . . . is it . . .?' Sasha by now was seriously worried, thinking Caroline's worst fears were finally realized. 'Is it something to do with Greg?'

'Yes it is. I saw his face so vividly last night that I knew immediately he was dead. He was saying goodbye to me.' There was a sob at the end of the phone.

'But, Caroline, have you actually *heard* he is . . . or is it just like . . . the knock on the door?' she finished lamely, not wanting to use the word 'imagination'.

'I know,' Caroline continued in a jerky, tear-filled voice. 'I just know. It was him, Greg, like a vision. It was his way of letting me know, saying goodbye. I have been very poorly with flu all week and now I feel so awful I can't get out of bed . . .' Her voice, getting weaker by the minute, trailed off again.

'Where are the children?' Sasha asked urgently, trying to stifle her own sense of panic.

'My mother has them. I managed to get the kids all ready and she collected them. She was so afraid of getting flu she didn't come in. That was a few days ago. My dreams at night are worse than ever, such despair, I can't sleep. I am so depressed I feel like doing myself in. I simply can't cope any more without Greg . . .' Suddenly the phone went dead. Frantically Sasha tried to call back several times but all she got was the engaged signal.

She was still sitting on the stairs with her phone pressed close to her ear listening to the repetitive tones of the engaged signal when her mother appeared, wiping her hands on a cloth.

'I'm just getting lunch,' she said, and then her expression

changed to one of concern. 'Whatever is the matter? Why on earth are you sitting there?'

'I'm afraid I've just had some very bad news.'

'Is it Ben?'

'Oh, no. It's a friend. She is very ill.' She looked up at her mother's anxious face. 'Mum, I'm very sorry, but I must go back to Redbury. I'm really afraid she might do herself in. I'll never forgive myself if something happened to her.'

It was almost dark when Sasha reached the house having driven, largely regardless of the speed limit, all the way from St Ives. Several times she had tried calling Caroline but there was no reply. She had sounded so dozy that she wondered if she was also under the influence of whatever pills she had and that she might have taken too many.

She was halfway there when she realized that she should have called the police, but it was too late and at the back of her mind she knew she had been aware of the panic it would cause and how upset Caroline would be if it was a false alarm. She only hoped she was in time.

Caroline's house was in darkness, as if deserted. Sasha got out of her car and, hurrying to the front door, pressed hard on the bell. As she expected there was no reply and she feared that already she was too late. Panic and fear took over as she hurried round the side of the house. The back door was also locked, and she returned to the front wondering if she should alert the neighbours, but that house was in darkness too.

She went round the house trying all the windows, finding them tight shut. Just as she was thinking she had no alternative but to call the police the kitchen window yielded a little and, summoning strength she didn't know she had, she heaved at it and managed to open it enough to try and wriggle through. Taking off her coat she pushed herself over the sill and, firmly grasping both taps of the kitchen sink, which was on the other side, pulled herself through the window. With a grunt she jumped to the floor, switched on the light and rushed through the hall, up the stairs and into the room where the door was open. From the light on the landing she saw Caroline lying on her bed. Heart in her mouth she walked towards her, switched on a light by the

side of the bed and looked fearfully down at the recumbent form
who lay, eyes closed, but breathing deep, irregular breaths.

Sasha sank on to the side of the bed and felt her brow, which
was very hot, took her hand and at that moment Caroline stirred
and opened her eyes, blinking as she looked around her.

Her eyes, finally focusing on Sasha, opened wide in surprise.

'Sasha, what are you doing here?'

'You called me, don't you remember?' Sasha looked at the
phone lying on the floor. She picked it up and replaced it in its
cradle.

'Did I?' Caroline put a hand to her head. 'I had a terrible
headache.' She tenderly touched her forehead as if seeing if it was
still there.

Sasha reached for a bottle of pills lying on the table and exam-
ined it.

'Caroline, have you taken anything?'

'Just for my headache.'

'How many?'

'Two or three. I can't remember.' She closed her eyes again
and sighed deeply, pulling the duvet closely round her. 'I'm terribly
cold.'

'It is *very* cold in this house.'

Sasha sat on the edge of the bed still holding her hand. 'I think
we should call the doctor or maybe NHS Direct. I can't think
why you haven't had the doctor before.'

Feverishly Caroline seized her hand. 'Oh, please don't. Greg
would be terribly upset.'

'Greg would be terribly upset to see you now, like this.' Sasha
picked up the phone.

'Please, Sasha, I *beg* you not to.' She struggled to sit up. 'I'll get
better. I had a very bad dose of flu but I have just had a long
sleep. I remember calling you now. I know I felt drowsy but I
just wanted to speak to you, someone who understands. I feel so
cut off from people who understand. I had this awful vision of
Greg's face. It was so vivid it seemed to fill the room and made
me think he was dead, but . . .' She sank back on the bed. 'No
one has been to the house so maybe it was just a bad dream. I
must have fallen asleep on the phone. I'm very sorry. Did I worry
you?'

'Of course you worried me. I've driven all the way from St Ives.'

'St Ives!' Caroline gasped.

'I was spending Christmas with my parents. I was just terribly concerned about you. I thought you were about to do yourself in.'

'Oh, I'm so sorry. I had no idea you were in *St Ives.*' This seemed to bring Caroline to her senses and again she pulled herself upright in bed. 'I would never have wanted you to come all that way. I just wanted to talk. I feel awful.'

'Well, I'm here now and I'm going to try to make sure you're alright. When did you last have anything to eat?'

'Can't remember, but I'm not hungry.'

'You must eat or at least drink. I'm surprised your mother hasn't been round.'

'She has enough to do. She doesn't want to get the flu too. Someone has to look after the kids. They have a houseful of kids. My sister, who is staying with her, has two. She said she'd come, but she hasn't been well either. There is a lot of flu going around. It makes you feel so low. They have enough to do without bothering about me. I said I was OK. It was naughty of me to let myself go to you, but I never dreamt you were in *St Ives.* You must go back and be with your parents and Ben.' Caroline paused. 'Was he there?'

'No, but that's another story. Look, let me go and see what I can get you to eat and at least make you a cup of tea.'

Caroline lay down again as if all the effort had exhausted her.

'You won't find much. The cupboard is bare.' She closed her eyes as if ready to go to sleep again.

Still deeply worried, and also understandably rather irritated, Sasha went downstairs where a search found almost no food in the house as far as she could tell, with the exception of a few tins which would hardly see them through Christmas because she knew she wasn't going back to St Ives. No eggs, sour milk, rancid butter, mouldy bread. She realized Caroline must have had nothing to eat for days. This lack of provisions was hardly the kind of thing you would expect from a woman with responsibilities, a family. She realized that Caroline in recent weeks must have been going through a slow process of breakdown, brought about by the intense, quite rational, worry about her husband and culminating in a bad bout of flu which may, in a way, have come as a life saviour.

This placed an additional burden on Sasha, who now had the responsibility of helping her recover physically and perhaps preventing a compete mental breakdown, with the consequences of the army having to be informed, and maybe even the children being taken into care. It was a prospect whose ultimate effects were too awful to contemplate.

It also placed a serious responsibility on her, which was the last thing she wanted. She had tried to avoid becoming too involved with her students and now she was in it up to the neck. But in a way she was glad. She may have helped to save a life and perhaps also a marriage and the break-up of a family.

Her first act downstairs was to switch on the central heating, which unaccountably was off, hoping the reason wasn't because it was broken. It was just seven o'clock and, hoping the supermarket would still be open on Christmas Eve, Caroline threw on her coat, unlocked the front door and hurried to her car to seek out provisions.

She was lucky. It was still fairly full with last-minute shoppers. She was even able to get a fresh chicken – she was in no mood to bother with a turkey even if there were any left – and vegetables, one of the last loaves of bread, milk, bacon, eggs, butter and enough of the necessities of life and one or two luxuries, including some bottles of wine, to see them through the holiday. Finally she staggered back to the car with a laden trolley whose contents with some satisfaction she was able to stuff in the boot.

Back at the house she first unpacked her carrier bags and stowed their contents away, poured herself a glass of wine, had a large gulp and hurried upstairs see how Caroline was faring.

Caroline was still sleep, lying on her side, but even in sleep looking more relaxed and peaceful, maybe because she was now sharing her burden with someone else, although her breathing was still heavy and laboured. The room was beginning to heat up although it was still cold and Sasha pulled the duvet more securely about the patient, covering her shoulders. She wondered if she should seek medical help and resolved to keep an eye on Caroline through the night. With that thought in mind she went into the adjoining rooms, which were remarkably tidy with beds made and, selecting one of them, decided to sleep there for the night and, as she was dead tired, not bother about remaking the bed. Tossing back the duvet she saw that it even appeared to have clean sheets. This reassured her about Caroline's state of mind. Even feeling ill, she had cared enough to tidy the kids' rooms and perhaps even change the bedclothes.

In a more cheerful frame of mind Sasha returned to the kitchen, drank some more wine and cooked herself bacon with two eggs, tomato, and opened a can of baked beans, which she had previously noted in the kitchen cupboard. These, plus a large quantity of toast, she scoffed almost without pause, realizing, when she had finished, how hungry she had been as it was seven hours since she had left home. With a guilty start she remembered her parents and, getting her mobile phone from her handbag, called her mother, prepared for the usual onslaught of reproaches. To her surprise her mother was surprisingly sympathetic, mainly concerned about her daughter's welfare and relieved she had got there safely. When Sasha explained the state she had found Caroline in, the absence of a husband in Afghanistan and so on, she agreed that it was out of the question to leave her until she was better. Sasha promised to try and make it for New Year.

This done she felt much more relaxed. She finished her wine as she washed up and tidied the kitchen and then went upstairs to see Caroline, who opened her eyes as she approached the bed and extended her hand towards her. 'You are so good to me,' she said, as Sasha sank down on to the bed. 'I can't think what I'd have done without you. I feel so guilty to take you away from your parents and Ben.' She looked towards the window. 'I didn't even know what time it is but it is too late now. You must go back to them first thing tomorrow.'

'Everything is under control,' Sasha said, placing a hand on her forehead. 'Don't worry about a thing. Just get better. I phoned my mum and I'm not going back until you are well enough.'

'But there is nothing to eat.'

'There is now. I popped out and did some shopping. Luckily the supermarket was still open. In fact I just cooked myself bacon and eggs. Do you feel ready to eat something now?'

Caroline pulled a face. 'Not really.'

'You must drink lots of water. I bought some bottles.' Then she looked at her gravely. 'Caroline, I am seriously concerned about you. Your forehead is still very hot. It is clear you have a temperature. If I don't think you are considerably better tomorrow I am going to insist on calling the doctor. Is that clear? You have neglected yourself and it is not fair on the children or Greg.'

Caroline's expression was sombre. 'I know. I have let myself go. I felt so absolutely lousy. But I am angry with myself for calling you and being such a coward when Greg is so brave.' Tears then started to roll down her cheeks and she lay back against the pillow once more.

'My dear woman you have been feeling low, but you are physically ill and have the flu, for goodness' sake.' Sasha got off the bed and stood up. 'You may have been low, but I'm sure even Greg can get the flu, and if he knew about this he would be quite understanding. Hasn't he telephoned you?'

'Yes, but I pull myself together and make an effort for him when he rings. He is on an important military operation. They keep moving so his calls are very brief. It is just to say he is OK really. The line is always bad. He doesn't know the kids aren't here. He can't call every day, which in a way is a blessing. Yet it worries me more now that I know he is on this dangerous mission which he can't talk about . . .'

Her voice trailed off and Sasha, fearing she was going to do another wobbly, and herself suddenly feeling tired and exhausted, said firmly, 'Caroline, it is getting very late. I am going to get you some tea and toast, since we now have milk and bread. I will give you a bottle of water and more headache pills, fetch you a flannel to wipe your face and hands, help you to the loo and back, and then tuck you up. I have looked at a room next door, which is fine, and I'm sleeping there. Tomorrow we'll have a fresh look at things. Is that all quite clear?'

Caroline managed a weak smile. 'Yes, thank you, nursie.'

Despite her intention to keep an eye on her patient during the night Sasha fell into such a deep sleep that it was dawn before she woke and, with a start, she jumped out of bed and went into Caroline's room where she tentatively, almost fearfully, approached her bed. To her intense relief she saw that Caroline was sleeping peacefully, breathing much more regularly, and when she gently put a hand on her brow it was warm but had nothing of the fever of the night before. The crisis, it seemed, was over. Careful not to wake Caroline she went back to bed and slept again until after nine.

This time Caroline was awake, propped up on her pillows, and gazing out of the window. She turned and smiled as she heard Sasha.

'I feel much better,' she said. 'Much.'

'I know.' Sasha perched on the side of her bed. 'I looked in on you at about six and could see there was a change from last night.' She put a hand on her forehead again. 'Still warm, but yesterday it was like a furnace. Happy Christmas,' she concluded.

'I've even forgotten it was Christmas,' Caroline said. 'Isn't that awful? Well, you've made mine and I've ruined yours.'

'Not at all. It's good for once to do something useful for someone,' she said as she got off the bed. 'I'm going to bring you some tea and toast and then I'm going to get our Christmas lunch. I bought us a chicken and some smoked salmon to start.'

'I must get up.' Caroline began to throw aside the duvet but Sasha pushed her back on her bed.

'You stay exactly where you are. You don't want a relapse, which is what happens with flu. You can have a bath if you can manage it, or a good wash or whatever, and then I'll bring your lunch up on a tray and have it here with you.'

'I'm going to come down,' Caroline said firmly. 'You can spoil me if you like with breakfast in bed, but I'm having Christmas lunch on a table!'

And as it was so nice to hear that old familiar ring of resolution once again in her voice, Sasha decided not to deter her.

'It's not exactly Christmas lunch with all the trimmings,' Sasha said as she started to carve the chicken.

'It looks very good to me.' Caroline had, with some effort, got herself downstairs, but the sight of food cooked and served by someone else began to make her feel almost hungry. Her mood bolstered by a very brief phone call from Greg, which finally put her fears to rest, she felt unusually cheerful.

Sasha had gone to some trouble to make the table look festive.

She had bought Christmassy paper napkins, red candles and a little Father Christmas, which stood in the middle of the table between the candles. She herself felt buoyed up by the improvement in Caroline's condition after her apprehension of the night before. As she cooked during the morning she thought that it wasn't such a bad way to spend Christmas after all – away from her parents and actually helping someone who needed her. People went to special refuges at Christmas to help the disadvantaged. Well, she was doing something like it and there was no doubt that it gave you a lot of satisfaction, probably through a variety of reasons, not all of them altruistic.

Caroline sipped at her wine but left most of it. She also left some of the smoked salmon and most of the chicken, and eventually, carefully put her knife and fork together and pushed the plate away from her. With a deep sigh she sat back in her chair and closed her eyes.

'That was lovely,' she breathed at last. Then, opening her eyes, she looked at Sasha who was still finishing her main course. 'Sorry, I can't eat any more.'

'Why don't you go back to bed?' Sasha said. 'You look done in.'

'It seems so ungrateful to you for all you've done – the lovely table . . .' Caroline gestured helplessly.

'It's not a bit ungrateful to me. I've had a very good meal and frankly I have enjoyed myself.'

'But shouldn't you be getting back to your parents and Ben?'

'Ben isn't there to get back to.'

'Oh.' Caroline looked surprised. 'Is he with his family?'

'Yes, at least I suppose so. I don't really know where he is.' As if wishing to put an end to the conversation, Sasha got up. 'Look, let me help you back to bed.'

'No, really, I don't need help. You haven't even finished.'

'I'll see you into bed and come back and finish.'

'And all the clearing up . . .'

'Come *on*,' Sasha said, and took her firmly by the arm.

Caroline stayed in bed the rest of the day. She had a phone call from her mother, who she assured she was getting better, without mentioning the presence of Sasha, and spoke to her children. Most of the time she slept.

Sasha, after clearing up, rang her parents and then took her wine into the sitting room and promptly fell asleep over a block-buster film on TV.

When she awoke it was already dark. She switched on the lights, drew the curtains and idly went over to the table which was littered with Caroline's paintings, and inspected them. They were very grim, littered now with dead bodies and wounded soldiers with gaping wounds, much worse than when she'd seen them before, all an indication of Caroline's morbid state of mind.

She felt in a way that the flu, by fastening on the physical, had saved Caroline from a nervous collapse, as well as her spontan-eous decision to call her and thus unwittingly summon aid.

In the evening she took Caroline up some supper of cold chicken, which to her gratification she ate, pronouncing herself much better, and both of them had an early and peaceful night.

Sasha woke late the next morning and found Caroline already awake, greeting her with a broad smile.

'Did you sleep well?'

'Like a top. You?'

'Great. I woke at dawn, spent a penny and then went to sleep again. I am going to get up today. At some stage I'm going to have to return to normal life and get the kids back here.'

'I'd give it another day, at least. See how you feel this evening. I thought today if you really feel up to it and the weather isn't too bad we could have a drive to the coast. Maybe take some notepads and draw a bit.'

'Even you?' Caroline looked at her in astonishment.

'Even me. I am quite an accomplished artist, you know. I always keep a pad in the car.'

'Well, you'll show me up. I can't draw at all.'

'I'll make sandwiches – more chicken, I'm afraid, though I think some smoked salmon is left – and maybe if we still feel up to it, round about lunchtime, we can be off.

And so it worked out. By noon they were parked on the cliff overlooking the bay. Caroline enviously watched Sasha, who already had her pad on her knee. With a few deft strokes, in no time she had an outline of the scene before them: the gleaming expanse of sea, the cliff rounding on one side. She even put in the few people on the beach who were walking their dog, plus a couple of yachts in the harbour, which was an act of imagination, as they didn't actually exist.

'There,' she said at last, sitting back. 'Not bad?' She glanced at Caroline.

'Bloody good, I'd say. Now would you go back and paint that?'

'No, I won't this one; I just did it for you, and for an exercise. But I have neglected painting and I might take it up now that Ben is no longer around. I shall have more time and, you know, I'd like you to take it up too.'

'What?' Caroline looked alarmed. 'Sketching?'

'No, painting scenes like this, peaceful, pastoral landscapes. If you like after Christmas when things return to normal, I can take you out with an easel and encourage you to start painting outside. It's what I'm going to do in class in the spring, so you'll have a head start.' She looked at her gravely. 'Caroline, I want you to stop those awful war scenes. I was looking at them last night and, frankly, they are doing you a lot of harm. You know that, don't you? They are deepening your depression and that is no good to you, the kids or your husband. By the time he comes back I want you to have a whole portfolio of cheerful, optimistic paintings and I'm sure that will be an indication of a new and more cheerful you. You must work on it.'

For a while Caroline remained silent and Sasha was afraid she had offended her. After all this was very personal stuff, dangerous ground and maybe an area that she had no business treading on. She looked at her anxiously and when she replied Caroline's tone was subdued.

'You're right. I let myself go down too far. I felt at one stage I was staring into an abyss. I can't explain it. I've always been so strong . . .'

'You must be strong again, and I'll help in any way I can.'

'Why are you so good to me?' Caroline looked at her curiously. 'You have done so much for me these last few days, driven up from St Ives on Christmas Eve and really taken me out of myself. If only for you I am determined to make a go of things.'

'That's my girl.'

More relieved than she could say, Sasha put away her pad and went round to the boot of the car to get out the picnic.

She sensed Caroline was tiring again and they would soon have to return home.

'Tell me about Ben,' Caroline said, munching a sandwich. She looked across at Sasha. 'Or shouldn't I ask you? You seem to have avoided it. Did you have a tiff?'

'More than that, much more. Ben has left me. In fact the night I went home after supper with you he had cleared out. Everything gone. I knew it was permanent.'

'But I don't understand. I realized things were not going well. You made that plain, but as drastic as that?'

'It shattered me at the time, I can tell you. Everything cleared out except a few paintings left in the studio. Completely un-expected. He left a letter saying he was doing it to me before I chucked him out. I don't think I ever would have. In fact I know I never would. Not in that cruel way without talking or attempting to talk about it and sort things out as they could have been. I realize Ben had been bottling things up in himself and I was too outspoken, unsympathetic, even harsh. No wonder he felt embit-tered and left me. Since he has gone I have thought a lot about what happened to make things go wrong and what I could have done to correct it. Anyway, now that it's all in the past, good riddance to him I say.'

She had been on the verge of telling her about Martin but decided not to. It was a bit too soon and Caroline, that loyal faithful wife, might have thought she was a bit of a slut falling into bed with a bloke she scarcely knew and knew even less about. For Martin remained something of a mystery, always careful to reveal little of himself.

Caroline, rather surprised by Sasha's acceptance of what seemed like a disaster, looked over to her. 'Maybe, you know, in a way, it is for the best.'

'Oh yes, I think so,' Sasha said cheerfully. 'Let's get back, shall we? You look all in and must be careful not to overdo it.'

Alice sat by the window of her flat waiting for Vanessa to pick her up. She was already late. She kept glancing out for the sight of a car and then she'd go and look in the mirror, make sure her hair was OK, give it a little pat and go back to her place. The hairs were almost glued to one another with hair lacquer, so it was unlikely that a single hair had been dislodged, but you could never be too sure, especially if you were nervous and she was, incredibly so, and sorry now that she had accepted Moira's kind invitation. They couldn't possibly really want her. It had been a misplaced act of kindness. A lunch party with people she didn't know, had never met, seemed now a daunting prospect. But Christmas on one's own wasn't much fun. The alternative was an occasion for forced jollity in the communal dining room with other similarly lonely residents. She had spent days deciding what to wear, had hair and nails done and tried different outfits, discarding one for another. Finally she opted for a jersey two-piece, without a blouse, and on the collar of the jacket was pinned a cameo that had once belonged to her mother. Round her neck was a string of small fine pearls, a treasured, much cherished present from Bernard on their engagement.

People had such fixed ideas about the elderly. It was horrible to be old. If one was slightly deaf, as she was, people thought you were stupid and, if you forgot anything, that you had Alzheimer's. It suddenly seemed to overtake one without warning and was hard to accept, especially after such an active life, and in herself she still felt middle-aged, if not actually youthful. If the afterlife existed, and she was not sure it did, it would be nice to have somewhere that you passed from one world to another without pain, suffering or fear. Just ascending some stairs to a door, through which you passed effortlessly, to be greeted at the other side by all those who loved you and who you had loved. These were her parents, her sister, one or two intimate friends from her school days, and Bernard her fiancé; but that love affair had been so very long ago that she could scarcely recall what he looked like or even now much about him. And there had never been anyone else after Bernard whom she had taken in any way seriously. It wasn't that she had considered Bernard irreplaceable, much as, at the time, she had loved him, but she had simply not met anyone else.

It was not even possible to envisage what life might have been like with Bernard, the children they might have had. As a teacher she had loved children and was close to them; but she knew she and Sybil had missed out on that magical moment when you discovered that you had a new life growing inside you, with the endless potential for joy and of course sorrow that entailed.

A ring at the doorbell interrupted her reverie and, suddenly flustered as she had not been looking out of the window, she went slowly to the door and reached it, just as the bell sounded again.

She opened it to find a quite stunningly beautiful woman on the other side who greeted her with a bright smile, head on one side:

'Alice? I'm Vanessa. I'm so sorry I'm late. We had a bit of a crisis in the kitchen. Put the turkey in too late.'

Alice took the hand of the young woman, who was dressed in a flowing grey trouser suit of some exotic lightweight material over an open-necked yellow satin blouse. On her feet were high-heeled gold sandals. She must have wowed the men as an air hostess, and even for a woman it was difficult to take one's eyes off her. Finally she let her hand go.

'Oh dear, I could have got a taxi. You should have telephoned.'

'Not at all. No worries, it is all sorted now. Are you ready?'

'I just have to put on my coat.'

Vanessa helped as she shrugged herself into it. 'And my stick.' Alice reached across to the hallstand. 'I had a hip replacement and I'm afraid I'm still a bit unsteady.'

'Don't worry about it at all,' Vanessa said soothingly, and glanced round. 'Have you got everything?'

'Yes.' Alice made a move towards the door then stopped. 'Oh dear, I've forgotten the presents! How *stupid* of me.'

'Oh, don't worry about those.'

'No, they are on my bed all ready. Would you mind?' She pointed towards a door and that nimble, perfect vision of agile young womanhood sped towards it, collected an assortment of parcels and brought them with her.

'*And* my bag,' Alice said. 'Oh dear, I must seem so silly.' She looked apologetically at Vanessa. 'Would you mind? It is by the window in the sitting room.' And she pointed her stick in the direction of the room as Vanessa once again made her way down the hall, emerging with the bag in her hand, which Alice grasped almost feverishly.

'I've been ready for ages. There is no excuse. I should have had everything by me.'

Yes she was old. Now she felt old, very old compared to this beautiful young creature beside her.

'My fault for being late,' Vanessa insisted and, taking her arm, still with the parcels in her other hand, steered her carefully to the door of the lift, as if fearful that she might lose her way.

Once at the car, which was a very expensive sporty model as one would expect to belong to such an apparition of style and distinction, Vanessa put the parcels in the boot and eased herself behind the wheel while Alice, still pink from embarrassment, stared fixedly ahead. All the things forgetful old women were expected to do she had done and she hated herself for it.

'There,' Vanessa said, looking enquiringly at her as if half prepared for another hitch. 'Ready?'

'All ready,' Alice said with a firm nod of her head. 'I feel I have given you such a lot of trouble.'

'No trouble at all,' Vanessa said breezily, engaging the gears.

'It is very good of your mother to have invited me to a family party.'

'Oh, it's not all family. The young man who teaches my children swimming is staying with us. We asked him out of pity as he was lonely and had nowhere to go, poor soul.'

'Like me. How kind of you,' Alice said, and then added unnecessarily, 'You are a very kind family.'

'He's playing golf with my husband. They get on like a house on fire. I hope they are back in time for lunch and don't spend too much time at the bar in the club.'

'I'm looking forward to meeting everyone. I've heard a lot about you.'

Vanessa glanced at her anxiously. 'Nothing bad I hope?'

'On the contrary. Your mother is full of praise for you.'

'That's a relief.'

By now they had turned into the drive of the house and there was Moira on the doorstep smiling and looking relaxed.

'Vanessa will have told you we had a crisis in the kitchen,' she said, going to the car and greeting Alice with a kiss. 'The turkey was larger than I remembered and we put it in a bit late. So she was late. I am so sorry.'

'I made it even worse by forgetting everything,' Alice said, as Vanessa emerged from the side of the car with an armful of parcels in her arm. 'She must think I am a stupid old lady.' She lowered her voice, 'Nervous, you know, at meeting you all.'

Moira clasped her arm affectionately. 'There is nothing to be nervous about, my dear. Ian and Tim are still playing golf; the children are watching television, needless to say. Only my son Toby, who you haven't yet met, is here.' She led her into the house helping her off with her coat in the hall.

A large fire burned in the grate of the drawing room, which seemed to stretch from one side of the house to the other. In front of it stood a very tall young man whose looks, if she didn't know, would have told her at once who he was. He was strikingly handsome, the male equivalent of his sister with thick, rather untidy blond hair and well-defined, almost aristocratic features. He was casually dressed in jeans and a T-shirt and had a glass in his hand, which he replaced on a table as his mother introduced him to Alice. He gave her a charming smile and said how pleased he was to meet her.

'Mum met you at the art class, I hear.'

'Yes.' Alice took the chair proffered by him close to the fire, which she was grateful for, though she didn't expect it was cold in the room. 'Very lucky for me.'

'Can I get you a drink? Sherry?'

'That would be very nice. A small one,' she said cautiously.

Vanessa came in and looked at her brother. 'Oh, you're up?' she said in the kind of bantering tone adopted by siblings.

'Yes I made it.'

'Good thing we didn't need you in the kitchen.'

'I knew there was nothing I could do. You girls are so capable. Drink, Van?' he asked his sister, but she excused herself saying she had to see if her mother needed any help.

Toby handed Alice the sherry and she took a nervous sip, not wishing to get drunk and make an ass of herself again. She said it was delicious and placed it carefully on a small table by her side.

'Your mother said you live in Oxford.'

'Yes.' Toby took the chair opposite her and stretched long limbs towards the fire.

'My sister was a staff nurse at the Radcliffe.'

'Oh, when?'

'Long before your time.'

At that moment there was a disturbance in the hall, the sound of a door opening and a sudden draught blowing into the room, mingled male and female voices in the hall. Vanessa entered, followed by two men, also immensely tall, and Alice felt that, except for herself and Moira, and presumably the children, she was in a house of giants.

Vanessa took the hand of an engaging-looking man of about thirty-five. He too was casually dressed in a check shirt under a pullover, tweed trousers, and had a healthy outdoor look.

'This is my husband, Ian,' she said.

'How very nice to meet you.' Alice held out her hand, which he clasped firmly. He had thick, slightly curly, dark hair, twinkling brown eyes, a tanned face and a charming smile. He told her how pleased he was to meet her in a voice that made you think he meant it. She took to him at once.

'Did you have a good game?' she asked.

'Excellent. Tim as a sportsman has a very high standard.'

He looked with approval in the direction of his partner while Vanessa, all smiles, and keeping well apart from him, was ushering a young man towards Alice.

'And this,' Vanessa said without a shadow of guilt on her lovely face, 'is Tim, a friend of ours who teaches the kids to swim. He is staying with us for Christmas.'

Alice tried hard not to look too interested as she shook hands with Tim, someone who really should not have been there. To Alice Tim was a very different proposition from the rest of the family. He was tall and exceptionally good-looking, with the build and physique of an athlete. Although he looked older than nineteen his appearance could not have been more different from Ian, who looked what he was − a successful, prosperous, self-assured professional man nearing middle age, someone with class. Tim did not have class. Whereas Ian was urbane, clean-shaven, Tim had fashionable designer stubble and the sort of spiky, greasy, contemporary hairstyle which always made Alice, as a member of the older generation, think the person concerned could do with a shave and a comb through their hair. Tim was everyman with a frank, engaging but essentially boyish smile showing an amazing set of even, shining, white teeth, which he flashed at her as he took her hand, and a firm handclasp. It was easy to see how he would have attracted someone like Vanessa for whom, in common with so many beautiful, and some not so beautiful women, one man was not enough.

After a little perfunctory chat with her, Tim joined Toby by the drinks table, helping himself to a bottle of beer, which he opened and put to his mouth, swinging round to survey everyone else in the room with the proprietary air of someone who clearly thought he belonged there and felt at home. It was impossible to know what was going on in his mind, but undoubtedly there was an air of self-satisfaction in the knowledge that he was cuckolding a man, years older and socially his superior, in the presence of his wife.

Moments later Moira, by now looking hot and a bit flustered, came to the door and announced that lunch would be served in about twenty minutes and anyone who needed to change or wash their hands should get on with it.

In the end, despite all the drama, it was a most enjoyable, even relaxing lunch. The table looked lovely, with crackers, candles, funny hats and streamers. The turkey, ceremoniously carved by Ian, was cooked to perfection, the flesh simply falling away from the bones. The Christmas pudding was carried in aflame, to cries of admiration. The wine flowed freely but not too freely; no one got drunk. The children were beautiful and delightful and, as ex-headmistress Alice noted with approval, very polite and well behaved.

Altogether it was a happy day and in the end she was glad she had come. She did not make any more gaffes, joined in the fun and party games afterwards, and was especially good at guessing charades, though didn't actually take part. In the early evening she was eventually driven home by Moira who was not keen on alcohol, had drunk only half a glass of wine, and welcomed the opportunity to get out anyway.

They stopped at the door of Alice's block of flats and sat there silently for a moment, each wrapped in their thoughts.

'It really was a lovely day.' Alice broke the silence. 'I was rather nervous about coming, seeing so many people I didn't know, intruding in your family life, but I am so glad I came.'

'I'm so glad you did too,' Moira said sincerely. 'It made a difference having you there. Frankly I didn't enjoy the day. I really resented Vanessa inviting Tim for lunch with us and I'm afraid at

times it showed. In fact to be truthful we had a little tiff in the
kitchen, which again explains the delay to lunch. I thought inviting
Ian to go off to play golf with Tim was just about the end, taking
it a bit too far, making a fool out of her husband, an innocent,
poor man. Almost playing with him. But if I had refused I think
she might have had Christmas lunch at her house and I couldn't
bear the thought of that. It wasn't necessary to have him at all.
She is very stubborn.'

'And how did Ian react to Tim's presence in their house?'

'Vanessa said he took it completely at face value, a young man
on his own for Christmas, which she tried to pretend even to
me was all it was.'

'I liked Ian so much.'

'Oh, he is a sweetie. A really nice, good man, a loving husband
and father. He deserves better than my daughter, although he
absolutely adores her.' A note of bitterness entered Moira's voice.
'I will be glad when Boxing Day is over and we can get back
to normal and not have to pretend all the time. Tomorrow I have
to go to them and we have lunch at a hotel. For me the stress
has been almost overwhelming and I think it showed.'

'Oh, I don't think it did at all. Cooking Christmas lunch, and
Christmas in general, is stressful for anyone, particularly for the
hostess. But tell me, how do you think Ian really took to Tim?'

'Oh, he liked him. He was good with the children, who adore
him, and he did all the right things. He was polite, helpful. Brought
me a magnificent bouquet of flowers. Exuded charm. But I felt
all the time Ian was being deceived and it upset me. Fancy deliberately having your lover in the house under the same roof as
your husband! Quite preposterous.' Moira almost snorted with
indignation. 'Ian assumed he is one of Vanessa's good causes. She
has so many. She behaved beautifully – detached, serene. Never
for a moment did I notice any untoward intimate sign or gesture
between her and Tim that would indicate they were anything
but casual friends. Oh dear, I hope all this hasn't really shocked
you?' She looked anxiously at Alice.

'My dear, as I told you before, nothing can shock me. Don't
forget I was headmistress of a large inner-city comprehensive
school for over twenty years. In a way I was slightly intrigued,
though I realize that's a bit naughty of me.'

'I think the other side of Vanessa *is* that she is genuinely sorry for him and wants to help him. Of course Tim is so good looking, and sexy I suppose, and . . . well, things just happen, don't they? I hope it will pass. It must pass. I know she is devoted to Ian, absolutely. She is married to him and wants to stay married. She likes her comfort and has everything she wants. Tim has nothing.'

'She is certainly very beautiful. I don't wonder men are so attracted to her. And she is kind too. She was exceptionally nice to me. She is socially accomplished and must have been a marvellous air hostess. I went round the place forgetting things and she was so patient and tolerant.'

'Oh, she's used to it with me. I forget things all the time.' Moira patted her hand. 'There, I must go. They'll think I've forgotten the way home and send out a search party!'

'Won't you come in for a coffee?'

'No, there is still a lot to do at home. Thanks for being such a perfect friend.' She got out of the car and escorted Alice to the door of her flat where the two women embraced fondly.

When the door closed Alice went into her bedroom, kicked off her shoes, went to the kitchen to make a cup of tea and took it into the sitting room. There she fell asleep in a chair and dreamt of a large, handsome, above all *interesting* family, like the Cunninghams, to which she so much wished she could belong.

Six

Pauline collected Rusty from her migraine-prone friend and walked with him to the park. It was that awkward time of the year between Christmas and New Year when some people fervently wished the holiday season was all over, and others thought it could not be long enough and dreaded gloomy January and a return to work.

Pauline was one of those who would liked to have spent more time with her family, but her parents were going on a cruise and her brother was a hospital doctor and had to resume his duties the day after Boxing Day.

It was her first outing for two weeks with the dog, who she had come to love as if he belonged to her, an affection that seemed mutual. Rusty didn't get enough walks with his owner and once inside the park he bounded away after he was taken off his lead, sniffing familiar haunts, relieving himself against favourite trees, as if he had come home.

Pauline loved these walks in the park with the dog and there were several other dog owners with whom she was on nodding acquaintance. They would gather by a bench near the pond rather as another group, mothers with prams or young children, tended to congregate in the playground where they could keep an eye on their charges while exchanging news or indulging in gossip.

It had been a good holiday break. Pauline was devoted to her parents who were supportive, generous and proud of their daughter. She and her elder brother Vic, who was there with his wife and three children, were close; so it had been a busy, happy time, so much so that she had not really wanted to come back.

The truth was that, despite her pretence to her family that all was well, Pauline was lonely. She did not make friends easily. In fact she hadn't really made any, and the watercolour class had been a disappointment thanks largely to her blunder at the first meeting when her thoughtless remark to Caroline had engendered a hostility that seemed to have continued all term. People avoided her and it served her right.

She walked towards the pond, conscious of the couples strolling arm in arm, mothers, and sometimes fathers as well, with children playing with balls, flying kites, all happy, normal family activities. She thought about Vic and his happy fulfilled life and how, this time in particular, it had come home to her that she might be missing out on something, not only on children, which she was in two minds about, but a loving relationship such as Vic had with his wife Anne.

She passed the field where a football match was in progress and there among the small crowd gathered on the touchline she saw a familiar figure, his back to her, hands thrust deep in his pockets: Roger. She had almost forgotten about him, and she didn't particularly wish to see him now in case he mistakenly thought she had deliberately come to the park to engineer a meeting, so she hurried on.

There were one or two people she knew chatting by the park bench, but Rusty was already in the water so she started throwing the sticks she had been gathering as she walked, grateful, at least, for the company of the lively dog and the pleasure he gave her.

'Hello Pauline.' A voice interrupted her train of thought and she turned to see Roger standing beside her. 'We meet again.'

'Why, Roger,' she said, feigning surprise, 'are you here again with your boys?'

He nodded. 'Did you have a good Christmas?'

'Absolutely wonderful. Did you?'

'Well . . .' He pulled a face. 'Wonderful, no. I entertained myself to a solitary lunch at a hotel. In general drank too much. Watched some pretty awful TV and was glad when the whole thing was over. One of the few things I regret about the break-up of my marriage is spending Christmas by myself. My wife always insists on having the boys.'

'Don't you have parents?'

'I'm afraid I would be bored out of my mind staying with them for Christmas. Don't get the wrong impression. I do see them from time to time, but they live in Scotland so you can't just go for a day or two and I always have to have the boys afterwards, and want to anyway. However, the boys came yesterday and I do like to be with them. The Christmas holiday always seems too long to me. And you?'

'Well, I usually spend the whole break with my parents, including New Year, but this year they are treating themselves to a cruise on the Caribbean. I have a brother who is a hospital doctor and he had to get back to work.'

'Are you doing anything for New Year?'

'No. Not as far as I know.'

She saw that Rusty was getting bored with his sticks so, summoning him and standing well back as he shook himself, she dried him thoroughly and put him on his lead.

'I must be getting back,' she said.

'To the sick friend?'

'Yes, she's OK today, but I wanted to go for a walk so offered to take Rusty. Nice to see you, Roger. See you again at the art class. Happy New Year.' And with that she turned to go.

'Pauline,' Roger called after her, 'my firm is having a dinner dance on New Year's Eve. I know it is late notice, but I wonder if you'd like to be my partner? It is usually a good bash at the Hotel Continental.'

His expression as he looked at her was rather comical, almost as though he was fearful of her reaction.

'Well . . .' Startled, Pauline hesitated. 'I don't know if I've anything to wear.'

'Oh, don't dress up. I mean a frock, yes, but nothing fancy. I'd collect you and bring you home, of course.'

'Well . . .' She hesitated again. 'Well, why not? Thanks,' she concluded lamely.

'Oh good. That's settled then.'

'I didn't mean to sound ungracious, but it did come as a surprise.'

'Of course. I understand.'

'But I must warn you, I'm not a very good dancer.'

'Neither am I.'

'OK then. Thanks,' she said again, managing a smile. 'Give me your home number, in case. I mean I do want to come but you never know – colds and things.'

'Of course.' He produced a business card from his wallet and handed it to her. 'And yours too. Just in case. Also give me your address again.'

This she did and he duly made a note at the back of his diary.

'I'll pick you up about seven. Dinner is at eight and dancing afterwards.'

'Sounds great. I look forward to it.'

'See you on Wednesday.'

Roger looked rather good in a tuxedo, even distinguished, and Pauline had made a special effort to temper the image of a hard, rather bitchy woman who got people's backs up, and looked attractive, even sexy, instead. Not that she was normally a sloppy dresser. As a businesswoman she took care to dress well and had dozens of outfits and plenty of suitable dresses. However, she splashed out on rather an expensive new one in black velvet, which she thought would be suitably dressy without being fussy. She had her hair done in a different style on the day and took special care with her make-up. She didn't want to let him down.

She was quite surprised at the change in Roger when he came to the door, hair neatly combed, the faint whiff of expensive aftershave. He always looked well turned out, but tonight there was a special quality, something she hadn't noticed before. Hard to define, but it suddenly made him appear more attractive. He in turn appeared delighted by what he saw on the other side and gazed at her for a moment. She hoped she hadn't gone too far. For a split second she thought he was going to attempt to kiss her cheek, and stepped aside at the same time as he seemed to have had second thoughts and drawn back.

'Drink?' she asked.

Roger consulted his watch.

'Actually,' he said, 'we are a bit late. We'll have plenty to drink tonight. I have a taxi outside.'

'Fine. I'll get my coat.'

It wasn't a coat but a velvet cloak, which Roger helped to drape round her shoulders. 'You look smashing,' he said.

'Thanks.' She smiled at him. 'You don't look too bad yourself.' And at that moment the rather tense atmosphere between them seemed to dissolve.

★　　★　　★

The function room of the hotel was crowded with well-dressed people most, but not all, quite young. Inevitably Pauline felt nervous as Roger escorted her in and they joined the throng. A waiter immediately appeared with glasses of champagne on a tray, one of which Roger handed to her before taking his own.

'Cheers.' He held up his glass.

'Cheers,' Pauline replied and put the glass to her lips. 'This is nice,' she said after a quick sip. 'Do all these people work at your firm?'

'Oh, no. Most of them are clients.'

Seeing that people were already starting to move towards an open door he wandered up to a notice board and consulted lists pinned on it, running his finger down until he came to his name.

'Here we are. Table seven. It seems that people are already making their way there.'

They joined the stream, Roger nodding to one or two people as they passed, stopping to introduce Pauline to the Managing Director, a prosperous looking, rotund man with an elegant wife, and exchanging a few words.

'Glad you could come, Roger.'

'Last minute, I'm afraid. I managed to persuade this beautiful lady to partner me.'

'Weren't you lucky?' Both looked at Pauline with smiling approval.

Each member of staff had a table so they were mostly strangers to Roger, though one or two were his clients. He went round exchanging a few words and introducing Pauline as he did. Roger always seemed so awkward and diffident in class that Pauline rather marvelled at this self-assurance, revealing a completely new side to him. Together with his changed and enhanced appearance it was like discovering what someone was really like. A changed man indeed, maybe more at home in his own environment than among strangers, yet there were plenty of strangers here.

Pauline, used to meeting people, easily held her own, conversing knowledgeably with the men on either side, one who was a solicitor and the other a businessman in the town.

When the dancing started the businessman, whose name was Tony, leapt to his feet and asked her to dance, excusing himself to his wife who was sitting next to Roger who, as if on cue, asked her to dance.

By now, well fed and reasonably watered, with two glasses of good wine, Pauline glided effortlessly on to the floor and, to her surprise, Tony danced quite well and even she was better than she let on to Roger.

At the end of the dance they strolled back to their table at the same time as Roger politely escorted the wife back and then held out his hand to Pauline.

'Shall we?'

She smiled happily at him as the dance began. 'I am really enjoying myself,' she said.

'Glad now that you came?'

'Oh yes, very glad. I see you are a better dancer than you let on.'

'You too,' Roger said, drawing her closer, his arm tightening around her. To her surprise it seemed quite natural and she responded, their bodies touching as they glided round the floor in perfect harmony. He was indeed a much better dancer than he had suggested and so, as she quite well knew, was she. At the end, instead of returning to their table, they waited for the next dance, feet tapping on the floor, and when it started he took her in his arms again.

Once again his hand tightened on her back, drew her closer and finally he placed his cheek against hers.

'People will think we're in love,' she murmured.

'So what's wrong with that?'

She drew herself away from him. 'Well, we're not.'

'Only kidding. Look, everyone's doing it.'

'But I would think most of them are dancing with their wives.'

'Come on, don't be silly.' He drew her playfully towards him, and she pressed herself up against him again.

She had her chin resting on his shoulder when, glancing over, she saw across the room someone she knew. She straightened up.

'Roger.'

'What?'

'That's Martin, look.'

He slowed down and looked in the direction she had indicated. 'Well, I don't know.'

Martin and his partner were not dancing cheek to cheek but rather formally, well apart, as Roger and Pauline drew nearer until collision was almost inevitable. They stopped just as Martin saw them, surprise showing on his face. At that moment, the dance came to an end, making conversation possible.

'Why, hello,' Martin said.

'Hello, Martin, isn't it a small world?' Pauline disengaged her hand from Roger's.

'Very small.' Martin drew the women he was dancing with forward. 'This is my wife, Sarah. Two fellow students from the art class,' he explained to her, 'Roger and Pauline.'

'Oh, it does exist then?' the wife said with a chilly smile.

Roger looked puzzled. 'I beg your pardon?'

'Of course it exists,' Martin said tetchily.

'Oh, the art class certainly exists,' Roger said, 'and he is one of the best students. And I'm one of the worst.'

'No, *I'm* the worst,' Pauline interrupted him playfully, anxious to start dancing again.

The conversation clearly made Martin uneasy as his wife continued to stare fixedly and unsmilingly at Pauline and Roger.

'How come you're here?' he asked.

'I work for the firm. I'm one of the hosts. And you?'

'Warrington's,' Martin said as the music started up again. Then dismissively, 'Very nice to see you,' and he turned back to his wife.

'And you. See you in class,' Roger replied, then to Pauline, 'Dance?'

He swept her once again into his arms as Martin, firmly taking his wife's arm, led her back to their table at the far of the room obviously, from his manner and the expression on his face, busy remonstrating with her.

'What a curious encounter,' Pauline said as they sat back in the taxi taking her home. Their hands were loosely clasped. It had seemed natural after the intimacy on the dance floor.

'What, with Martin?'

'He was clearly very uneasy.'

'And so was she. The whole thing was very odd.'

'What do you suppose she meant by saying "oh, it does exist then?" She had a very sceptical expression on her face.'

'Maybe she doesn't trust him.'

'They were an odd couple,' Pauline continued thoughtfully.

'Somehow they didn't seem to fit.' Sarah had been attractive, fair, of medium height, younger than Martin, wore a lot of make-up and had the firm, set expression on her face of an unhappy woman. Her smile had been perfunctory.

'Certainly not what you'd call a loving couple.' Roger's hand tightened over hers.

Pauline responded, her fingers intertwined with his, conscious now of their own intimacy and what it might possibly lead to, aware of a growing feeling of excitement. Of course they were both slightly drunk.

'I thought he seemed uneasy seeing us,' she said.

'Certainly surprised. Warrington's is one of our most important clients. They are big builders in Southampton. I wonder if Sasha knows he's married.'

Pauline looked at him in surprise. 'Why?'

'Because I think she fancies him, and maybe he fancies her. Perhaps that's why he looked so unhappy at seeing us.'

'How do you know she fancies him?'

'I can sense it.'

'Because you fancy her yourself?'

Roger abruptly let her hand fall. 'What a thing to say. I don't fancy her at all. Whatever made you say that?'

Pauline could sense in the darkness the surprise on Roger's face. His whole body had somehow stiffened beside her. She longed once more for the feel of his hand in hers, a resumption of that intimacy engendered on the dance floor by the whole tone of the evening, but it remained where it was, by his side.

'Sorry,' she said contritely, 'it was a silly thing to say. She is so attractive. I thought maybe you did.' She tentatively reached for his hand again, but it remained by his side, unresponsive.

'Well, I don't. Besides, she has a partner.'

Pauline decided it was wiser not to ask how he knew.

The taxi stopped abruptly outside her door and the driver turned to look at them enquiringly.

'It's been a lovely evening,' Pauline said, as she opened the door, 'I did so enjoy it.'

'Good,' Roger said. 'Me too.'

Once outside the cab she leaned towards him. 'Would you like to come in for a quick coffee?'

'No, I must get home. I have a babysitter for the boys. She'll wonder where I am.'

She had forgotten about the boys.

'I'll wait until you unlock your door,' he said.

'Thanks again.'

He gave her a wave as she turned, and as she put her key in the lock she looked back and waved, but the taxi had gone.

Pauline opened the door suddenly feeling tired, despondent, but above all angry with herself. The bloom of the evening, the promise it had seemed to contain had vanished completely. Once more she had put her foot in it, said the wrong thing, and maybe done herself out of a pleasant, perhaps even important relationship. On the other hand, why would Sasha fancy Martin if she had a partner and, besides, how did Roger know that?

Seven

Caroline finally got the call she had so dreaded, not in the middle of the night as she'd expected, but halfway through the morning, as she was doing housework and Adam was having his morning nap. The doorbell went and when she opened it a non-commissioned officer stood on the other side.

'Oh no,' she gasped, and was tempted to shut the door again. Then she knew that this was the moment and she must face up to it.

'Come in,' she said, stepping aside, her lip trembling, and the sergeant removed his cap and entered the hall.

'Is it Greg?'

'Oh, Mrs Baxter, no,' the sergeant said quickly, a note of apology in his voice. 'Corporal Mark Dean has unfortunately been killed in action and I wondered if you'd go round and comfort Mrs Dean, who specifically asked for you because Corporal Dean is in your husband's platoon.'

Caroline, still trembling, asked the soldier into the sitting room and offered him coffee, which he declined.

'I'm very sorry I gave you a shock.'

'That's OK,' Caroline said. 'You see I have been dreading something happening to Greg; we all live in this fear and now it's Sharon's turn. I'll go at once. I'll have to take my son to my mother's and then I'll go straight to Sharon.'

'I can give you a lift.'

'When did it happen?'

'Yesterday. I'm afraid we had to tell her this morning and she is, of course, terribly upset.'

'She's got three young kids.'

'I know.'

Caroline spent the whole day with Sharon, suffering with her, a woman to whom she had never been particularly close, but now they were sisters in grief as their husbands had been comrades in arms. It was as if Greg had gone and she was experiencing vicariously, through her, her own grief, her own sense of loss.

'It's all so bloody pointless,' Sharon kept on saying. 'What does this war mean? No one wants it. Mark didn't want it. Didn't know why he was there. Hated the fucking place. Didn't believe in it. Who does? None of us. Do we?'

Caroline shook her head, her arms still tightly round the grieving woman's shoulders.

'No, none of us. I begged Greg to leave the army.'

'The boys in the battalion think so much of Greg. If he goes they'll all go. What sort of life do I have now? And the kids. How do I tell them? *What* do I tell them? Is all this suffering worthwhile for something we don't believe in? It is one thing to fight for your country, as people did during the Second World War, really protecting us from invasion and occupation. It is quite another to fight in a country thousands of miles from here for people we don't know and causes we couldn't care less about, whatever they are. Do you know?'

Caroline shook her head. 'They say it is to protect us from terrorists, but who is supposed to believe that?' She lit another cigarette for Sharon who smoked incessantly all day and even made her start again, though she had given it up a number of times.

Much coffee had been drunk and pots and pots of tea. Little had been eaten. The number of cigarettes smoked would have shocked the health watchdogs. People came and went, mostly other army wives who had heard the news by text or the army grapevine. Sharon's mother was on her way from Manchester. Her brother, also in the army, had been given compassionate leave and was flying home. Everything possible was being done, but nothing would ever, could possibly ever, make up for the loss of a partner who was supposed to be there for life.

When Sharon's mother arrived Caroline, completely exhausted, left, promising to return the next day if needed. She picked up the kids from her mother and drove home. They all had tea together and, after the children were in bed, Caroline went down to the sitting room and sifted through her recent paintings lying on the table, still-lives or fantasy pictures of beautiful, peaceful places, some that never existed. Angrily she tore them up, threw them in the waste-paper basket, got out fresh sheets of paper, her paint box, fetched clean water and commenced a savage depiction of men lying mangled and dead on a battlefield. To hell with what Sasha had said; this was real life.

When she finally went to bed she found it impossible to sleep. The terror she had imagined of what might happen when the doorbell rang and a soldier stood on the other side had happened that day, only for another woman. All the time she spent comforting Sharon she was aware how easily it might have been her, and how the next time it might be, and all the army wives would descend on her house to help her try and fill that awful chasm that had suddenly opened, which she had always dreaded, and that they would also dread happening to them.

Yet she had surprised herself by the way she managed to sustain Sharon, the calm and strength she had summoned up from nowhere, that she didn't know she had, the words she had found which somehow seemed to help the poor woman. Even now she had forgotten what she said and how she did it. She knew she must be ready for the next time, the time it really might be her.

'Today I want to consider further techniques in painting with watercolours.' Sasha began addressing her class. 'I want to begin with masking, which is intended to preserve certain areas of your picture while you work on another. You can do this using fluid of which there are two types, or masking tape. Let me show you what I mean.'

She went across to her easel on which she had already placed a half-finished painting of the busy marina with yachts entering and leaving, a small motor cruiser passing, and swans swimming, all against a background of buildings surrounding the harbour.

Some of the class watched the demonstration with more attention and interest than others. There was a rather sombre air about its members today, perhaps due to post-Christmas gloom, or the weather, it was hard to tell. It was still quite cold in the room, as though the heating had not been fully turned on, and most had kept on coats or jackets. Roger, who obviously had a cold, even had his scarf tightly round his neck. Numbers were reduced perhaps owing to sickness. It was flu time and it was a bitterly cold, frosty night.

The most cheerful person was Alice, smiling and serene as always, elegantly dressed, coiffed, made-up. She could have given away twenty years had it not been for the deep marks of age etched on her face. Even then she could have shed about fifteen, making her look nearer a well-preserved and healthy woman in mid-seventies. Both she and Moira had produced good home-work; some hadn't brought any, blaming Christmas; and one, Caroline, hadn't yet dared show hers to Sasha. At the last moment when Sasha had come round on her inspection, her courage stalled and she mumbled some excuse about showing it to her later. She had just returned from accompanying Sharon to watch the coffin containing Mark's body being unloaded from the aero-plane and anger was still at boiling point, but she remembered how good Sasha had been to her over Christmas, what a lot she owed her, and thought she owed her more of an explanation than she could give in the classroom.

Pauline had done nothing, Roger a little, which Sasha said she would look at later, recalling her promise to assess his work. Others in the class varied, but on the whole the output was small. It often happened in the second term, as if students had somehow lost interest.

As the class came to an end – Sasha having completed her lecture, while students got down to attempting to apply the tech-nique she had suggested – Caroline beckoned to her and, as the room emptied, produced her paintings from her portfolio and showed them to her wordlessly.

'Oh,' was all Sasha said as she studied the horrifying scenes depicted, mangled bodies lying on desert sand against a smoke-filled background.

'The horrors of war,' Caroline said, defiantly.

'I can see that. Well . . .' Sasha replaced them on the table and looked at her friend.

'I owe you an explanation,' Caroline said. 'Which is why I didn't produce them before. And I want you to know, Sasha, how really grateful I am for what you did for me over Christmas, but I have spent most of the past week comforting a woman who has just lost her husband, a member of Greg's battalion, and I got so angry at what had happened to a nice, decent guy, a father, who was just obeying orders, didn't even believe in the bloody war, which has left three young kids who will grow up without ever having known him, or forgetting most of what they knew. I tore up my paintings in a fury one night on an impulse; they were so unrealistic. And I did these, and have been doing them ever since, after I get home at night from an exhausting day.'

'I understand,' Sasha said gently. 'They are actually very good. Objectively speaking, your technique has improved enormously. The important thing is, how are *you*?' She looked at her anxiously. 'I have tried phoning you but . . .'

'I was with Sharon, day in, day out, and you know what? It was like going back into the deep end after nearly drowning. Compared to what Sharon was going through, the actual experience of losing her husband, I forgot about myself and found strength from her, more confidence in myself, and my own fears sank into the background. I was thinking of someone else for a change. I have spent too much time thinking about myself. All the time in the background was the possibility of it happening to Greg, and watching his body, which I had last seen so alive and vigorous, being brought off the plane. I saw not only Sharon's tears, but also those of the other women around us and thought that nothing seemed worth it, no amount of support or compensation you could ever hope to get. But for me personally the extraordinary thing is that that experience, horrible as it has been, has done me good. Made me braver, more worthy of Greg and the boys with him. I am sleeping better and I think it has prepared me for whatever happens.'

'Good,' Sasha said, pressing her arm. 'I'm glad. Come and have coffee.'

Roger had been behind Pauline in the coffee queue.

'Hi,' he said into her ear, and she turned, feigning surprise.

'Hi Roger. How have you been?'

'Fine, and you? Here, let me.' He reached ahead of her and produced the cash to pay for both of their coffees.

'That's very kind of you.' Gratified, she followed him to the table.

'I'm sorry I haven't been in touch,' he said, sitting down. 'But I took the boys away for a few days to see my parents in Scotland. Kay hasn't been well and was glad to get rid of them.'

'Nothing serious, I hope?'

'No, only the seasonal flu. She gets it every year.'

'I thought you might have been rather annoyed with me,' she said.

'Annoyed?' He looked surprised.

'The stupid thing I said . . .' She paused, and looked round surreptitiously, 'About Sasha,' she whispered. 'You fancying her.'

'Yes, I was a bit annoyed,' he admitted, 'but it passed. It was silly. I think we were both a bit tiddly.'

'And silly of me to say it. I do put my foot in things.'

'That's part of your charm,' Roger said, stirring sugar into his coffee.

'Oh?' Pauline's face flushed. 'Do you think so?'

'Yes I do. I also think you underrate yourself. Oh,' he said, looking up, 'here are Sasha and Caroline.'

Both women had paused by the side of their table, rather wanting somewhere else so that they could continue their conversation, but there being no other empty spaces they sat down next to the couple.

'Move up,' Caroline said.

Obligingly, Roger moved up, staying next to Pauline, but leaving room for Caroline to sit next to him while Sasha was on the other side. Across the table were Moira and Alice.

'Did you have a good Christmas?' Roger asked chattily.

'Well . . .' Sasha glanced at Caroline who was staring into her cup. 'Different, shall we say, and you?'

'Boring, but I invited Pauline to my firm's New Year's Eve dance and we had a good time, didn't we, Pauline?'

'Very,' she said.

'Oh, and you'll never guess who we saw?' He paused dramatically while the others looked at him expectantly.

'Martin.' Roger sounded like a conjuror producing a rabbit from a hat.

'Martin?' Caroline asked, perplexed.

'Yes. The Martin who comes to our class; he was with his wife.'

'With his wife?' Caroline glanced at Sasha. 'Was she nice?'

'Well, we didn't chat. It was in the middle of the dance floor. Yes, she seemed OK. Quite attractive, tall, elegant, rather aloof. She didn't say much, and then they just walked off and we got on with our dancing.'

'What a coincidence.' Moira, listening with half an ear from her position across the table, butted in. 'Did you know Martin had a wife, Sasha?'

'Why shouldn't he have one?' Sasha replied as calmly as she could, yet she felt the heat first rush to her cheeks and then drain away. 'I know nothing about Martin. Besides, he hasn't been to class for ages.'

'Did he say why he never comes to class?' Moira seemed keen to pursue her questioning.

'I didn't ask him,' Roger replied. 'He seemed quite keen to get away. Anyway it was very noisy. Oh, his wife did say, "oh, so it does exist," when he told her he knew us from the art class.'

'Which made us wonder if *she* thinks it is an excuse,' Pauline put in.

'For what?' Caroline asked.

'Who knows? It was the way she said it, that's all.'

'As though he might be leading a double life.' Roger sniggered. 'Crafty old Martin.'

'Crafty old Martin.' Still mentally reeling, Sasha hung back to wait for Caroline who had stopped to talk to someone else she'd met, a fellow army wife, who was taking another course at the centre. She had got away from the table as soon as she could in case her shock at the news about Martin became too obvious. As it was Caroline had already noticed that something was amiss.

'What's up?' she asked as she joined her. 'Don't you feel well? You're as white as a sheet.'

'No, I'm not OK. In fact I feel physically sick. Let's go and sit in the car. I promise I won't be sick there!'

'I haven't got my car,' Caroline said. 'I thought I'd walk and get some exercise. My mother is babysitting.'

'I'll take you home. We can talk on the way.'

'Fine,' Caroline said, shivering as they emerged into the night. 'It's so bloody cold anyway.'

Once inside the car Sasha set off in case anyone else saw them sitting chatting. When they were clear of the centre she slowed down.

'Martin and I started an affair,' she said. 'Or rather, we slept together, just before Christmas. I haven't been able to think of anything else since. I've been obsessed by him, by the thought of being in love again.'

She glanced to see her friend's reaction, but Caroline was staring grimly in front of her, taking it all in.

'Go on, I'm listening.'

'I asked him if he'd ever been married and he said he had briefly, a long time ago. He also said . . .' Sasha almost choked on her words. 'That he thought we'd be together for a long time.'

'The bastard.'

'I think he is a bastard. I can't believe it, but maybe he's done this kind of thing before. He just appeared at the college one day and asked me out for dinner as he was going away. I suggested Luigi's in the High Street but he was very keen to choose a place out of town, which he said would be "discreet". It didn't occur to me at the time to wonder what we had to be discreet about if we'd nothing to hide.'

'You did fall for him, didn't you?' Caroline said.

'I did rather, I admit it. I did. I think it was a reaction to Ben.'

'You quite fancied him at that lunch you had in London.'

'I know. What a fool I was.'

'Maybe he's unhappy? Maybe the wife doesn't trust him either, from what she said to Roger about the art class existing after all. Maybe it's an unhappy marriage.'

'That doesn't make it any better, does it?'

'Not really. I can see his attraction though. Trouble is, bastards are often like that, or so I'm told. Happily I've been spared the experience.'

'He could have told me the truth – that he is married and it is an unhappy marriage. *If* it is. Now I feel I don't trust him at all.'

'Perhaps he would have told you eventually.'

'I'm not going to give him the chance. I don't want to see him again. He said he wouldn't be returning to the class as he is away a lot. His business is having a bad time because of the recession. Anyway I now feel I could never believe anything he says. And I don't want to get into such a dodgy relationship any deeper, thank you. I've enough problems in my personal life.'

'Can't say I blame you.' Caroline patted her back consolingly. 'But I did wonder why you were so calmly talking about Ben at Christmas, as though you didn't care about him any more.'

'I didn't want to tell you about Martin yet,' Sasha admitted. 'I thought it was too soon. Anyway I also thought you might consider me a slut for slipping into bed with him so easily.'

'You a slut!' Caroline exclaimed, putting a hand on her arm. 'The last person I'd think of as a slut.'

'You see I've been so restless. I feel I want to start something new and I don't necessarily mean an affair. Though perhaps that's why I was such a pushover for Martin. You know, go away somewhere, do something different.'

'Go away? From the art class?' Caroline looked shocked. 'We should miss you terribly.'

'Oh, I won't go just like that, but an idea has been simmering at the back of my mind for some time and now maybe I should do something about it.'

'We've already gone past my mother's,' Caroline said abruptly. 'You'll have to backtrack I'm afraid.'

Roger and Pauline were still sitting at the table deep in conversation after most of the students had left and the staff behind the counter were noisily clearing up. They had almost naturally resumed the rapport they had enjoyed at the dance, and as soon as they were left alone at the table Pauline said: 'Did you notice the way Sasha reacted to the news about Martin's wife?'

'I thought she seemed surprised.' Roger tried to sound offhand.

'I thought she looked upset. She went all pink.'

'I think you're imagining it. Rather as you imagined I fancied her.' He looked towards the counter and waved a hand at a member of staff signalling to them. 'I think they want us to go. We're the last ones here.' They both got up, shrugging on coats and, as they reached the door, the lights in the canteen were turned off.

'Have you got your car?' Roger asked as they stood by the main door preparing to face the elements.

'Yes, thanks.'

'See you on Sunday perhaps, in the park.'

'Perhaps. I don't know if I'll have the dog.'

'Come anyway. I'll have the boys. I'd like you to meet them. Maybe have lunch afterwards?'

'Well, maybe.'

They strolled together to the car park and Roger saw her into her car. 'See you Sunday,' he said, shutting the door.

'I'll see.' And with a wave Pauline drove off.

It wouldn't do to seem too keen. In fact she didn't know exactly how she did feel about Roger. Initially she had not been at all attracted to him. He had a bland, almost instantly forgettable face, and fair hair thinning at the temples. In fact rather the stereotype of what his wife had regarded as a 'boring accountant'. However, when he'd appeared in a tuxedo to take her to the dance she had seen him in a different light. His height was an advantage, his features, if not memorable, at least were not unpleasant. He was the kind of bloke one could easily introduce to one's mum and dad and expect them not to be disappointed, especially with an unmarried daughter in her thirties. He certainly had an air of confidence that night she had not noticed before, and they had danced very intimately. She'd thought he might want to kiss her in the taxi taking them home and then perhaps they might drift into bed, something she was not averse to, having been without a sexual relationship for far too long. But then she had made that utterly stupid remark about him fancying Sasha, whereupon his manner changed completely and he said he had the boys staying with him, so it would never have been bed anyway.

Just as well. She imagined Roger was the kind of man who might have rather old-fashioned views about women who 'gave themselves' too easily. Besides, because it was such a long time since she'd had sex, she would have to fit herself up with some kind of contraception. She didn't imagine that Roger would carry condoms in his wallet, but one never knew.

However, now there were fresh overtures and it would be really stupid to reject them, so, the following Sunday she didn't even ask her friend about Rusty because they could hardly take him to a restaurant for lunch. She made her way on a sunny morning to the park and there everything was repeating itself: the boys were playing football and Roger was standing watching them, hands thrust deep in his pockets.

'Hi,' she said.

'Oh, hi,' he turned and looked at her. 'So you came.'

'I came and I thought if we were going somewhere for lunch, as you suggested, we wouldn't want Rusty.'

'Oh, good thinking.' He consulted his watch. 'The game will have finished in a few minutes. Hungry?'

'I could always eat.'

'It's McDonald's, do you mind?'

'McDonald's is fine. I look forward to meeting the boys.'

At that moment the final whistle blew and the teams came off the field to where parents were waiting with coats and scarves.

'This is Kevin, he's the youngest, and this is Oliver,' Roger said, bringing them forward. 'This is Pauline, a friend of mine from the art class.'

'Hi.' Pauline smiled as both boys politely shook hands, unable to conceal their curiosity about her. She thought that Kay must have been very attractive because, although having a slight resemblance in build to their father, Kevin and Oliver were extremely good looking, with jet-black hair, unlike Roger's insipid blond, and limpid brown eyes.

'Hungry?' asked their father.

The boys enthusiastically nodded their heads.

'McDonald's it is.' And Roger led the way to his car parked on the edge of the park and they drove into town.

McDonald's was crowded, busy, noisy. The boys were clever, articulate, exchanging banter with their father, good company. It was a long time since Pauline had had a hamburger. Seeing Roger in the role of a father was an altogether new experience. He came alive in their company – playful, argumentative, above all talkative, not at all the reserved man she'd first known in the art class, but one familiar to her from the New Year dance – a split personality. But then perhaps so was she. Normally outgoing, she was shy at first, not used to this atmosphere, but gradually she relaxed, became more involved and joined in the banter and the fun.

Above all she felt the same sense of camaraderie she had when she was with her brother and his children, part of the family, a feeling of belonging she was unaccustomed to, had longed for, and if she was not in love with Roger – and she wasn't – she felt she wanted to be, and would work on it.

He drove her home en route to taking the boys back to their mother. She and Roger remained silent, the boys chatting in the back. She knew, however, that the rapport had continued, and when he stopped in front of her house she said, 'Thanks *so* much, Roger. I've really enjoyed the day. Your sons are lovely.' She got out of the car and leaned across to look over at the boys. 'Bye, Kevin and Oliver. See you soon I hope.'

'Bye,' they chorused in union.

Roger leaned across the passenger seat towards her, half whispering, 'We must see more of each other.'

'Yes, I'd like that.'

'I'll give you a ring during the week.'

He watched her thoughtfully as she put her key in the lock and, as she turned and waved, all three waved back. Putting the car into gear he headed towards the motorway.

'Is she your girlfriend, Dad?' Kevin asked.

'Kind of.'

'Are you going to marry her?'

'Well, not yet. I hardly know her. How did you like her?'

'OK, a bit quiet at first.'

'That's because she probably felt awkward in our company.'

'But quite nice. Not like Mum.'

Which, Roger thought, although the boys didn't mean it that way, was a strong point in Pauline's favour.

Eight

Alice stood with her back to the window of her little studio, her easel in front of her, putting the finishing touches to a painting she was doing of a favourite scene remembered from the past: the woods above the village of Milton Abbas in Dorset. It was part of a series of scenes which she had called Remembrance of Things Past, after a favourite novel, and some of which she had already submitted to Sasha who had praised them in the gentle, caring way Sasha always did.

How grateful she was to Sasha and the watercolour class which had given her not just a new lease of life, but a new friend, Moira – so much so that now she almost felt part of Moira's family. Although Moira was much younger she felt that she was sincerely fond of her and enjoyed her company, and that the attention paid to her wasn't just out of pity. The Christmas lunch had been followed by many more, but she tried to reciprocate by taking them all out occasionally to Sunday lunch at a pleasant hotel with facilities for the children to escape and run about. Or she would just take Moira to lunch in town followed perhaps by a trip to the cinema. Then there were many outings with Moira in the car to paint, mostly the scenic coastline, the bay and the distant hills towards Dorset and Lyme Regis.

So much for the present. Her past life was recaptured through the medium of paint, reliving those days when she and Sybil lived in the Blackmore Vale, their time pleasantly enlivened by excursions to places like Milton Abbas, reached by a long tree-lined road with, in season, white garlic massed on either side, filling the air with its pungent smell, and in the adjacent woods, a mass of bluebells. They would sometimes take a picnic and put down a rug on a slope overlooking a beautiful valley, or one with a view of the public school, formerly the home of the earls of Dorchester. Joseph Damer, the first earl, or 'the wicked earl' to the locals, had an entire village submerged, rebuilding it higher up, so that he could have an uninterrupted view of the surrounding countryside. Or they would lunch at the pub halfway up the main street of the village and, afterwards, walk down to the lake and around the fourteenth-century church with its historical connections and the beautiful white marble monument designed by Robert Adam to Caroline Damer with the effigies of her grieving husband stretched alongside his dying wife.

Alice always drove while Sybil exercised her right to tell her what to do and where to go with all the authority and stubborn ignorance of an elder sister.

In her mind's eye Alice visualized the bluebell wood when a ring on the doorbell interrupted her happy memories and, paintbrush still in her hand, she went to the door and opened it.

'Moira!' she exclaimed with pleasure, but then the welcoming smile faded as she saw the expression on her visitor's face. 'My dear, whatever is the matter?' she said, drawing her inside and shutting the door. 'You look terrible. Are you not well?'

She ushered her to a chair and Moira sat down without even unfastening her coat.

'It's Ian,' she gasped. 'He has had the most terrible car accident in Kenya and is being flown over by air ambulance.'

'Oh my dear, how dreadful.' Alice sank into a chair beside her. 'You don't know the details of course?'

'I know he is very badly injured. Vanessa has gone to the airport to meet him and I have the children downstairs in the car.'

'Then you must bring them up.' Alice got up and looked out of the window.

'No.' Moira shook her head. 'I feel I must be with Vanessa. My dear . . .' She paused and looked appealingly at Alice. 'I know this is a terrible thing to ask, but I wonder if you would look after the children for me at least until this evening.'

'Of course I will. They are lovely children.'

'And they know you. Thank goodness they do. Would you mind, would it be too awful to ask you to come to my house? They have all their things there and it is not too unsettling for them. I can make up a bed for you. Then if I am late back I won't worry and I know Vanessa will have peace of mind. It has all happened so quickly, my mind is in a whirl. I just couldn't think of anyone else to ask at such short notice.'

Alice crossed the room and stood in front of her stricken friend. 'Then you have come to just the right person. I'll quickly pack an overnight bag and I'll be ready. The children will be fine with me and you will want to be with your daughter. Have the children . . .?' she paused. 'How much do they know?'

'They know Daddy's had an accident. We don't know how bad. However, from the little we *do* know I think it is very bad.' She faltered again. 'He may be paralysed. Oh dear.' She put her face in her hands and her voice cracked. 'Isn't it all just too awful?'

Although it was a responsibility being in a strange, or relatively strange house in total charge of two very young children, Alice had not been a teacher all her working life for nothing. She loved children and her confidence and ease of manner soon attracted them to her, and on this occasion made Vanessa's two feel at ease even though they knew that there was something seriously amiss with their father. Freddie was five and Helena three. They were both lively and attractive with Vanessa's brilliant colouring and fair hair. Moira had tried to conceal her unease as much as possible, to appear relaxed, even calm as she had explained the situation to them and how she wanted to be with their mummy while Aunt Alice looked after them. They all arrived back at the Cunningham house early in the afternoon and Moira took Alice to the pleasant first-floor bedroom she had hurriedly prepared for her, and then introduced her to the intricacies of an unfamiliar kitchen, showing her where everything was kept and what she suggested they might have for tea. She described the children's routine and, after being assured that everything would be alright, she left just as it was getting dark, phoning Vanessa to tell her she was on her way.

'Now don't worry about a thing,' Alice assured her as she was getting into her car. 'Not as far as we are concerned anyway. You look after yourself and Vanessa and phone me with news as soon as you can. Or maybe after the children are in bed.' She betrayed her anxiety for a moment. 'I'll leave it to you.'

Nevertheless, for all her composure, it felt strange watching the car drive away and realizing her responsibilities, for she didn't know how long. But Helena and Freddie made everything easy for her. They were very self contained, enjoyed puzzles and games, and only watched television while Alice got their tea, which she shared with them.

It was a simple tea of baked beans on toast which Moira told Alice Vanessa would not consider nutritious but, naturally, was a favourite with the children for this very reason.

'Their mother is very conscious of their diet,' Moira had told her. 'Five helpings of fruit and vegetables a day, no caffeine or white bread, Coca-Cola strictly taboo, that sort of thing. Everything must be organic, fair-trade or free-range, but when they are with me I sin horribly and we have sausages and chips or baked beans and I never feel guilty about it because I know it is a treat. If I am to look after the children for any length of time I'm sure I shall have full dietary instructions from Vanessa.'

Alice liked baked beans too and was less concerned with a correct diet, having the opinion that at her age it was too late to give it any serious consideration. Accordingly she ate what she wanted, her only concession being that there should not be too much of it, as being fat was almost as bad as being old and the two in conjunction were best avoided.

The children were very helpful in the kitchen, telling her where everything was kept, as if she didn't already know, and stacking the dishwasher for her. After tea they were allowed half an hour's children's television while she went upstairs to prepare their beds and put out their night things. As soon as she called they were on their way to bed, anxious to please as well as impress by being on their best behaviour. She then supervised their bath routine, and after reading them a story tucked them up in twin beds. It was then that Helena became tearful and clung to Alice as she bent to kiss her goodnight.

'Do you think Daddy will die, Aunt Alice?'

'Oh, darling, no.' Alice sank on to the bed and put her arms round the stricken child. 'Modern medicine can do wonderful things. Doctors are very clever these days. They will look after him well.'

'Then why are Mummy and Gran with him?' Freddie chipped in from his side of the room. Obviously the pair had been discussing the event in some detail.

'Because he is very sick and naturally your mummy wants to be with him and your grandma wants to be there too for extra support. They have had a shock. We all have. It is perfectly natural, but it doesn't mean for a minute that eventually he will not recover.'

She wasn't certain that this remark comforted Helena, who sobbed quietly for a while, but she was also obviously very tired and eventually her eyes closed and Alice gently let go of her hand. Crossing the room she saw that Freddie's eyes were wide open. He wasn't crying but his face was creased with anxiety, so she sat on his bed and leaned towards him, whispering, 'OK?'

He nodded but didn't speak so she put a hand on his brow and gently stroked it.

'Daddy will be alright,' she whispered.

'Promise?'

'Promise.'

He raised himself in the bed and put his arms round her. 'I love you, Aunt Alice.'

'And I love you too,' she said, scarcely able to contain her own emotion. As he sank back she also held his hand until eventually his eyes closed and his breathing became steady. She stayed for a while longer and then, after putting the light out by the side of his bed, crept quietly out of the room. She went down the stairs to the kitchen where she cleared things away, then she sat in the sitting room with only one light on, reliving the events of the day, momentous as they had been.

She always thought that at times like this it would be helpful to have the consolations of religion, but she was no longer religious and didn't think the children were either. Sybil had been a very keen member of the established church and as long as she was alive Alice had conformed.

She had been very touched by the attitude towards her of the children and thought this was a tribute to their parents. At a very trying time they had behaved in an exemplary manner which, considering their ages, was almost incredible and quite moving. Yes, she did love them. She loved the whole family who had given a new dimension to what had been a solitary, even self-centred, life and she would do all she could to help them bear the unbearable. It was very satisfying to be trusted, but above all wanted and useful and to feel that this had somehow set the seal on her full integration into the family circle. Now she belonged.

But if Ian did die she hoped the children would forgive her for her deception and would understand – if not immediately, then one day – the reason for it.

Moira must have returned in the early hours because Alice, quite exhausted from her eventful day, had fallen into a deep sleep and heard nothing. She had left her door open in case either of the children called – they were only two doors away – and felt sure that in that event instinct would have awakened her; but the first she knew about her presence was when the door was quietly opened and Moira crept across the room with a cup of tea.

'Oh!' Alice, still half asleep and disorientated, looked at her visitor as though she didn't know who she was or how she had got there, and then pulled herself up in the bed. 'What time is it?'

'Don't worry. It's early, only seven, but I wanted you to know I was back.'

'And . . .?' Alice looked at her anxiously and Moira perched on the side of her bed.

'Ian is extremely ill. It is early days but he might be paraplegic. He all but died in the air ambulance. Was resuscitated twice and is in intensive care. Of course Vanessa is beside herself with grief, and guilt I'm afraid, having been with Tim, she confessed, when the call about Ian came. Even then she had her mobile switched off which delayed her response. I came home because there is not much I can do. She has a bed at the hospital and I have to take Freddie to school.'

'I'll look after Helena.'

'You are an angel. Are you sure you have the time?'

'Freddie told me he loved me. Poor Helena was in tears and

asked if I thought her daddy would die. Of course I had to say that I was sure he wouldn't, as the doctors were so good. Naturally they are both concerned and unhappy and need a lot of love and support, which I hope I am able to help give. In my many years as a teacher I often had to comfort children who lost parents or a parent, even grandparents who they were close to.'

Moira leaned across the bed and embraced her. 'I can see you are going to be of great comfort to me because Vanessa is grief stricken and wracked with guilt about the way she has deceived Ian. How relieved I am that I told you about Tim, that you know the truth. It will give a whole new meaning to their relationship. And what if he is paraplegic?' She stopped abruptly and, putting her head in her hands, started to weep.

'Oh, it is all too awful,' she whispered between sobs, 'seeing Ian lying there, the tubes coming from all directions, utterly inert. He has not recovered consciousness, which is perhaps a blessing. Who knows what is going to happen now?'

And what – a thought Alice kept strictly to herself – if he died?

The talk at the art class was all about Moira's son-in-law and the terrible accident he'd had. Alice and Moira had both been absent from the art class the previous week, but as it was the time for illnesses of all kinds, colds and seasonal flu, not much notice was taken of it. In fact that week numbers were altogether diminished and Sasha wondered if it was sickness or because people were beginning to lose interest or, so preoccupied as she had been with her own problems, that her teaching wasn't inspirational enough. It was that part of the term when she had more or less taught the beginners all they needed at that stage to know and the advanced students were showing signs of wanting to move on. After Easter and lighter days it would be outings to the surrounding countryside or coast to move on to the trickier subject of landscape painting.

This week Alice had arrived late at the class and, apologizing to Sasha and giving her reasons, did so in a voice loud enough to be heard by the whole class, most of whom stopped working to listen.

'Moira has two grandchildren,' Alice continued, 'and I have been helping to look after them while she went to the hospital to be with her daughter.'

'Oh, that is terrible news,' Sasha said while individual voices were raised in sympathy. 'How is he?'

'He is still very ill and it is too early to give a prognosis. His wife Vanessa spends most of her time at the hospital, so I have been staying over at Moira's house to help with the children and enable her to support her daughter. Oh . . .' Guiltily Alice stopped, realizing the whole class was listening to her. 'I mustn't go on. I'm holding up proceedings.'

'We quite understand,' Sasha said. 'Give our love to Moira and say we are thinking of her.'

'I will.' Alice had not been neglecting her painting as, in fact, while Freddie was at school and Helena at her nursery school, she had been able to use Moira's studio to produce work which she extracted from her portfolio and put on Sasha's desk. She was particularly attracted by Moira's beautiful garden and the large, almost ornamental holly tree which dominated it, setting it off to perfection and which now formed the centrepiece of some of her paintings.

However, the interruption seemed to unsettle the class, some of whom were still struggling with newly acquired techniques – sponging, drying and blowing, and scratching. There was such a lot to learn and, in fact, according to Sasha it never ended.

After the class Sasha stopped by Alice's table.

'Can I give you a lift, as Moira isn't here?'

'That would be very nice.' Alice began to put her things together, 'But I'm afraid I won't stop for coffee.'

'I don't want to much either. I'll explain to them I'll be taking you back. See you by the front door.'

'No problem,' Sasha said as she joined Alice minutes later. 'They quite understand. Excuse me a second, I just had a text on my mobile.'

She stopped and looked at it, lingering on the message for a moment, her face gradually changing colour.

'Not bad news, I hope?' Alice asked anxiously as Sasha stuffed her phone into her pocket.

'Oh no.' Sasha's smile was forced as she led the way to the

car, but it was too dark for Alice to notice it. 'Nothing important. It's great for Moira to have you,' she said as they settled in.

'It's great for me to be able to help. She has done such a lot for me. Transformed my life in many ways. And, really, tragic as the circumstances are, it has been a delightful experience for me. The contact with young children is very precious to me, you see, having had none of my own.' As they stopped outside Moira's house she put a hand on Sasha's arm. 'My dear, don't think it impertinent of me, but if I may be allowed to give you some advice it is not to delay a family, because the time might come when you realize, as I do now, what you have missed.'

'I'll remember that,' Sasha said, making an effort to look cheerful.

'How is that young man of yours?'

'Oh, he's fine,' Sasha said, 'and give Moira my love.'

'I'd ask you in, but I think she might have gone to bed early. She gets very tired. I'll see you next week.'

'Take care,' Sasha said, and watched her enter the house before, still sitting in the car, she reread the text message: '*Darling I'm back. I've missed you so much and am longing to see you. Lunch tomorrow?*'

After a while she texted back. '*OK.*'

To have refused to see him would have been to deny her the chance of telling him just what she thought of him.

'*Same time, same place. I'll pick you up,*' he had texted back. When he arrived at the college she was waiting for him in the porch and slipped into the seat beside him.

He looked at her eagerly.

'You look fantastic. You don't know how much I've thought of you and how I remembered last time. By the way,' he said with a meaningful glance, 'I have the rest of the afternoon free.'

'Last time,' Sasha thought grimly to herself, staring straight ahead, 'and there will be no next time.'

'Is there anything the matter, sweetie?' he asked anxiously.

'There's plenty the matter, Martin,' she said, as they stopped in the hotel car park. 'And I honestly don't want you to go to the expense of buying me lunch, because I don't ever want to see you again.'

The expression of contentment on his face disappeared in a trace.

'Last time we met,' she went on icily, 'you forgot to tell me you were going to take your wife to a New Year's Eve dance before you went abroad.'

'Oh.' Martin seemed resigned rather than shocked, as though this was something he had ben expecting. 'Roger and Pauline, I expect. I feared as much. I wanted to tell you, but I did have to fly on New Year's Day to Dubai. There was no way I could contact you. Somehow I just hoped it wouldn't come up at the class. There was no reason to think it would. Bad luck really.'

'I don't think I can believe anything you say, Martin.'

'I did. I promise. I've been there a month. Desperate negoti-ations because everything is falling apart and we have some massive projects there. Millions of pounds are at stake.'

'Why didn't you tell me you were married?'

'Because I didn't want to lose you. Look, let's have lunch and I'll explain. We both have to eat, after all. And if it's the last time . . .' He looked at her appealingly.

Sasha was indeed hungry and it was hard to give full vent to her indignation in such a public place. So she shrugged, nodded silently, and followed him into the restaurant where they were given the same table they had occupied before.

'Is this where you bring all your girlfriends?' she asked as they studied the menu.

'I see you want to be difficult, Sasha.'

'I want you to understand I am very hurt, desperately. I don't usually fall into bed with men I hardly know, and I feel you made a fool of me. You told me you were once married, which implied you weren't any longer. That was a deliberate lie meant to deceive me.'

She paused as the waitress reappeared and took their orders. Sasha no longer felt hungry but she ordered spaghetti and he ordered the steak plus a bottle of Beaune. He looked very agitated and kept fiddling with the cutlery on the table. Then, when the waitress had gone, he leaned over so that his voice could scarcely be heard.

'Look I am very, very sorry. What I did was wrong and now I am paying for it. I was telling the truth in the sense that my real marriage was over a long time ago. But you see I was so afraid of losing you. I desired you madly. Have for ages.'

'And you couldn't resist the chance of a shag, knowing I was vulnerable after what happened with Ben.'

'No, it wasn't like that at all. I didn't know we were going to go to bed. I think it was something we both wanted. I know I should have told you about Sarah at dinner that time. I meant to, but it wasn't because I just wanted to get you into bed. You see, it is a very complicated situation with my wife. We have been married for twenty years and she is not a well woman. She suffers from clinical depression and has been hospitalized several times. She is on heavy medication. I do not love her and she doesn't love me. Yes, she is very suspicious of me. Always asking what I'm doing and where I'm going. She hangs on.'

'Roger and Pauline had that impression. She said something about the art class being genuine.'

'Yes she did. She wouldn't even believe I knew them from the art class. It was a horrible evening altogether, but it is one of the few occasions we do go out together. We hate being alone with each other. This is another reason I am so keen on going abroad on business, and she doesn't even believe that. I am trapped in a nightmare situation. We sleep apart and haven't had sex for at least ten years and, yes, I have had one or two affairs, but you were different.'

'Sounds like a story, Martin,' she said sarcastically.

'It is *not* a story.' He thumped the table so hard that people having lunch nearby stared at him.

'Sorry,' he said, lowering his voice as Sasha frowned and jerked her head in their direction. 'I told you I had fancied you for a long time, and I did and still do. And not just in the sexual sense. You are my ideal woman – strong, clever yet very feminine. I wanted to discuss with you the possibility that I might leave Sarah, but it is a very difficult thing for me to do. We have two grown-up children who I think might be quite sympathetic to my situation, but they are also very attached to their mother and concerned about her.'

If true (could she really ever believe Martin now?) it was a heart-rending story, but her instinct for self-preservation was strong and Sasha knew what she must do.

'I don't want an affair,' she said firmly. 'I want to make that plain. I mean I don't want an affair with a married man, whatever his circumstances. Too many people I know have got themselves into this situation and can never get out of it. I am sorry about your wife. As for you leaving her, naturally I don't want that either, so I think it's goodbye for us, Martin.'

'So I meant nothing to you?' he said, with an air of desperation.

'Yes you did, you meant a lot. I felt strongly attracted to you, but in this case my head rules my heart. I don't want to go from one unsatisfactory situation, my relationship with Ben, to another. As people know you're married we would always have to be furtive, meeting in out-of-the-way places like this, and I'd hate that. I can see no future for us. Dear Alice said to me the other night that I should not miss the chance of having children and I think she's right. If I go into a relationship with you too deeply it will be the end, and I'd be trapped for good.'

Sasha had a class that afternoon of advanced art students taking their finals in the summer and she didn't know how she got through it, the events of her lunch with Martin reverberating over and over again in her head. By the end of the day it was throbbing and she couldn't wait to get home.

There she took herself immediately to bed and lay in the dark thinking, wondering if she'd done the right thing, if burning her boats with Martin was really what she wanted. Hadn't she had him continually on her mind since the meeting at the National Gallery, and since they had made love? Hadn't he seemed to light a fire inside her, and hadn't she really thought they had a future? There was something that seemed so sincere and genuine about Martin that it was hard to believe it was all an act.

Had she thrown away a small chance of happiness? And would she ever know? Yet there was also something very definite about the way they had said goodbye. They had both left their food unfinished and walked silently to the car, maintaining the silence all the way back to the college, which became unnerving. There was simply nothing left to say.

'Goodbye, Martin,' she'd said, glancing at him as she got out of the car.

'Bye,' he'd replied, and immediately put the car into gear even before she had shut the door. She didn't watch him as he drove off, but went straight through the college doors.

No turning back.

Nine

Vanessa sat by the side of Ian's bed looking at his inert form with all the tubes and life-giving appliances attached to him; the oxygen mask that was essential twenty-four hours a day was clamped firmly over his nose and mouth, while his eyes remained tightly shut. She was given a room to sleep in at the hospital but when his life still hung in the balance she only left his side when Moira came and took over for an hour or two while she tried to have the rest that she so desperately needed.

Watching Ian it was hard to recall what he had been like – lively, active, good looking, someone she had grown so accustomed to that eventually the relationship grew stale and she started an affair. But at the beginning it had all been very different. She had been madly in love with him, apart from the fact that he was so very suitable as husband material, with family money and a job that enabled her to live in the style she had been accustomed to throughout a pampered life. Her parents had adored him, and now she remembered more than ever those heady days of first love rather than the way they had degenerated as they settled down into domestic routine, the trivia of day-to-day life and the advent of two children.

The rot really began when Ian was promoted in his job and spent so much time travelling abroad, thus leaving a lonely restless woman with too much time on her hands despite the number of good causes she had espoused in an effort to placate a guilty conscience. But here again she knew she was venerated for her style and what she looked like rather than what she was able to do. As a figurehead she was always being invited to adorn functions, glamorous and beautifully dressed, of course, and open things rather than getting into the nitty gritty of hard work or even the dreary tasks of writing letters or stuffing envelopes or, horror of horrors, baking cakes for fêtes and open days.

Vanessa knew she had been spoiled by her father, then her husband, borne aloft by the universal admiration that her looks caused, the way people stopped and stared at her, their open admiration. She had never suffered loss or deprivation of any kind and when she became bored with her marriage, which, with hindsight, seemed inevitable, she had quite easily drifted into an affair with someone who was younger than Ian and much better in bed, made sex more adventurous and exciting once again.

Almost a stranger to introspection, the days during which Ian lay in a coma had made her examine herself and her life in a way she never had to before and inevitably what she found was not pretty. Unused to calling on the Almighty, she found herself praying and vowed that if Ian ever recovered she would reform and make herself into a good and faithful wife, a homemaker rather than a home breaker, and an even more loving and devoted mother to her children.

And then there was the day his eyes opened, focused on her with difficulty, but eventually his face cracked into what was a kind of smile. She got up and, leaning over him, looked into his eyes trying so hard to focus.

'I love you, darling,' she said, her voice breaking with emotion, and Ian made an effort to move his lips in a way that suggested that he wanted to say he loved her too.

Vanessa rang the bell beside his bed and summoned a nurse who called the doctor who shone lights into Ian's eyes and pronounced that he was in fact showing the first real signs of a sustainable recovery.

Throughout the day as Ian continued to try and fight his way back into the living world and daylight, Vanessa remained by his bedside, holding his hand which remained mostly in inert, but occasionally it seemed to respond to her with a very slight, gentle squeeze. When her mother arrived late morning she gave her the joyful news, together with the revised medical prognosis, and for a while her mother sat on the other side of the bed watching him. However he didn't open his eyes again and seemed to have sunk into an easy, more normal kind of sleep, nothing like the deep, rather frightening, almost complete withdrawal of a coma.

Vanessa whispered that she wanted to go home and get a fresh change of clothes and, after brief consultation with the nurse, they left and Moira took her daughter back to her house in her car.

'You look absolutely beat,' she said as they entered the house. 'You really must get more rest.'

'I think when they confirm he's really out of danger I'll come back and sleep here at night,' Vanessa replied. 'The hospital will probably kick me out anyway. They've been very good.' She paused. 'Where are the kids? There is a strange silence.'

'Freddie is at school. Helena at the nursery. Alice may have gone home to get some things or gone to town for a break. She is very independent. She's almost completely in charge now.'

'She's wonderful,' Vanessa murmured.

'She certainly is.'

'We must find a way of showing her how much we appreciate her.'

'She knows, don't worry, and I think she truly enjoys it. She loves children and ours especially.'

They were in the kitchen where Moira had put on the kettle while Vanessa sat at the table sorting through the mountain of accumulated post, a lot of which was to do with Ian's accident, the details of which were slowly surfacing due to the remoteness and inaccessibility of the area in which it had happened.

'That's funny,' Vanessa said, looking up from the letter she was reading.

'What's funny? Do you want anything to eat?' Moira asked.

'I wouldn't mind some toast. I didn't have any lunch. There's bread in the freezer. Honey in the cupboard above the stove.'

'What's funny?' her mother repeated.

'This letter is from the solicitor in London dealing with the case. He says someone was in the car with Ian, but this person – he doesn't say whether it was a man or woman – escaped injury, managed to get him to hospital, and so saved his life. We must find out who it is and thank them.'

She looked up as her mother laid two slices of toast in front of her.

'Tell me if you want more. You must eat, Vanessa. You are getting terribly thin and pinched looking. Not you at all.'

Vanessa reached up and took her mother's hand.

'Isn't it marvellous? About Ian.'

'Really marvellous.' Moira sat opposite her daughter, a mug of warm tea clasped in her hands.

'I must start sorting out things for when he comes home. Getting his room ready. We'll need a nurse. Mum . . .' Vanessa paused. 'I expect you're wondering about Tim?'

'It did cross my mind how you feel now,' Moira replied diplomatically.

'I feel dreadful. I feel a horrible, base little swine. Ian is such a good man and I am not worthy of him. Obviously I've been doing a lot of thinking, self-examination if you like, all the time I've been sitting by him wondering if he was going to live or die. It makes you reassess your priorities. We have a very good marriage, we have lovely kids, live in a nice house, no financial problems in a time of deep recession because Ian works so hard, and all I can find to do is have an affair with a young student ten years my junior. That's all it is. There is no love there at all, at least not on my part.'

'Have you been in touch with him?'

'Occasionally he texts me to ask about Ian, but he'll know how I must feel and I think respects it. I won't even see him to tell him it is all over. Basically Tim is a nice guy and I'm sure he'll understand and maybe even despise me for the way I've behaved, as I do myself. But as for the affair, it was nothing, a fling, and it is over. End of story, Mum.'

Moira looked for a long time at her daughter, saw the anguish in her face, the pain in her eyes and, oh, how she hoped she meant it.

So, having hovered for days between life and death, in the end life won and Ian made rapid progress. He began to resume some feeling in his body and what had at first appeared to be paralysis turned out to be caused by the extensive fractures to his legs and serious internal injuries, which was why he had spent so many days on a life-support system.

But he was a young, fit man previously in good health, and two weeks after he had arrived in hospital he was moved out of intensive care into a private room off the general ward, though he was still closely monitored. Whether he would ever completely be able to return to his former level of fitness was still a matter of conjecture, as the damage to his legs was quite severe and there were some internal injuries still unresolved. He was frequently taken down to the theatre for surgery and minor repairs. The consultant in charge of his case had told Vanessa that he would almost certainly not have survived had he remained in Kenya. As Alice had told the children, doctors could do wonderful things these days and they certainly did in a modern well-equipped hospital, bringing Ian back from the dead.

It was now March and the days were lengthening. Ian had been in hospital for over a month and the day would soon come when he was able to return home – and what then?

A routine had now been established by which Alice remained almost permanently at Moira's house, only going home occasionally for a change of clothes, allowing Moira to come and go as she pleased. Vanessa now went home only to sleep, and still spent most of her days at the hospital helping Ian to get better, being there for him when he came back from theatre. In a way it was as though their romance was starting all over again and this was an unexpected blessing of the accident. Meanwhile Alice had indeed become to the children almost a permanent fixture in their lives. Occasionally she would even pick Freddie and Helena up from their respective schools by taxi. Moira however always tried to be home in the evening to see the children, put them to bed and read them a story.

Moira valued Alice as someone in whom, knowing the full facts of the situation, she was able to confide and they often sat and discussed what was happening in the hospital and the many conversations she had had with Vanessa about her guilt and determination to reform her life.

One day after Alice had picked the children up she saw Vanessa's smart sports car in the drive and when she told the children their mother was there they ran into the house and she followed slowly. Moira had occasionally taken the children to visit their father in hospital, as his recovery progressed, so they had not been altogether cut off from their parents. It was, however, the first time Alice had seen Vanessa and she realized she was quite apprehensive. So much had her life changed that she began to wonder what she would do when she was no longer needed. Maybe the moment had now come? As she entered the hall Vanessa ran to greet her and hugged her warmly, putting an arm through hers as they moved into the sitting room while the children raced upstairs. Alice had been concerned about the way recent events might have changed Vanessa's appearance but, although appreciably thinner, her face a little gaunt, as usual she looked and smelled delicious. One would never have imagined that her life had been so recently smitten by tragedy.

'Darling Alice,' she cried, seemingly reluctant to release her. 'Whatever would we have done without you?'

'I'm quite sure you would have coped,' Alice said prosaically.

'I don't know that we would have found someone to come and live in the house or indeed cope in any way as well as you. The children adore you.'

'And I adore them. No problem there,' Alice smiled. 'Besides, selfishly, I am able to use your mother's studio and have done some paintings. I particularly love the holly tree,' she said glancing out of the window, 'and have incorporated it in some of my work.'

'Yes, we all love it,' Vanessa replied, following her gaze. 'Mum's studio used to be my bedroom, and as a child I was mesmerized by it.'

'Did you know some see it as a symbol of friendship?'

'No I didn't. Fancy that.'

'So much a symbol of how I feel about your family.'

'And how we feel about you.'

Vanessa kissed her lightly on the cheek, finally releasing her tight grip.

'How is Ian?' Alice asked, moved by her conversation with this troubled young woman.

'He is making the most wonderful progress. There is such a change from when I first saw him, bruised, broken and shattered. He is almost, but not quite, back to his old self. He walks with crutches and is itching to get away from the hospital. The consultant is reluctant to let him go, but might agree if we have a full-time nurse in place, which of course we shall. I can't wait to get him home.'

She paused and looked at Alice as if wondering how much she knew, but Alice merely gave her sweet, calm reassuring smile

and said, 'Of course you are. You know that I am available whenever needed.'

'But you will be dying to get back to your own home and
have some peace and quiet, and when Ian comes home the children will be back with me and we shall all be able to resume
our normal life.'

Alice was not at all sure, at that moment, that she was so
anxious to resume hers.

Sasha rang Caroline's doorbell and stood waiting, rather appre-
hensively. She knew how Caroline felt about unexpected visitors,
but she had not been to the class for two weeks and it was nearly
the end of term.

She was about to ring again when the door slowly opened
and Caroline peered nervously round the side.

'Oh,' she said, relief flooding her face, 'it's you.'

'Sorry,' Sasha said apologetically as Caroline stood back,
inviting her in. 'I don't want to worry you, but I wondered if
you were OK?'

Caroline didn't look OK. Her normally handsome face was
worn and haggard and she looked a wreck.

'I've rung you a couple of times and left a message but you
don't ring back so as I was just on my way to the college I
thought I'd pop in. I felt a bit concerned as we haven't seen you
at the class for a couple of weeks and there is only one more
session before the end of term.'

'I know, I should have rung you, but . . . I don't quite know
how to explain because you'll think I am such an idiot.' Caroline
led the way into the kitchen where there was a pile of washing
in a basket and the washing machine was going full tilt. The sink
was full of dishes and the table covered with dirty plates, jars and
bits of leftover food.

Caroline ran her hands through her mass of untidy hair, which
looked as though the roots badly needed re-tinting. 'Sorry,' she
said, 'this place looks such a mess but . . . well . . .' She sank on
to a chair. 'I have been feeling awfully depressed again. Really
worried and out of sorts.'

'Why, has something happened?' Sasha perched on a chair
opposite her.

'No, on the contrary, it should be good news. Greg will be home for Easter – that is, he is supposed . . . well you see I am so terribly worried, convinced in fact that something will happen to him. I have had this awful feeling of doom. You know, just as I did before. The knock on the door . . .' Her voice trailed off. 'I feel I keep on hearing it and sit bolt upright in bed in the middle of the night, heart pounding, covered with sweat.'

'But nothing happened then. All that worry was for nothing.'

'I know, but do you read the newspapers? Blokes seem often these days to be killed just when they are due home. There was something the other day about a man who was about to leave for home and the day before . . .' Caroline's eyes filled with tears which began to trickle down her cheeks. 'Can you *imagine* just how the family feel? Getting all excited as the tour of duty was over and then this . . .'

This time the tears ran unhindered and she put her face in her hands. 'I can't really stand the suspense. Sometimes I feel I am going out of my mind and,' she gestured wildly round, 'look at all this mess. I can't seem to get a grip and my mother has had the kids for a night or two. I spend most of the day lying on my bed staring at the ceiling and I've started smoking again. Mind you, it started with Sharon. I don't want the children to see me like this and they are all excited about their dad . . .'

'You should have called me,' Sasha said in a practical tone of voice. 'I would have tried to get you out of yourself.'

'As you did last time. You were brilliant; but I don't think painting can help me any more.'

'Caroline,' Sasha said gently, 'you don't want to greet Greg like this, do you? He will have had an arduous six months—'

'*If* he survives,' Caroline said grimly.

'Well, I'm taking it for granted he will and he won't want to be greeted by someone who has let her fears get the better of her; someone who looks a mess and, frankly, whose hair could do with a makeover.'

'Sharon still hasn't recovered. She is on pills all the time.'

'Yes, but Sharon's husband did die and yours won't.'

'How can you be sure?'

'I'm sure,' Sasha said robustly, getting up. 'Now look, I'm going to help you to get this place straight, and then we're going somewhere nice for lunch. I don't have a class until three.'

They had just got the place straight and, better still, Sasha thought she had got Caroline in a more cheerful frame of mind when the doorbell rang and Caroline's expression changed abruptly to one of fear and Sasha knew what she was thinking.

'Now don't worry. I'll go and get it. Probably the postman. You go and get ready,' she said and went to the door where a pale faced, rather tense looking young woman gazed at her uncertainly.

'Oh, is Caroline not in?'

'Yes she's in. I'm a friend, Sasha.'

'I'm Sharon,' the woman said, 'a friend of Caroline's. I think I've heard of you. Aren't you in charge of the art class?'

'Yes, that's me.'

'It seems to be a great help to her. She has been so wonderful to me. I lost my husband recently and I don't know how I'd have got through it without Caroline. She is so strong and supportive.'

'We were just going out to have a bit of lunch but I'm sure she'll be glad to see you.'

'Hi Sharon,' Caroline said brightly, coming down the stairs. 'You OK?'

'I'm OK,' Sharon replied in a far from OK-sounding voice, 'but I was a bit worried about you, not having seen you for a few days.'

'I'm sorry. There is such a lot to do,' Caroline paused as if thinking of an excuse.

'I know, Greg will soon be back. I've been thinking of you, envying you I guess. In a way the return of the men will make it worse for me.'

Sharon's voice faltered and Caroline hurried down the remaining steps and put her arms around her.

'We'll all be here to support you.'

'I don't know what I'd have done without her.' Sharon turned to Sasha.

'She's been a fantastic help to me. Never thinks of herself, only others, and she must have been going through doubts and torments like the rest of us. We all have.'

'Yes, she's a wonderful person.' Sasha smiled encouragingly at Caroline. 'So brave and strong.'

'And Greg is an amazing man too. His men adore him. Did you ever meet him?' As Sasha shook her head she went on, 'Heaven knows where they'd be without him. He keeps them all together.'

'I'm really looking forward to meeting him.' Sasha glanced at her watch. 'Look, I have an afternoon class. Why don't you come with us and have some lunch? We thought we'd just go to the pub.'

'That would be great. I could do with cheering up,' Sharon said. 'I don't know how I'm going to cope when the battalion comes back without Mark.'

'You'll cope,' Caroline said, hugging her again. 'We'll all be here with you.'

Watching Caroline in the pub was like witnessing a different woman, Sasha thought, to the nervous, fearful creature on the verge of a breakdown she had seen just a couple of hours before. Now she was smiling, comforting, resolute, strong, a woman she didn't recognize and she thought that there was a lesson here: a lesson that in helping others one was definitely able to help oneself.

How true.

She left them in the pub in a cheerful, but thankfully still sober mood, Caroline giving Sharon the support she was unable to summon for herself. The mood even affected her and she got back to college just in time for her class.

No man is an island. Sasha was reflecting on the events of the previous day, the arrival of Sharon and how it had introduced her to a Caroline she didn't know, bringing out the very best, the finest, in her friend. After all, as the poet said, we are all inter-connected with one another, part of the main.

Sasha would have been the first to admit that she was not as good an artist as Ben. Nevertheless, she was accomplished and had been awarded prizes for her work. One of the reasons she had got the post at the art college was the quality of her work, largely abstract paintings, and yet in encouraging Ben and his career she had sacrificed her own creative energies. She had had to work to support them both, and to what little effect. Small thanks she had got from him.

Maybe he would flourish better on his own? By spoiling him she had done him no favours, but she would love to know how he was doing. She often thought of her ungrateful lover, a partner of ten years, a friend for longer, but resisted the impulse to contact him, not to try and persuade him to come back to her, but to see how he was doing. You couldn't just banish from your life someone who had been part of it for so long.

When it had finally dawned on her that he had left for good – not even a Christmas card from him – she decided to adapt his studio for her own use and the development of her artistic career as a sideline. Knowing too well the perils of trying to strike out as an artist, she felt she would never be tempted to give up the day job. Yet Ben had been too confident of his own genius, spurning offers of commercial work or even teaching at the college part time as Sasha had suggested.

The studio was at the top of the house with good light and all the paraphernalia that an artist could need. He had even left a few of his canvases now stacked against the wall, and the day after the meeting with Sharon she went up to inspect the studio again and also take a look at the few efforts she had made to execute work of her own. She taught watercolour painting because it was what she had specialized in, and she was also an accomplished draughtswoman. However over the years, in the little time she had to do any of her own work, she had drifted over to abstract work in bold, vivid colours as she became more in tune with the development of her own mature feelings and ideas.

That blustery March day as the wintry sun struggled to penetrate through the clouds her thoughts were also full of the impending return of Greg from Afghanistan and the effect it would have on the life of his wife and children, but also of the men in his battalion who loved him so much, should he decide to leave. It seemed to her that Sharon had thrown down a kind of gauntlet, a challenge that Caroline would find it very difficult to deal with.

Sasha idly looked through Ben's canvases and decided that his unique style did indeed have merit, and wondered if she should somehow try and contact him and remind him that they were there and see if he wanted them back. Or was she just looking for an excuse? Did she, in her heart of hearts, want to see him again, maybe even resume their relationship? For the fact was that, despite her extensive workload, the people she knew and her many interests, she was very lonely. She did not like living on her own. She wasn't used to it and it was alien to her.

On the easel she had a half-finished abstract and she wandered over to her palette and work materials, hurriedly abandoned – she couldn't remember how long ago – as all the things intervening in her life kept on clamouring for her attention.

Yet her thoughts kept on wandering. Indeed no man was an island. Caroline had helped Sharon and she had helped Caroline, and even dear Alice seemed to have been of enormous help to Moira, and who would have expected an octogenarian being called upon to do something like that and, above all, being so willing and able to do it?

Upstairs, engrossed in her thoughts and the task in hand, she wasn't sure whether she had heard the doorbell until it sounded again. Still with her overall on she went downstairs, flung open the door and was surprised to see Caroline just about to turn away.

'Come back, come back,' she called.

'Oh you're in,' Caroline said, retracing her steps. 'I saw your car and wondered. I hope I'm not interrupting anything?' She gazed curiously at Sasha's stained overall. 'Are you working?'

'I am, but come in. I was just looking for an excuse to have coffee.' She shut the door after Caroline and took her into the kitchen. 'I decided I was too involved in myself and had neglected my own work.'

'You mean your painting?'

'I mean my painting,' Sasha said, plugging in the kettle. 'I am, after all, a trained artist and I do too little of my own work.'

'Too busy helping others,' Caroline said, sitting down. 'I felt awful about yesterday.'

'But why on earth should you feel awful? I am full of admiration for you.'

'Oh, you can't mean that.'

'But I do. Look what help you have given Sharon and what a high regard she has for you.'

'Yes, but she doesn't *know* me, does she? As you do.'

Sasha spooned coffee into the mugs, filled them with boiling water and put one in front of Caroline as she sat opposite her.

'I only know a bit of you as you only know a bit of me. I was thinking just now of how we are all connected, helping one another. Do you know the poet John Donne and his poem with the words "no man is an island"? It came to me very vividly when I heard how highly Sharon thinks of you.'

'And Greg,' Caroline said solemnly. 'As well as wanting to apologize to you for yesterday, that's what I came to see you about. What on earth do you suppose I am to say to Greg if he tells me, as I suspect he will, that he can't leave his men and wants to stay on in the army? I think I've always known that's what he'll do, despite his promises. He has never convinced me about his protestations, that it is his last tour of duty. He is too ingrained as a soldier. It is all he knows. And frankly, Sasha, I don't think I could take any more. I'd crack up completely. And what would Sharon think of me then?'

Ten

It was a wonderful, sunny spring day when Ian was eventually allowed home, in an ambulance with a nurse in attendance, and one waiting for him at the house. The doctors had wanted to send him to a convalescent home, but Vanessa had convinced them that she would ensure he was properly and professionally looked after. His room was beautifully prepared, not as a sick room but as a 'get better' kind of room with flowers and the open window letting in the sunshine, his bed neatly turned back. Next was the room he normally shared with Vanessa so that she was close at hand if needed.

She was at the door when the ambulance arrived and Ian was carefully lowered on a stretcher and borne into the house like a Roman emperor making a triumphal entry.

'Your room is all ready, darling,' Vanessa said, bending to kiss him. 'Welcome home.'

'*My* room?' He looked at her in surprise. 'Not our room?'

'The doctors thought you should have your own room for the time being, but I am only next door and a very nice nurse is waiting for you upstairs.'

Ian was still very weak, as was demonstrated by his willing-ness to be put straight to bed, and he lay there as people fussed about him making him comfortable. He bade goodbye to the ambulance men and the nurse who had accompanied them and thanked them for their care.

'This is Rosie,' Vanessa said, bringing the new nurse forward.

'Hello Rosie,' Ian said, smiling. 'I feel a bit of a fraud.'

'I'm sure you're not, Dr Fleming,' Rosie replied, professionally smoothing the duvet across him.

'Drop the "doctor" bit. My name is Ian. I'm not a proper doctor anyway, just an academic biochemist.'

'Ian then,' Rosie said with a smile. 'The point I'm making is that you've had a very bad injury and will be convalescent for a long time. The doctors have sent me all your hospital notes.'

'I'm sure it's not necessary,' Ian said, 'but for the time being . . .' He held out his hand towards Vanessa. 'You've been fantastic and it's very good to be home.'

'And it's very good to have you home,' she said, perching on the side of the bed.

He clung on to her hand as though afraid of letting her go. 'Sometimes I thought I'd never see home, or you and the kids again. Now we can begin our lives all over again.'

Rosie was standing in the background, anxious not to be obtrusive, but she gave a delicate cough as though to remind them of her presence.

'I think Dr Fleming – Ian – should have a little rest,' she said. 'He has had a very tiring day. You don't want to overdo it.'

'You're quite right, Rosie,' Vanessa said, slipping off the bed. 'I'll go down and get lunch. Are you hungry, darling?'

'Not really.' Ian sank back on the pillows. 'Too excited.'

'Just some soup and an omelette?'

'I'll toy with it.'

'Rosie?'

'I'm OK at the moment, thank you, Vanessa. I may slip out a bit later if that's OK.'

It was rather awkward having another presence in the house, Vanessa thought, as she busied about the kitchen heating soup and breaking eggs for Ian's lunch. There was something unnatural about it. She liked Rosie, but rather hoped her tenure would be brief. After all she herself had nothing else to do but look after him. The thing was he still had to have various medications and painful injections that would have been impossible for her to do. Like Ian all she wanted was to get back to normal life, just them and the kids. But would that ever be possible?

She took Ian's lunch up to him on a tray, chatted for a while and then left him after Rosie said she would bring down the tray and settle him for his afternoon rest. She was still in the kitchen when Rosie came down with the tray and asked if Vanessa minded if she popped out for an hour or two.

'I've given him his injection and medication and he will

sleep. He will probably sleep much better anyway now that he is home.'

'That's great,' Vanessa said, looking up from her soup. 'How do you think he is? I want you to be honest.'

'He seems to have made really good progress, but I can see there is still a problem with his legs. He had so many bad fractures it's a wonder they didn't have to amputate. So it will all take time to heal.'

'Do you think he will ever completely recover?'

'Oh yes. He might have to walk with a stick, and I don't know that he will ever be able to travel as much as he did, as I understand he was an overseas manager. But he is young and strong-spirited. What sometimes concerns me is that occasionally in bad accident cases there is psychological damage, post-traumatic stress, and you often can't tell that for a long time. But don't worry, it doesn't affect everyone, and Ian has a lot of support from you and a loving relationship. I can tell.' She smiled kindly at Vanessa. 'I just want to pop home and leave a note for my husband. I haven't had time to tell him about this job. I had to fill in for someone who was ill.'

Vanessa looked concerned. 'I don't want to keep you from your home.'

'Not at all. That's what I am supposed to do – or rather, I try not to, but if the agency is short of nurses they can call on me. I'm here for as long as you want me.'

'Any idea how long that might be?'

Rosie shook her head. 'Time will tell.'

Rosie's words left Vanessa feeling rather depressed and she wondered if she was indeed telling her the truth about the prognosis for Ian. After lunch and clearing up she popped her head round Ian's door to see if he was OK. The curtains had been drawn and he seemed to be asleep so she didn't disturb him.

She returned to the lounge to sort through the stuff that had come back from the hospital with Ian, which included a case with spare pyjamas, washing and shaving kit, and a bulging briefcase which to her surprise opened. In it were various papers, a camera, his passport and travel documents and his mobile phone, which she was sure must need recharging. It was an indication of the extent of his illness that he hadn't asked for it before as, like most men and some women, it was a piece of vital equipment that seemed to be almost permanently attached to his ear. She switched it on and it lit up indicating that there were several unanswered messages waiting for him. She opened the first text message and stared at it for a long time, almost not comprehending, as if thinking it was for someone else.

Darling, it read, *am so anxious about u. I know it is difficult for u but text me if u can 2 let me no how u are. M*

Scrolling through Vanessa found several others in the same vein, the first beginning a few days after his accident, the last about a week ago.

Ian frantic with worry. Hope u got back safely. No news this side. Lovingly M.

Really darling try and let me no how u are. The airline will tell me nothing except that u got back alive. So terribly anxious.

For a moment in her confusion she had wondered if they had come from her, until she realized her name did not begin with an 'M' and, anyway, she had never texted him after she heard about the accident, but had rushed to the airport.

In a state of severe shock Vanessa sat there for some time, the mobile in her hand, before realizing that it was essential to be practical and that it was almost time to go and pick up the children, and wishing that she had reminded Rosie to be sure she was back in time.

The messages were from someone, obviously a woman, who either didn't know that he was married, or didn't care.

It was quite a long time since she'd had the leisure or, above all, been in the mood, to return to her painting, Moira thought as she placed her prepared paper, carefully stretched, washed and mounted on plywood, on her easel. The preparation for painting in watercolours took time, but if done properly the process had its own satisfaction. She had already arranged her still life on a table in the centre of her studio and, as she began mixing her paints on her palette, there was a gentle tap on the door which opened and Vanessa put her head round.

'Am I disturbing you, Mum?'

'Not at all,' Moira said a little reluctantly as she put down her palette and wiped her hands on her overalls. 'I hadn't really started. I was thinking that now things have settled down I should start work again. Sasha will be expecting some home-work from me.'

'I'm sure she will understand,' Vanessa said, but there was something in her tone of voice that disturbed Moira, who peered closely at her daughter. 'Are you OK? Is there something wrong? Ian OK?'

Vanessa flopped in one of the easy chairs and peeled off her gloves, flinging her head against the back of her chair.

'Ian is having an affair, or was, in Kenya with a woman who was in his car when he crashed. Her name is Marion Kronge and whatever I feel about it or her, she saved his life. Whether it was worth saving I don't know.'

'Oh, *Vanessa.*' Moira threw herself into the chair opposite her daughter. 'How on earth did you find out about it? Did Ian tell you?'

'Oh no, Ian didn't tell me. You bet your life he didn't. Anyway I haven't asked – yet.' She told her mother about the texts and her efforts to find out who this 'M' was in view of the compro-mising messages on the mobile.

'The obvious thing was the solicitor who is dealing with the case. It wasn't easy as Mrs Kronge kind of disappeared so I don't know much about her.

'I just asked him if he could find the name of the person in the car as I'd like to thank him, or her. I didn't say I knew the passenger was a woman. All he could find out was her name, which she had left at the hospital. No address. It must have been chaotic as they rushed him into A and E or whatever equivalent they have in Kenya. I just thanked him and said if he found out her address to let me know. He asked me why I didn't ask my husband, to which I had no answer. I knew it was a woman because of the nature of the messages. They all began with "darling" and left one in no doubt.'

Vanessa leaned against the back of the chair again and closed her eyes. She looked drained.

'Isn't it a bugger, Mum? All that time I spent lashing myself with guilt about Ian because he was so good, and now I know he is not good at all, no better than me.'

'She may work with him.'

'She well may, but if she is a mere colleague she would hardly send those loving frantic messages, would she? It never occurred to me, even though he spends so much time away, and in Kenya too where they have a plant.'

'I must say it would never have occurred to me either,' Moira said. 'Oh, darling, I am so sorry. It is deeply upsetting for you.'

'Just when I was going to reform. All those good intentions.'

Moira leaned forward urgently and looked her daughter in the eyes. 'Vanessa, you must reform.'

'I don't know whether to have it out with him or not.'

'And would you tell him about you?'

'About *me*?' Vanessa looked shocked. 'Of course not. That would stir things up.'

'Well then.' Moira sat back, her expression firm, her hands clasped tightly in her lap. 'You don't want to break up your marriage, do you?'

'No, I don't, not unless I discover that the husband I respected and thought so upright is a serial adulterer.'

'I'm sure he isn't. It's probably a fling, the sort of thing you said you had.' She got up and, going across to Vanessa, gently stroked her head. 'If you want my advice, do nothing. He sinned. But so did you. So you're equal. Try and start a new life with Ian all over again, recapturing the excitement and the passion of first love.'

'That's what I intended to try and do as I spent all those hours by the side of the bed reflecting on our past lives,' Vanessa said. 'But it will be very hard. Believe me, Mum, it will be very hard. How much do I know about the extent of his relationship with Marion? For all I know he may be longing to get back to her. There are too many unanswered questions, too many imponderables. One day the truth will have to come out.'

'Incidentally, what has happened to Ian's mobile?' Moira asked, as they both made for the door. 'Has he not missed it?'

Vanessa paused on the threshold. 'Funnily enough he only asked for it the other day and I said I didn't know where it was. Maybe, I suggested, he'd lost it in the crash.'

'What did he say to that?'

'Nothing. Just shrugged. I chucked it away and told him I'd get him another.' Vanessa smiled wearily. 'So you see we can have a clean sheet to begin again.'

The first thing Sasha saw as she entered the classroom was a tall upright figure sitting at the back of the class: Martin. There was no time to pause or go back and she felt a wave of anger and irritation that he should put her through this. As she made her way to her table there was a buzz which gradually subsided as she took her place, sorted through her papers which included sheaves of artwork and, finally, perched on the end of the table. There was an end-of-term feeling about the class, an air of restlessness in the room.

Deliberately avoiding Martin's gaze, which she knew was fixed on her, she smiled round at the rest of the class, noting that as well as the renegade Martin, Moira was also back in her place. She bestowed a special smile on her.

'Well, as you know, it is the last class for this session and I would like to congratulate all those who have done such sterling work. Some of you I know have found it more difficult than others. Others are ready to move on to Advanced next year.' She studied the upturned faces in the row in front of her. 'You, clearly, Alice, and you too, Moira.' She addressed the others in the room. 'Sally and Frances.' She paused, and looked directly into his eyes. 'And obviously Martin, who it is very nice to welcome again. That is if you're going to stay on, Martin?' Now there was a slight edge to her voice.

'I hope so,' he said. 'I am really very sorry, Sasha, for my absence all term, but I have had a number of personal difficulties and have also spent a lot of time abroad on business.'

'It's entirely up to you, Martin,' Sasha said, surprising herself by her calm, her air, she hoped, of detachment. 'Now, the summer term is slightly different. It is my custom to have a few sessions out of doors to see how we deal with landscape painting. There is also an exhibition at the end of term of the work of all the art classes in the Institute and I hope we can submit a number from this class.'

For a moment she studied some of the paintings on the table. 'For example, I have some really excellent work here. Among them Alice, Moira and possibly Caroline, whose portfolio is a bit lean and who could do a bit more if possible. I also think Pauline has made great progress.' She smiled approvingly at Pauline whose face flushed with pleasure. 'Roger incidentally might be able to move on to Advanced next year if he cares to. Also Caroline if she has the time.'

'It sounds as though you want to make a clean sweep,' Roger said, with a wry smile.

'Not at all. But this is only the beginners' class and it shows what a good job I have made getting most of you this far. Now those of you who have work to finish, please get on with it, and those who want to discuss work with me, now is the time.'

She got off her table and began to distribute the artwork she had to their owners. The first to come up to her was Martin.

'I think I left some work here from last term, Sasha.'

'Oh? Did you? Well, then I don't know where it is.' She crossed to one of the cupboards and rummaged through the accumulation there. 'You can go through this lot if you like, Martin, but really stuff is not supposed to be left behind.' She knew she sounded rather prissy and schoolmistressy, but she didn't mind. 'Now I've got rather a lot to do.'

'See you later perhaps,' he whispered, but she ignored him and returned to her table where a small queue was forming.

Sasha felt tired, weary, depressed, and lingered only long enough in the canteen after class just to say goodbye to people. Seeing Martin again, and so unexpectedly, had unsettled her, but she was pleased that her reaction had not given too much, if anything, away. After a passage of several months she remembered his attraction, but could still find no real justification for that moment of madness when, after what was essentially a very brief intimate acquaintance, she leapt into bed with him and for a time imagined herself madly in love. Now she felt nothing but coldness towards him, and regret for what had happened.

It was still partly daylight as she crossed the car park and immediately saw him standing by her car, or rather leaning against the bonnet as if he had been there a long time. She slowed her pace to try once again to collect her thoughts, but he had already seen her and, straightening up, started to walk towards her.

'Really, Martin . . .' she began, but he held up a hand.

'Sasha, please don't say anything until we have had a chance to talk.'

'There's no point, Martin.'

'But I think there is a point when you hear what I have to say. Can we go for a drink? Please.'

It seemed absurd to be standing in the middle of the car park engaged in what to any passing student was obviously an altercation, so she nodded and, opening the car doors, indicated he should get in.

'You don't want to eat?' he said.

'No thank you. I have eaten and am seriously tired so this must be very brief. There is a pub just across the road.' Putting the car into gear she edged out of the car park just as Roger and Pauline came past and, seeing her, waved. She waved back.

'Damn,' she said.

'Damn what?'

'Roger and Pauline saw us.'

'So?'

'So I don't want them to see me driving off with you.'

'Are they an item?' he asked, turning his head.

'I have no idea.' She drove to the pub which was almost opposite the Institute, parking in a street alongside. 'We shall probably see the whole of my class there.'

'Then if you care so much let's go somewhere else.'

'I don't care so much, Martin. I really see very little point in this meeting which, as far as I am concerned, can be said in a word: "goodbye".'

Martin got out of the car and went round to open the door for her.

They went silently into the bar, which was half empty, and found a seat in the corner. She asked for a white wine and while he was at the counter she watched him, wondering why she had even agreed to this. He returned with her wine and a glass of beer for himself.

'Well,' he said, looking at her. 'You *are* very angry with me.'

'I'm confused.' She took a sip of her wine. 'I don't know why you have come back to a class you have been absent from all term. You should have realized that it would take me unawares and be embarrassing for me, and I don't know how you could even consider doing such a thing. You must have known that, apart from anything else, it would make me very cross. Also, knowing me, even a little, I can't understand how you can even think there is any chance of us resuming a relationship again.'

'Because things have changed, circumstances have changed, and I remain very attracted to you, Sasha. I may have handled this badly and I see now I have, but the fact is I can't get you out of my mind. I have thought of you so much these past months, but they have been very tense and difficult for me both person-ally and business-wise. Because so many building firms have gone under I am severely threatened with redundancy. We have had to lay off a number of staff. Then Sarah became seriously ill and is now in residential care. It may be that she will stay there as she is suffering from very severe depression.'

'Oh.'

The silence between them was prolonged as Sasha considered the import of what he had said, and he waited for her reaction.

It was Martin who spoke first.

'I am really in love with you, Sasha, and I would do anything to turn the clock back to that time when I thought you loved me too.'

'I don't know that I ever did,' she said. 'Really love you I mean, to be brutally honest. I spent a lot of time when you were just one of my students actively disliking you, as you know, thinking you were offhand and arrogant. But it changed in London. Quite honestly I think it was a reaction to Ben. You were, or seemed, so much more mature and sophisticated than he was and then, of course, he left me. That was a real jolt to my self-esteem. Well, you know the rest. I don't think it was that important. I was lonely and very vulnerable, so when I discovered you had lied to me about being married, I was able to put you quite easily out of my mind. And that is how I remain. Detached. Not interested. I am really sorry that you have had all these difficulties – your job, your wife. It must be very hard for you. I accept that, but I don't see how it possibly changes the situation for us in any way. In fact it would make it even more complicated. I must emphasize you are not part of my life and never will be.'

'And that is your final word?'

'Final.' She finished her wine and looked at the floor.

'Would anything change it?'

'No.'

'Can we be just friends?'

'We could try.' She gave a bleak smile and got up. 'I would personally be very glad if you did the decent thing and kept out of my life for good. If you do intend to go on with your art classes, anyway, next year you should go to the Advanced class.'

'Well, don't forget there is another term to go,' His voice took on a stubborn edge. 'I am not molesting you and I have every right to be there if I want.'

Sasha stared at him with unconcealed dislike.

'It is your right to do as you like. I am merely the teacher. Now, Martin, I am dropping with fatigue and want to go home. Is your car in the Institute car park?'

'Yes.'

'Well, you had better go and get it before it closes and you won't be able to get out.'

It was with some satisfaction that she watched him scurry out of the pub with the briefest of goodbyes, anxious, she imagined, not to have to walk home.

'Trying it on again, Martin,' she thought and, feeling desperately despondent, unhappy, and somehow a bit false, made her way slowly to her own car.

The children were huddled close beside her as, on a cold and cloudy, almost wintry day, Caroline waited with the other women outside the barracks to welcome their men home. Crowded round them were wives, mothers, girlfriends, small children, babies in arms – some of whom had not yet been seen by their fathers – who had waved them off six months ago on a cold, dark winter's morning. Now it was spring, a time full of hope, and Caroline knew without any doubt that Greg was on the plane bringing him home.

The faces were different too, only now they were excited,

joyful. There had been no mistaking the fear and anxiety when they saw the men off, all of them tightly under control wondering if they would ever return. And some of them hadn't. The regiment had sustained too many losses and several women who had been there on that October day were absent, among them Sharon, still grieving for her dead husband.

There was a babble of excited voices as the first of the buses rounded the corner, stopping outside the barracks, followed by a sudden hush as the doors opened and one by one, carrying their cumbersome kit, the men started to emerge. There were tears, of course there were tears, and then laughter and joy, cries, screams of excitement from the children who rushed into their fathers' arms, kisses, many deep and prolonged.

Greg was not on the first bus, and Caroline experienced an irrational spasm of fear until the doors of the second opened and he was one of the first off, looking anxiously round until he saw her and his family, and his face broke into smiles as he hurried towards them.

She looked on benignly as he hugged the children, taking Adam into his arms and then their eyes met and she came up to him and kissed him lightly on the cheek. They had been married too long to show affection in public.

'Hi,' she said. 'Welcome home.'

'Missed you,' he said, his arms tightening round Adam, one hand on the head of Jenny who was clinging to him while Christopher, still a bit shy, hung back.

They broke up to allow Greg to greet other wives while Caroline chatted to the men whose wives she knew.

Finally everyone began to disperse and, after a word to the commanding officer, Greg signalled to Caroline that it was time to go home; the family reunited at last.

But she knew immediately there was something different about Greg. He looked older, almost haggard, and his close-cropped hair was much greyer than it had been before he left. He didn't smile very much and when they were home, he roamed around the house as if looking for something that he had lost. Caroline had prepared a stew for lunch and as the two elder children had the day off school they all sat down at the table together, but the conversation was stilted, awkward and Greg said very little. He also ate very little which surprised Caroline after a long journey. She sensed from his mood that the best thing was to go along with it. The children kept up an endless babble of chatter, eager to tell their father what they'd been up to in his absence, but Caroline could tell his mind was elsewhere. In Afghanistan without a doubt, or with the wives whose husbands had not returned.

As she rose to clear the dishes she said, 'My mother will have the children this afternoon if you like. I expect you could do with a good sleep.'

'No, I'm OK.' Greg pushed back his chair and lit a cigarette, something he was not supposed to do in front of the children. 'I like having them around, real life.'

'By the way,' Caroline said, 'I invited Sharon for supper tonight. She is very anxious to see you. Is that alright?'

'Ah, yes.' Greg sank back in his chair with a deep sigh. 'Mark. I want to talk to Sharon.' He looked over to his children who were hanging on every word and Caroline could sense him perhaps, despite his sadness, beginning to relax.

'Come on, kids,' he said, 'let's go to the park and mess around with a ball.'

That evening it was Greg who opened the door, while Caroline remained tactfully in the background. Sharon stood on the threshold staring at him as though she had seen a ghost. Then she threw herself into his arms and laid her head on his chest weeping. As he put his arms round her and hugged her Caroline withdrew to the kitchen.

It had not been an easy day, not quite the homecoming she had looked forward to, not like the others, different. The stress of the war and separation was obviously affecting Greg more than in the past. He seemed to have withdrawn from her and was trying very hard to communicate naturally with the children, who also felt the tension as though it had penetrated their bones and they took a long time to settle.

She left Greg and Sharon alone for about half an hour and when she returned to the sitting room he had given her a drink and they were sitting on the sofa, he still with an arm round her. Her face was puffy, swollen with tears, and Caroline thought Greg might have shed a few too.

'Supper is ready,' she said. 'That's if you're ready.'

Sharon, bleary eyed, looked up.

'I feel so awful spoiling your homecoming. Greg has been wonderful, but seeing him again . . .'

'Of course, of course,' Caroline murmured, sitting down on the other side, her hand resting on one of Sharon's.

'And Caroline,' Sharon said, looking at Greg, 'she's so strong. She has been a wonderful support to me. I don't know how she remained so brave. You see, I knew Mark wouldn't come back. I feared it so much. I used to imagine I heard the knock on the door at night. I'd sit bolt upright in bed sweating and I could see his face looking at me.'

The tears began to flow again while Greg's arm strengthened round her and he and Caroline exchanged glances over her head.

'Oh, Greg,' Sharon said jerkily, 'you must never leave the men. They rely so much on you and here we women rely on Caroline.'

None of them ate very much supper, but quite a lot of alcohol was consumed as Sharon relived over and over again her fears, resisting any effort to comfort her. Eventually Greg called a taxi and took a still tearful Sharon home.

When he returned Caroline was in bed and she lay listening to him moving around downstairs, and wondered if he would have something more to drink and fall asleep in the chair downstairs before creeping up to bed at dawn, as had occasionally happened before. In a way it was like a stranger living in the house.

However, soon she saw the stair lights go out and he came into their bedroom, sitting down heavily on the bed beside her.

'You still awake?' he asked.

'Of course.' She held out her hand. 'Come to bed.'

She watched while he undressed and went into the bathroom, and when he returned she had the duvet turned back. He sank into bed and lay there silently, still keeping a distance from her, staring at the ceiling.

'What a night,' he said. 'What a day. Still. I had to see her.'

'Of course you had.'

'She said you were so brave.'

'I wasn't brave at all. I spent my whole time worrying about you, thinking I heard the knock on the door, sitting up in bed in the small hours just like her. I only made an effort to help Sharon. In fact I think if all we women had been open and honest with one another and confessed our deepest fears, just how worried we were, instead of keeping to ourselves, the stiff upper lip and so on, we might all have been better off.'

Greg's hand reached for hers.

'I wasn't brave either. I had moments of sheer terror, more so than ever before, but I knew I should never show it because everyone else felt the same. Those improvised explosive devices are sheer hell; you never know where you are going to find one and when you do often it is too late. It was a hell of a tour, this one. The number of casualties was out of all proportion. I actually watched Mark die before the helicopter could get to him. It was one of the worst moments of my entire army career.'

Caroline squeezed his hand.

'We must try hard and return to normal,' she whispered. 'For our sakes and we owe it to the kids who have missed you so much.'

'I know. It's going to take a long time. I am all stressed out, but you know, Caroline . . .' He turned his face to her and she could feel his warm breath on her face. 'I wasn't going to tell you so soon, but I have to say it, get it out of the way. I can never leave the army now, not as long as the blokes need me. I know I'm going back on a promise I made to you, but, frankly, I feel I need them as much as they need me. There is a stronger bond than ever before. You know that, don't you?'

'Yes,' she said after a long, long silence. 'Yes, I do now.'

Eleven

Easter

Camping was not Pauline's thing. She was a woman who liked her creature comforts: a good hotel, soft warm bed, and an en suite bathroom with a loo that flushed. She couldn't see why they could not have gone to a hotel for the weekend, but if Roger wanted to camp, she would camp. Despite all the overtures he had been surprisingly resistant to settling into an affair. There had been a lot of heavy petting, mostly in the car after the art class, or a visit to the cinema, but when she invited him in afterwards, or they had a meal at her house, there was always an excuse until she began to think that maybe there really was something wrong with Roger's sex drive, something he was ashamed of, a reason why his wife had been glad to get rid of him. So their relationship had reached a kind of impasse which, although it involved a considerable degree of intimacy, was neither an affair or not an affair.

In fact, she would do anything to propel Roger into something she thought he wanted and she certainly wanted, because her sex drive was quite normal and seriously underused.

The thing was that in everything else Roger was such eminently suitable husband material. He had a good job, his finances were sound, he was not bad looking. An accountant might sound a bit dull but it was a good, solid profession and her parents would be pleased. There would be no need for her to work and she could play bridge and give afternoon teas for charitable causes or for raising funds for the Conservative Association. There was no doubting his intelligence and they had a lot in common. They liked the same kind of films, the same programmes on TV, discussed world issues, were politically compatible and generally enjoyed each other's company. One of his drawbacks, apart from the sex thing, was that he was on the mean side and would save whenever he could on eating out, which was probably why they always went to McDonald's with the boys, and to some cheap eatery on the few occasions they ate out, and maybe he never suggested a hotel in case he had to foot the whole bill.

Then of course there were the boys. He adored his sons and Pauline was determined to share this enthusiasm, as much as someone who was not a blood relation could. And she did like them. They were bright, articulate, intelligent, old in a way for their years and seemed quite happily to accept her because she was now regularly included in the weekends in the park or jaunts to the coast, and by now she had an easy, natural relationship with them to the extent that she seriously considered she would like children of her own.

In fact Pauline wanted to settle down, be a wife and mother, with a large house and a nine-to-five husband who mowed the lawn at weekends, be like other women. Roger, she had decided, was just the man to bring this about – after all he had somehow fathered two children – so when he suggested camping over Easter she had immediately agreed.

The camp was in Dorset by the sea, a lovely position with a heavenly view of Lyme Bay and the surrounding coastline. It was a well-appointed site with electricity points for light and heat and a decent, if not luxurious, facility with running water and proper toilets. Thank heaven, she thought as she was shown round, there would be no need to creep into the hedges under cover of darkness.

'Lovely,' she enthused, 'heavenly spot. How clever of you to find it.'

'We've come here for years,' Roger said as he and the boys erected the tents, adjusting the guy ropes while she held the pegs steady. She had never camped in her life, but decided that if this was part of the price she had to pay to get Roger, camp she would – until, that is, she had him firmly enough under control to demonstrate to him her superior way of thinking, her enjoyment of comfort and a modest degree of luxury.

There were three tents, which was what she had expected, had even resigned herself to. This was a chance to establish real familiarity both with him and the boys, over a number of days spent together in the healthy outdoors surrounded by beautiful countryside.

The first night they ate out at a nearby pub. They were all tired from the journey, though it was quite short, but there was the general excitement of setting up camp and having a look round; introducing Pauline to what was familiar to them but strange to her. This included a walk on the pebbly beach and a hunt for fossils, it being part of the famous Jurassic coast.

Even though she was completely unaccustomed to sleeping in a bag on hard ground, she was sufficiently exhausted to have a good night's sleep and woke to the welcome smell of cooking. Peering through the flap of the tent she saw they were hunched over the butane gas stove, by the side of which a table had been laid and chairs set up. She hurriedly pulled on jeans and a T-shirt, deciding a wash would have to come later, and joined them.

Roger looked at her approvingly. 'Sleep well? We left you as long as we could but we're starving.'

'I'm starving too,' she said, rubbing her hands in eager anticipation. 'Here, let me.' She took the handle from Oliver's hand and pushed the sausages around the pan.

'We're lucky with the weather,' Roger said, looking up at the sky. 'The forecast is good.'

'Oh, I am going to enjoy it here,' Pauline sighed, sitting down to a plate full of fat greasy food which normally she would abhor. 'I think I could take to this lifestyle.'

She smiled at Roger and his expression of satisfaction seemed to engage them in a moment of intimacy which, if it had the desired result, would make her sacrifices, sleeping bag and greasy breakfast – and this was only the beginning – well worthwhile.

After the breakfast things were cleared and Pauline had done her ablutions, not with her customary care but this was the outdoor life after all, they set off to climb up the nearby hill from which there was a superb view of the Dorset countryside on one side and the sea on the other. With packs on their backs they began to trudge along the coastal path from which there was a nauseatingly steep descent to the sea. They had a pub lunch – Pauline insisted on paying – and walked even further until Pauline began to feel quite exhausted, whereupon Roger solicitously suggested they should turn back.

'No, I'm fine,' she bravely insisted, but he looked at her with concern. 'Come on, I can see you're all in. Frankly I am too. You've done splendidly.'

'Have I passed the test?' she asked, with a smile.

'How do you mean?' Roger looked puzzled, but Pauline shook her head.

'Nothing. Just a joke.'

They perched for a few moments on a stone while the boys went ahead and, when he pulled her up, he gazed straight into her eyes and she thought he was going to kiss her. At that moment the boys turned back to see where they were, so instead he took her hand while they set off after the boys and they continued to walk, hands tightly clasped, while a feeling of anticipation ran through her.

'I know what you mean,' he said, after a while, as though he had been giving the matter a lot of thought. 'You think I'm testing you by introducing you to camping?'

'In a way.'

'Well, I'm not. I thought you would genuinely enjoy it. Besides I wanted us both to spend a few days together and see how we got on, especially with the boys. I think so far we're doing fine. Really fine.'

'Then it is a test,' she insisted.

'Not at all,' he replied. 'Not at all. Aren't you enjoying it?'

'Very much,' she said, and strangely it was almost true.

They cooked the evening meal over the stove having bought provisions at the camp shop and afterwards walked down to the beach and watched the sun sink over the horizon before going to the pub for a nightcap. The boys were tired and so was she. Very. She couldn't believe that by nine o'clock she was quite ready for bed.

'Lovely day,' she said, as he saw her to the entrance of her tent. Roger smiled complicitly and blew her a kiss.

Pauline had no idea of the time when she woke suddenly aware of a presence in the tent, and then Roger flopped beside her panting heavily.

'Sorry, did I frighten you?'

'Kind of. A bit.'

'Are you alright?'

'Yes.' She felt rather breathless too.

'I want you, Pauline, you know that.'

'What did you think I wanted?' She quickly unfastened the sleeping bag.

'Are you protected?' he asked as he slipped in beside her and turned to her.

'Of course I am, you silly boy. I've been protected for months. I was beginning to think this would never happen.'

When she awoke she could hear the birds singing. It was strange, but not unwelcome, to have the warm body of a man slumbering beside her. Their lovemaking was not exactly cataclysmic, the earth didn't move, but what else could she expect on a cold night in a dark tent, sharing a narrow sleeping bag on hard ground? But still it had happened. It was complete. She stretched with satisfaction, aware that he was suddenly awake.

'Sorry I wasn't much good,' he murmured. 'Kay always said I was a lousy lover. Besides, I'm out of practice.'

'I am too.' Pauline squeezed his hand tenderly. 'Don't worry. We'll work at it.'

'You're lovely,' he murmured in a voice full of emotion, and promptly fell asleep with his head on her breast.

Lovely, but not 'in love', Pauline thought, not yet, but then neither was she. It would come. She'd work on it too. A new life, a man of her own.

She could already hear the lawnmower going on a Sunday morning and the children laughing as they ran alongside their father, while their mother was in the kitchen of the large house preparing Sunday lunch, just like so many other women up and down the country, all around the world.

Sasha hardly noticed the cold and the wind as she took her usual walk along the steep coastal path in St Ives. Deep in thought, as she was, she was also well wrapped up against the elements. She'd decided she owed her parents a longer visit than the two days she usually allotted to them because she had not seen them since Christmas, and owed them an explanation as well as more of her time.

She was the only child of parents who had been steeped in convention all their lives and couldn't quite understand the motives of the offspring they had hatched. They acknowledged her gift as an artist and undoubtedly appreciated her attainments, but felt she had taken a wrong direction in her personal life, which had so far deprived them of grandchildren and any chance of a normal life: a son-in-law, family visits and outings and the chance to boast to acquaintances that such things provide. In fact moving to St Ives and forsaking their life in suburbia had perhaps been a mistake. In many ways they were as lonely and cut off as their daughter, which made her feel guilty that she didn't visit them more often, or even try to understand them better.

Sasha felt there was a great gulf between herself and her mother and father, which she deeply regretted, especially now that she herself felt so isolated and alone, somehow cut off from the world in her emotional life and to some extent her professional life as well. She was not involved in any sexual relationship, her close friendships were few and her work seemed to have become humdrum and stale. She even felt that she had not tried hard enough to understand Ben, his frustration and how he felt about his career. After all he was a man to whom she had been committed for over a decade and maybe she could have made more effort to help him, instead of letting the relationship sour and degenerate into mutual recriminations. By leaving her he had made a point, establishing his independence and to some extent his masculinity.

In the course of the many solitary walks Sasha had taken along this beautiful coastline during this short Easter break and the occasions they offered for reflection and introspection, she had found a lot wrong with her own life and attitudes and was now somehow bent on changing them. She was nearly thirty-six and felt that life was passing her by, which was perhaps why she had yielded so eagerly to Martin, as a way of clutching at straws. However there was not much you could do about the past, but you could try and point yourself in a new direction in the future.

For one thing she did far too much teaching and didn't pay enough attention to her own art. She had been considered at the Slade a pretty accomplished artist in her own right. In many ways her little history of art group interested her and was more rewarding than the undergraduate students. She even felt she was becoming tired of teaching art to people who would never make a career of it or even, many of them, use it to enhance their enjoyment and appreciation of art.

Above all, she had done a lot to make up to her parents for the neglect of the past. They had enjoyed themselves despite mixed weather, been on trips to Penzance and Land's End, and she had taken them out for several meals. She had done her best to be a dutiful daughter and felt to some extent she had drawn closer to them, especially her mother. So much so that the following morning as Sasha prepared to leave her mother was almost in tears.

'I really will miss you, Sasha. It has been a very happy visit and you have been very good to us. I do wish you were nearer. Your father is so silent. Sometimes he hardly speaks all day and he does the same dreary things like walk to the corner shop for his paper and fall asleep in front of the television every evening.'

'I will miss you too, Mum,' Sasha said, embracing her after she had put her case in the car along with the basket of goodies – fresh eggs, cheese and, of course, a large pot of Cornish clotted cream – her mother had pressed on her.

'I wish you'd come more often.'

'I will, I promise.'

'And I wish – I know I shouldn't say it – but I do wish that you'd get a nice man, be happy and settle down.'

'Yes, Mum. I'll try hard.'

They embraced warmly, clung together for a few moments and then, with her father watching from the window of the sitting room, more waves and Sasha was off, back to reality, for once feeling rather sad about leaving such lonely people trapped in their isolation. Maybe her life wasn't so bad after all. Was there any point in getting a man and settling down, as her mother called it, if this was all one had to look forward to?

Vanessa stood at the window of her bedroom watching Ian and the children together on the lawn. They adored their father and, if his accident had done little else that was good or positive, it had brought the family closer together. Or, more accurately, it had brought Ian and the children closer together; she wasn't so sure it had had the same effect on their own relationship. She couldn't recall a time when he had spent so much time at home, and even now he was restricted by his need to use crutches and the irritating lack of progress on the injuries to his legs which had made one shorter than the other.

Rosie had left, but Ian still remained in his own room and showed little desire to resume his place in bed beside Vanessa. Moreover, and perhaps more importantly, it was something they avoided discussing and this served, if anything, to increase the growing chasm between them, which was difficult to ignore no matter how much you tried. Maybe the lack of satisfaction in their sex life was one of the reasons Ian had developed a relationship in Kenya. It was certainly why she had turned to Tim, thoughts of whom increasingly occupied her mind.

She felt in some ways she and Ian were at a crossroads in their lives, with too many matters unresolved, even about their future together. In all the time she had spent by Ian's bed in the hospital and thought about their future, making all sorts of good resolutions, she had never expected an impasse such as the one in which they now found themselves. She had expected that, with his miraculous survival and her subsequent guilt, a good new life would begin again; but so far it hadn't. As far as she knew he wasn't so much depressed as frustrated about his lack of progress, but maybe a deeper depression underlay his reluctance to discuss anything of importance with her.

It was nearly lunchtime and Vanessa was about to turn from the window when she saw a car draw up in their short drive. Ian looked up at the car as an arm appeared from the driver's window and waved at him. He rose from his chair and limped over to the car while a man got out and shook hands and for a moment they chatted together enthusiastically. However what drew Vanessa's attention was the occupant who had emerged from the passenger seat, a woman wearing a white suit and a white hat, which partly obscured her face. For a moment she stood where she was, looking at the scene on the lawn, until the man beckoned to her and she slowly made her way towards Ian who first kissed her lightly on the cheek and then stood for a moment gazing at her, still clinging tightly to her hand. Finally letting it go he introduced the children who the couple fussed over, and then he gestured towards the house whereupon Vanessa hurriedly moved away from the window, glanced in the mirror to check her make-up and hair, and hurried downstairs, by which time Ian stood in the hall talking to his guests. He looked up as Vanessa appeared, making a gesture towards the couple standing beside him.

'Darling,' he called out, 'some very good friends of mine from Kenya have suddenly arrived. Let me introduce Arnie and Marion Kronge. My wife, Vanessa,' he said, pointing to Vanessa who stretched out her hand, a fixed smile, she hoped, concealing her astonishment.

'How do you do?' She shook hands with them both whereupon Ian led the way into the lounge, Vanessa following, almost in a trance-like state, taking in Marion's neat slim figure and realizing she was looking at her husband's lover, which was somehow hard to take in.

'We should have rung,' Arnie was saying. 'It was all very spur of the moment.'

'How long are you here for?' Vanessa gestured towards chairs while Ian perched on a stool because of his legs.

'Only a few days,' Arnie replied. 'Marion wants to take a trip to London to do some shopping. We were both anxious to see how Ian was as the firm could tell us very little.'

'Only that Ian was making a good recovery,' Marion said, smiling at him, 'which relieved us a great deal.' She spoke in a low, melodious voice with a pronounced Kenyan accent, as had her husband.

'Arnie is the managing director of the Kenya branch,' Ian said, looking at Vanessa whose eyes kept wandering to the children still playing on the lawn. The atmosphere in the room was very tense, nervous, and unnatural, something in addition to the unexpected arrival of guests.

'You must stay for lunch,' Vanessa said suddenly, glancing at her watch. 'We were just about to eat.'

'Oh, we couldn't put you to the trouble . . .' Marion began.

'No trouble at all,' Vanessa said, jumping up. 'It is cold, there is plenty of it ready and you must be starving. I just have to lay two extra places. Meanwhile Ian will get you both a drink.'

Marion in fact was beautiful, Vanessa decided, having had the chance to study her, now without a hat, across the table. She felt she managed to retain her charade of the perfect hostess entertaining business friends of her husband, something she had done often enough in that past which seemed so distant now. Marion was petite, with beautifully styled sleek black hair framing a pale oval face, lightly made up with blusher and a very pale pink lipstick. She had deeply recessed, mesmerizing dark blue eyes which seemed at the same time all-knowing. She seemed perfectly at ease, making a point of maintaining, as did Vanessa, an air of detachment with no obvious, or any way discernible, interest in Ian other than a professional one, no little surreptitious glances or evidence of affection that Vanessa was looking out for. In fact, if she hadn't the evidence of the text messages, it would be impossible to tell they had been anything but fleeting acquaintances. Marion scarcely looked at Ian and when she did it was in a way to which no onlooker could possibly attach any deep meaning.

It was a light lunch of cold meats and various salads of which there was, as Vanessa had said, plenty. The children were quiet and well behaved and allowed to leave halfway through to go to their playroom. The talk was fairly perfunctory, mostly about the global economic crisis and its effects on the pharmaceutical industry. These were mercifully slight as medicines were always in demand, and the recent alarming outbreak of a new influenza virus in Mexico, linked to pigs, meant that all the large companies were busy preparing a vaccine.

Ian was interested to hear about business developments in Kenya and, after lunch, he took Arnie up to his study for a chat while Vanessa and Marion were at last left alone to face each other across the table,

'Coffee?' Vanessa enquired, after the pause which followed the exit of the men.

'Coffee would be lovely,' Marion replied, 'but we mustn't stay too long. There is so much to do – and look,' she said, starting to get up, 'I must help you clear the table.'

'No, please don't. I never clear up when my guests are here. I'll take coffee up to the boys and then we'll have ours in the lounge.' She steered her guest firmly to the door.

When she returned a short time later Marion was sitting in a comfortable armchair looking elegant and sophisticated, legs crossed, seemingly completely at home. She greeted Vanessa with a smile.

'What a lovely home you have,' she said, 'and how beautiful your children are, and so well behaved. Unfortunately Arnie and I were never able to have any. I envy you.' A look of sadness temporarily marred her features, which made Vanessa feel almost sorry for her.

'Thank you,' she said, pouring the coffee from a side table. 'Milk and sugar?'

'No thanks. Black.' Vanessa passed her a cup and then, putting her own on a side table, sat down facing her. 'Yes, we are very fortunate. We are a very happy family and the kids adore their father and were so thrilled to have him home safely. By the way,' she said, turning to stir her coffee, 'I must thank you for saving the life of my husband.'

The mask of composure vanished and Marion's features registered surprise, almost shock.

'Oh, how did you know that?'

'I was told by the solicitor representing us that Ian had someone with him in the car. Naturally I was anxious to know who it was, so I could thank them, and he managed eventually to get your name from the hospital.'

'Oh,' Marion said, and paused as if not knowing how to proceed. 'Vanessa, I would rather you did not mention that to my husband. He doesn't know I was in the car with Ian.'

'I see.' Vanessa put her cup to her lips and then, after taking a sip, looked at Marion over the rim. 'Very well.'

'Have you told Ian this?'

'No. He has been too ill and doesn't want to discuss the crash because he says he remembers nothing. It is never referred to and I don't want to do anything to upset him.'

'Do you know what happened to his mobile?' Marion asked suddenly, taking Vanessa by surprise.

'I've no idea. It must have got lost in the crash.'

'No, it was not lost. I put it in his briefcase with the rest of his papers and made sure it was safe in the hospital. Did his briefcase return with him?'

'Yes.' Vanessa put her coffee down, taken aback by her question and aware that the pace of her heartbeat had quickened. She could have lied, but why should she? Anyway, now that it had come out she had a burning desire to know, and also to let

Marion know that she knew. 'But he thinks the mobile was lost. I took it out when he was still in intensive care thinking it should be charged and checking of course for any important messages.' She looked steadily across at her guest.

'I see. Then you know?'

'Yes, I saw your messages. And I know you were having an affair with my husband.'

'How much of this have you told Ian?'

'Nothing, and he might never have known if you hadn't turned up today. Frankly, Marion, it might have been much better if you stayed away.'

'I couldn't stay away. Arnie wanted to see how he was. Arnie is fairly new to the job and said he can learn a lot from Ian. Of course I was uneasy, but I did want to see Ian again for myself, find out how he was and be sure he is alright.'

'Are you in love with him?'

'I do love him, but I also love Arnie. It was an affair, something on the side. We live in Kenya, you know, which has a reputation for this sort of thing. You must have heard the phrase "Are you married or do you live in Kenya?" I think it goes back to the thirties. I don't know if you can understand that? Something important, but at the same time trivial. I would never leave Arnie for Ian, and I know Ian would never leave you. He talked about you a lot and said you were very beautiful, and you are. Naturally I was curious about you too.'

She stood up, clearly in the grip of some deep emotion. 'I think I ought to call Arnie and suggest it is time we left. I know he has a lot to do and this has got to a stage I never expected.' She paused and looked intently at Vanessa. 'I really am very sorry for upsetting you, Vanessa. But it may all yet come out anyway if there is any kind of enquiry.'

'Oh, there won't be. All Ian has said is that the crash was his fault and no one else was involved. He said he doesn't want an enquiry, and one can see why.'

'The roads in Kenya are very uneven and, going a bit too fast, he hit a tree. He got the brunt of the crash, but I was completely unscathed, though deeply shocked. I do think that if I hadn't been in the car with him he would have died because it was a very remote part and he might have stayed there for days, undiscovered. We'd had a few days alone together and were returning to Nairobi. Arnie thought I was staying up country with friends. Now you know the whole story.' She spread out her arms in a gesture almost of despair.

As if on cue the door opened and Ian came in followed by Arnie, who said breezily, 'We have had a very good chat, but we must go, darling.'

'Just what I was thinking.' Marion had easily resumed her carapace of relaxed sophistication, though her pale face had more colour than before.

'And you girls had a good chat?' Ian looked a little anxiously at them, Vanessa thought.

'Most interesting,' Vanessa said, smiling and slipping an arm through Ian's. 'We learned a lot about each other.'

'When you are in Kenya again you must come and see us,' Arnie said, as they walked to the front door. 'Maybe Vanessa would accompany you one day?'

'We'll see,' Vanessa murmured.

'I don't think I'll be returning to Kenya,' Ian said. 'With all the medical care I need, when I do return to work they are thinking of a home job for me, and all in all it might be for the best. I have missed seeing the children a lot, being away so often, and Vanessa too, of course.' They were still arm in arm and he pressed her close to him.

They walked with the Kronges to the car and all embraced warmly and shook hands, Ian kissing Marion lightly on the cheek, Arnie doing the same with Vanessa. They promised to remain in contact and perhaps in the future to meet again, in the insincere, artificial way that people do knowing it will probably never happen. Then Ian and Vanessa stood by the gate, still arm in arm, waving them off.

'Nice couple,' Ian said.

'Lovely,' Vanessa agreed, as they turned back to the house.

That night, just as Vanessa was about to turn off the light, Ian slipped into bed beside her.

'I love you,' he said.

'I love you too,' Vanessa replied, and that night they made love for the first time in many months.

Twelve

May

In a spring that had promised much, but didn't live up to that promise, May was a reasonable month in the West Country and, fortunately, the day selected for the landscape class was one of the best. They met on a hill overlooking the sea a few miles out of Redbury all armed with paints, paper mounted on boards, and Moira had even brought an easel. Not everyone in the class had come and Sasha was relieved to see no sign of Martin, the thought of whose possible appearance had almost wrecked her anticipation of a pleasant day. However, there had already been two evening classes since the Easter break from which he had been absent. Anyway, she reasoned, it was ridiculous to be afraid of Martin. What had happened between them was now a long time ago and he did not and could not be a threat to her equilibrium in any way at all.

She had bought her paints too and after a short talk, which complemented the lectures at the first evening classes of the summer term, she arranged her class in various positions so that they each had a different aspect of the harbour and bay. Besides Moira all the regulars were there including Alice, Roger, Pauline and Caroline. It was obvious to everyone, now, that Roger and Pauline were an item. Since Easter they usually came to class together, left together and today had arrived in the same car.

They all arrived late morning and, after lots of discussion on the places to select, which involved some friendly argument, sat around eating sandwiches and exchanging items of news before getting down to work. People often had the mistaken idea that landscape painting was easier than other subjects. In a sense it was, in that it might be more enjoyable, a change from the lectures and still-lives of the regular art classes which could, on occasions, be stultifying, and a challenge to the lecturer to keep his or her class both instructive and interesting.

They had been working for over an hour, everyone bent on their tasks, occasionally getting up to get a new perspective or standing back from their work to assess its effect, when a car drew up and parked beside those on the edge of the field. Sasha knew, with a sinking feeling in the pit of her stomach but also a sense of inevitability, exactly who had arrived.

'Hello, Martin,' she said casually as he emerged from his car, clutching his painting equipment.

'I'm sorry I didn't let you know I was coming,' Martin said, 'but I didn't know until the last minute if I'd be able to make it.'

'Find yourself a place,' Sasha said, offhandedly gesturing around. 'I'm afraid all the best ones are taken.'

'That's no problem,' Martin said. After looking around he selected a spot away from the others and, returning to his car, produced an easel, which he set up and began mounting his paper with the practised air of an expert. In a way Sasha was quite curious to know what he would produce, but after he had settled she went back to her own work, sketching with a pencil on a pad on her lap. She saw Caroline glance at her in sympathy and she gave a slight shrug, as if to ask what could one do about a situation, which, in the light of hindsight, was not altogether unexpected?

Allowing for the irritation caused by Martin's arrival the afternoon was, on the whole, a successful one and at five she walked around the group inspecting their work, lingering longer over some than others, making suggestions about perspective, the use of colour, the measurement of distance and other instances where outdoor work differed from that done inside.

Caroline had done a really good painting of the harbour and her work seemed to reflect a serenity of mood that Sasha, recalling the hideous images of war, had not seen in her work for some time.

'Very good,' she said approvingly, then, putting her mouth close to Caroline's ear, 'Will you wait for me at the end? I don't want to be left alone with him. He's hanging on.'

Caroline nodded. 'I'll say you're coming home with me. In fact, why don't you? I would like to talk to you.'

'That's a good idea.'

'Come and meet Greg.'

'Great.' With a smile Sasha moved on to Alice, whose technique had improved more than anyone else's.

'You do some beautiful work, very delicate and individual with a good eye for colour,' she said approvingly.

'I come here quite a lot with Moira.' Alice smiled up at her. 'It's a place I love, with such wonderful views.'

'It shows.'

As usual Pauline's rather resembled the effort that a schoolgirl without any knowledge of painting techniques might have made.

'Not very good, is it?' she said, looking anxiously at Sasha who stood examining her work.

'You have a long way to go, but you have definitely made some progress. And Roger . . .' She paused beside him. 'Roger has improved too. You will soon be ready for the advanced class.'

The last one was Martin. It would look too obvious if she left him out. She stood behind Roger, watching Martin, who had moved his easel even further away from the others, facing land rather than sea, and who was bent over his work. He always appeared at the evening classes in a business suit as if he had come straight from work. Today he was in casual clothes, jeans, an-open necked shirt, hair slightly tousled, an overnight shadow. This was a strong, powerful-looking Martin, a man in control, which was, she supposed, what had drawn her to him in the first place. She knew she was still attracted to him, which was the moment he happened to look up and saw her gazing at him, maybe her expression giving more away than she intended. For a second or two their eyes locked and then she turned her head quickly away.

When she reached him he was perched on his stool, head bent towards the painting on his easel. She stood behind him inspecting it, longing to reach out and touch him. If only he knew, she thought, what conflicting emotions were warring beneath her, she hoped, detached exterior. He hadn't done very much, some of it sketched in with pencil.

'You look as though you've done this before, Martin,' she said.

'I've done a bit of landscape work,' he murmured, still concentrating on the picture before him, perhaps deliberately avoiding eye contact. 'I'm sorry if I upset you, Sasha. I don't do it deliberately.'

'You seem to come late almost on purpose,' she replied, keeping her voice low, hoping her tone did not give her vulnerability away too much. 'Every time you're late as if drawing attention to yourself. That's what upsets me.'

'Can we talk about it?' he said, looking up at last.

'I'm going back with Caroline.'

'OK. Maybe next time?'

She didn't reply but, feeling deeply disturbed, moved away, knowing that he had sensed her weakness. So there would be a next time, and a time after that and . . . she could see herself ending up in bed with him again, compromising, giving in and the whole sorry business of recrimination and reproach starting all over again.

Finally it was time to pack up. As the last one to arrive, Martin seemed reluctant to go and dawdled over his work, while the others began the not inconsiderable task of clearing up, which included saving precious artwork, folding stools and tables, stacking them back in their cars and then gathering round Sasha as if unwilling to disperse.

'A good day I would say,' she said. 'We are terribly lucky with the weather. Some of you have done exceptionally well. Would you like another outdoor session before the end of term?'

Murmurs of eager assent followed.

'We'll discuss it at our next class when you can put some finishing touches to what you've done today.' She turned to Martin, who hadn't moved. 'We're off, Martin,' she said.

'See you.' He raised a hand without looking back.

Caroline was sitting in her car and waved when she saw Sasha go towards hers.

'See you at my place,' she called out.

Sasha nodded and got behind her wheel, glancing once more at Martin who sat in solitary isolation, his back to her, painting away. She felt an unreasoning and unreasonable tug of emotion, almost pity, at the lonely figure, again experiencing that tug at the heartstrings which would not go away.

As she arrived outside Caroline's house the door opened.

'Greg's not here,' she said. 'He's out with the kids, but come in. I wanted to chat anyway. Have a drink?

'Not as I'm driving. Coffee would be nice.' She followed Caroline into the house aware of how things had changed since she was last there. The presence of a man made a great difference, she thought, reflecting on her own tidy, silent but rather forlorn house since Ben had left.

'So,' Caroline said, putting on the kettle as Sasha sank into a chair by the kitchen table, 'is Martin a problem?'

'Not yet, but he will be. You see today I realized that I still feel attracted to him. To be perfectly honest with you the fact is I am lonely. I need someone. I wonder if I have been too hasty with him, but I know it is just a weakness on my part. Anyway let's change the subject. How are things with Greg?'

Caroline didn't reply for a while but concentrated on making the coffee. Then she put a cup in front of Sasha and sat down opposite her.

'Difficult,' she said. 'He has not been the same man since he came home. I have never known him like this all the time we've been together. He has often been away, you know, Northern Ireland, Iraq, Basra, but this is different.'

'How is it different?'

'He is very withdrawn, lot of silences, broods a lot. He spends a great deal of time with Sharon whose husband was killed. He'd nursed him on the field as he lay dying and seems to have a personal feeling of responsibility that he didn't save him or bring him back alive. Everyone says he risked his own life getting him to a safe place away from the gun battle that was going on. He goes frequently with Sharon to Mark's grave. She leans on him a lot and he feels guilty. It is almost like an obsession. One thing I know for sure, Sasha: Greg is not going to leave the army. He has told me so and when the battalion returns, which may be as early as next year, he will be there with them, with his boys as he calls them. They need him, so it doesn't matter so much whether or not I need him too. They have priority in his life, not me or his family.'

'And how will that affect you?'

'Well, does one ever learn?' Caroline looked at her with an unspoken question on her lips, to which Sasha did not know the answer any more than she knew it to her own personal dilemma, which this new revelation about Martin had created.

★   ★   ★

'That was a lovely day,' Alice said, leaning back against the seat of the car, sighing with contentment.

'Lovely,' Moira agreed, 'except that I didn't think Sasha looked too happy, did you?'

'No.' Alice frowned. 'Do you think there is anything between her and Martin? She always seems to change when he is around. I noticed it when he turned up in class before the end of term, and then today when he arrived her manner and attitude changed at once. She seemed to become more nervous, ill at ease.'

'He is a very attractive man,' Moira said.

'Yes, but he's married.'

'Then that may be the problem?'

'It certainly may.'

'I don't know much about her private life,' Moira went on, 'but I understood she has, or had, a boyfriend with whom she has lived for a long time.'

'If that is the case it does sound very complicated. What complex lives young people lead.'

'Different from your early days?'

'Very different. Oh, very different, but we were more repressed and I don't think that was a good thing either. I always regretted I didn't marry Bernard.'

'Or go to bed with him?' Moira looked at her. 'It may sound impertinent, but did you?'

'Well since you ask, no. It wasn't the thing. We always had the idea drummed into us that a man would think less of a woman, and I know Bernard certainly would have. He was very upright, religious too. He was anxious for us to get married and I always held back, as I told you, reluctant to give up my freedom so soon. Well in the circumstances I got plenty of that. Too much.' There was a definite note of regret in Alice's voice.

'Do you ever think of him?' Moira looked at her sympathetically, thinking how many long years Alice had had to regret her decision.

'I used to, every day, but not so much now. And, talking of complicated lives, how is Ian?'

'Ian is very much better. He goes to work now, not every day but two or three days a week depending on how he feels, and he still has treatment. A car collects him and brings him back.

I would say that he and Vanessa are now very happy together. I hope so anyway.' Her voice trailed off uncertainly. 'As far as one can tell.'

As close as Moira was to Alice she didn't feel like confiding too many of her family problems or secrets to her. Open minded she might consider herself, but enough was enough. 'By the way,' she said, 'have you any plans for a holiday this summer?'

'No, not really. I am quite happy where I am. I live in a nice place by the sea and I have my painting. Sasha was very kind about it today. I don't know that I would want to move on to the advanced class. I like her so much.'

'Well, the thing is, Ian and Vanessa have a house in the south of France. I go there with them every summer. Vanessa wondered if you would like to come with me this year? It will be for about two weeks. Vanessa stays there for most of the holiday with the children and Ian comes and goes. This year he will probably stay all summer to complete his recuperation. Then friends visit too. It is a large old farmhouse and there is plenty of room. We would all love to have you. Vanessa suggested it as we are all so grateful for your help this year.' She placed a hand on Alice's arm. 'Besides, it is not only gratitude. We like you and enjoy your company.'

Alice hesitated a long time before she replied.

'Well, my dear, I don't know what to say. It is very, very kind of you, but may I think about it and let you know?'

'Of course,' Moira said, 'there is plenty of time.'

Roger and Pauline drove back to her house both in a reflective mood, saying little on the way. He stopped outside her door and looked at his watch.

'Much later than I thought. But it was a good day.'

'Yes it was.' Pauline began to get her things together. 'Come up for a bite?'

'Why not? I won't stay though. I have to go on a course tomorrow and must do some work.'

'There's something I want to tell you.'

'Oh, sounds ominous.'

'Not really.'

She put the key in the lock and he followed her into the kitchen.

'What is it you want to tell me?'

'Can I tell you over supper? Open some wine.'

Roger was by now so at home in Pauline's house that he almost knew where everything was, certainly where the wine was kept.

Pauline busied herself putting together an omelette with salad while Roger poured wine for them and then sat at the kitchen table watching her. He now felt totally at ease with her, that finally he had found a woman who understood him and who he could relax with, above all in bed when nothing too much was expected of him. This was in contrast to Kay who fell on him like a hungry lion, increasing his sense of inadequacy because she always complained about him afterwards until she finally rejected him altogether.

Consequently he felt slightly uneasy at what it was Pauline had to tell him. He looked at her anxiously as she put their plates before them and sat down facing him.

'What is it?'

'Don't be so *worried*,' she teased, smiling at him. 'It's about the watercolour class. I want to give it up. Sasha still doesn't think much of me.'

'She said you've improved.'

'She has to say something. Don't be so patronizing, Roger. You know I'm no good. I don't even enjoy it very much. I'd have given up before but for you.'

Her gaze was so full of meaning that he felt overwhelmed, overjoyed because it seemed to reflect the way he felt about her.

'Let's get married,' he said.

Pauline stared momentarily at her plate as though she couldn't believe what she had heard. Then she raised her eyes and said rather jerkily, 'I didn't mean you to go *that* far to keep me in the art class. It's a bit of a drastic step, isn't it?'

'I want to keep you,' he said, putting down his knife and fork. 'Not in the art class but for me. I was terrified that you were going to say you didn't want to see me again, you had someone else, or you were going away. You seemed so grave. It made me realize how much you mean to me and how I feel about you.'

'But we don't have to get *married*.'

'Don't you want to?' His expression became anxious again.

'Yes I do. I want it more than anything, but I felt you were carrying too much baggage to ask me: Kay, the boys and so on.'

'The boys have taken to you. In fact when he first met you Oliver asked if I was going to marry you.'

'And what did you say?'

'I think I said I felt it was a bit soon. As for Kay you told me to forget about her and I have. I see her naturally when I pick up the boys. I do think of her from time to time obviously, not with love or affection, but as a person who did me a lot of harm, never tried to understand me, expected too much of me, whereas you,' he looked at her again, 'are just right.'

He rose from the table and went over to kiss her, a light kiss, one of love and affection rather than passion.

'I can't believe this,' Pauline said, when he had returned to his place. 'I can't believe it's happened.'

'I know we're meant to be together and I would like to fix up everything soon. Not hang about, a register office, something quick. How do you feel about that?'

'I'd like you to meet my parents,' Pauline said, prosaically. 'I want to be sure they approve of you as a son-in-law.' She gave him a smile that was full of love, understanding and desire.

'I think I'll stay the night after all,' Roger said. 'To hell with the course.'

Later, with her future husband lying asleep beside her, Pauline reviewed with some incredulity, a state of complete disbelief, the events of the day. She was overwhelmed with such joy that she felt she would burst. Everything was just right. Roger was just right. They would make an ideal couple. As for her dream of walking down the aisle in a lovely white dress on the arm of her father, in front of an admiring congregation, well, that could go hang.

Dreams were there to be shattered when everything else was right. She rather imagined that a few more might go and that, at least in its initial stages, Roger would set the pace of their marriage. He had already suggested moving in with her. No need, he said, for a big house, and she should go on working, to start with anyway. There was no mention of children and she felt it was too soon to raise it. She knew that Roger, being a person professionally connected with money, was cautious, some might unkindly call it mean. This was a weakness, however, that she accepted because of his training as well as his personality. She also thought that, because of the kind of person he was, he would be faithful to her.

Above all was the fact that at last she had a man, a man she wanted and who wanted her. She needed to fit in, to be with him and then she could gradually start to work on bringing him round to her way of thinking. Doubtless their honeymoon would be spent camping, and the boys would be there too.

In his sleep he gave a contented little sigh and she kissed him very gently on the forehead, holding him in her arms until she too drifted off to sleep.

Roger drove away from Pauline's house in the small hours of the morning still slightly befuddled by the events of the previous evening. He was both elated and bemused by the action he had taken, which had surprised him as much as Pauline. Roger was, by nature, a cautious man, completely lacking in spontaneity. He liked to weigh things out, balancing one against another before he made a decision, and last night he had not taken that decision until Pauline told him she had something to tell him and he had been quite sure it was the end of their affair. In his relief he had done an uncharacteristic thing: thrown caution to the winds and suggested marriage. Marriage. It was a very big step to take. Not only this, he had also decided where and when they should get married, soon, and where they should live. It had taken him months to decide to propose to Kay and, when he did, he had everything in place: the day, the time and the ring in his pocket.

For once in his life he had done something on the spur of the moment and the amazing thing was that the more he thought about it as he drove back to his flat, the less he regretted it. Not one bit. It had taken him an age to propose to Kay, seconds to propose to Pauline and because of this fact alone, this contradiction, he was sure he had the key to happiness and good fortune.

Sasha stood outside the door of her head of department and took a deep breath. She was feeling very nervous. When she finally knocked, a voice immediately told her to enter and she found Trevor Judge sitting at his desk working on his computer. He looked up and then smiled with pleasure when he saw who it was.

'Sasha,' he said, getting up, 'this is a nice surprise. Everything alright?'

'Fine,' she said, 'have you got a minute to spare?'

'Of course I have.' He indicated a seat. 'In fact,' he pointed to the screen, 'I was just thinking about you and wanted to talk to you.'

'Oh?'

'Shall I go first, or will you?'

'Maybe I should.' Sasha paused to get her breath. 'Trevor, I would like to take a year's sabbatical. I know it is late notice, but there are complications in my personal life and I feel it would do me good to get away from it all for a year.'

'Oh,' Trevor looked grave. 'Is it to do with Ben?'

'Kind of because of what happened with Ben, the way he walked out on me, but it is also about another person. Someone with whom I do not want to get involved and who won't go away.'

'Oh dear.' Trevor for a moment seemed lost for words. 'Is it a member of staff?'

'No. He is not a member of staff, but he is one of my students in my adult education class, an older man, and he is very persistent. It makes it very awkward for me.'

'I can see that.'

'I have done everything I can to discourage him, but I am attracted to him and I think he knows it.'

'Then?'

'He's married.'

'Ah.' Trevor sat back in his chair.

'He says he is not happily married and his wife is in a mental home, but the situation is too fraught, largely because of that. I can't cope with it. I don't want it to interfere with my life because I can see no happy ending.'

'I can understand that. It's a pity, Sasha, because I was going to tell you that Michael Stokes is leaving and I wanted to invite you to apply for his place as deputy head. You know we have to advertise everything, but I am pretty sure you would be a strong candidate.'

Sasha blushed with pleasure. 'That's very flattering, Trevor, but I'm not sure I'm ready for that either. I feel I've neglected my own painting and I thought I'd go to Italy for a year and combine that with study. Maybe at the Institute in Florence.'

'Won't he be here when you get back?'

'If he is I shall be stronger. Besides, things might have changed.'

'You might have found a virile Italian?'

'I might.' She smiled. 'You never know. I could do with a bit of luck.'

'Well, Sasha, that is very sad news, and, as you say, it is rather late to find a replacement, but I'm sure the board will consider your request sympathetically. I might persuade Michael to stay on. He hasn't found a job but is just restless.'

'You needn't tell them all the details.'

'Of course not, but we shall miss you. You must be sure to come back. You are very popular here and I don't wonder your students fall in love with you.' He looked at her as though he was half in love with her himself, but she knew that he loved his wife and family. He was a grandfather and not far from retirement and she had always found in him a good and wise counsellor; above all, a friend.

Sasha returned to her room, a great weight taken from her mind. The die was cast and with it came a sense of liberation that so often taking positive action can bring. She felt that at last a plan that had its germ during her Easter break in St Ives had been put in place, and she was free to get on with her life in a country she loved and far, far away from temptation in the form of Martin Oakshott.

Thirteen

June

There was an end-of-term feeling about the class, even though it had a few more weeks to go. They were all preparing for the exhibition, putting last-minute touches to half-finished paintings with an air almost of youthful excitement. Students bustled about from table to easels to cupboards, rummaging for work done ages ago and forgotten about. The weather had been so dismal that the landscape classes had been cancelled and it was doubtful if they would resume, given the weather forecast in a summer that had initially held out so much promise.

Alice had a stack of work and the difficulty was deciding what to show, a problem on which she consulted Sasha.

'Space is limited so a couple of your best,' Sasha said, looking through her portfolio. 'You and Moira have done more work outdoors than most people, so choose from your landscapes. You are definitely ready for the advanced class, Alice.'

'But I'll miss you so much,' Alice said.

'The tutor for the advanced course, a colleague of mine, is very good and a gifted artist. You'll like him. You need a challenge, Alice. In fact a lot of students in this class are due to move on.' Her gaze lingered for a moment on Pauline. 'Except one or two.'

It was difficult to know what to say to students whose work had shown very little improvement, if any. A few had dropped out and she had always been hoping that Pauline might. Anyway it wouldn't be her problem any more if Pauline did decide to return in the autumn term.

As Sasha had resumed her inspection Moira got encouragement too and Caroline was, next to Martin, one of the best in the class so there was no debate about which direction she should take. In fact Caroline had accumulated almost as much work as Alice, as if making up for lost time once she had more peace of mind following Greg's return from the war. She had now included one or two war pictures in her portfolio.

'How are things?' whispered Sasha.

'Good,' Caroline nodded. 'Greg's going to come to the exhibition.'

'Put in some of your war stuff. He'll be pleased.'

'I'm glad you're not annoyed.'

'Why should I be? Things are very different now from what they were a few months go. See you later.' Sasha gave her shoulder a squeeze and moved on to Pauline whose table looked suspiciously bare.

'Not exhibiting, Pauline?' Sasha asked her. 'I don't want you to feel too discouraged.'

'It's not that, Sasha,' Pauline said, with a glance at Roger next to her. 'But I have nothing to show that I'm proud of, and anyway I'm giving up the art class. You have been very, very good and patient but I know I am just not good enough. Besides,' she glanced at Roger, 'Roger and I have become engaged.'

'We want to get married in the autumn,' Roger said. 'There is so much to do, so I shan't be coming back either. You'll be rid of both of us.'

'Well!' Sasha stepped back and looked round at the class, most of whom had stopped working, ears pinned back. 'That's brilliant news – not to get rid of you, of course, but to know how happy you are. What a very satisfying, and I must say not entirely un-expected, outcome. Did everyone hear that? Roger and Pauline are to be married in the autumn.'

Everyone started chatting and smiling in the direction of the newly engaged couple. Hands were waved.

'At least if you didn't make an artist out of me you got me a husband,' Pauline said. 'So I can thank the watercolour class for that.'

Sasha stooped and pecked her on the cheek then crossed over to shake hands with Roger. She returned to her table thinking that the class were ready for her own announcement.

'Well, everyone, that is splendid news, a happy note to end the year on, and I know we all wish them every happiness. However I do have a little news of my own, not quite in the same cat-egory. I have applied to take a sabbatical from the college and there is every reason to think it will be granted. I want to develop my own painting and continue my studies in the history of art, so I shan't be here next year either.'

A clamour of consternation broke out, markedly different in tone from the pleasure that had greeted Pauline's announcement. Sasha raised a hand.

'I know some of you will be disappointed, and thank you for that, very gratifying, but most of you are ready to move on. I don't know yet who will be taking this class, but we have a lot of teachers and artists at the college every bit as well qualified as me.

'Now to practical matters. We have one more class before the exhibition. I think our landscape outings must be abandoned as the weather has been so unreliable, and we have already had to call off two. So at the next class I will take all submissions for the exhibition and give you final details of what to do and when to arrive. I hope that as many of you as possible, whether exhibiting or not, will come. So, I look forward to seeing you again next week.'

It was a subdued little group of regulars who gathered round Sasha in the canteen after the class. Alice looked the most stricken.

'I can't believe you're going,' she said. 'I can't bear it.'

'You will be absolutely fine, Alice. Besides, you will be in another group.'

'But you have brought out so much in me. You are so patient. I don't think anyone else could have done so much.'

'You're inspirational,' Caroline said, her voice breaking, 'and a very good friend.' She looked round the table. 'You don't know because we never told anyone just how good Sasha has been to me. My husband has been in Afghanistan and at Christmas I nearly cracked up and turned to Sasha who forsook her own holiday with her family – I didn't know she was in Cornwall – to spend it with me and she made a great differ-ence to my life.'

'It wasn't me,' Sasha said, gently. 'It was the power of painting.'

'Sasha encouraged me to work again. Took me out to intro-duce me to landscape painting. I will never forget it.' She put an arm round Sasha and hugged her.

'I feel really embarrassed,' Sasha said. 'I will miss you, but I'll be back after a year and if you are still around I'm sure we won't lose touch. There are always letters, cards, e-mails.'

Even Pauline looked upset. 'You have been very good and patient with me, Sasha. I hope you will be very happy during your sabbatical.'

'And what great news about you two,' Sasha said, turning to her.

'Dark horses. Although we did notice you seemed to be pairing off,' Moira said.

Roger appeared almost transformed by the change in his personal life. He had found someone who, by believing in him, had contrived to bring out the best in him, banish the sort of insecurity and awkwardness that had once caused him to make a fool of himself with Sasha. No longer shy and reserved he was bursting with a new-found confidence that even seemed to show in his appearance.

'We were brought together by a dog,' he said. 'Pauline walked a neighbour's dog in the park and I was there with my boys. We naturally came together. I think, actually, that she was stalking me.' Roger looked slyly at Pauline who gave him a sharp nudge and he put an arm round her and drew her close to him. 'Only teasing, silly.'

Sasha thought what a change there had been in this formerly rather tense, reserved man, who had once tried to chat her up. But as a pair they were well suited. The power of love, she thought rather enviously, remembering how relieved, and yet at the same time disappointed, she had been that Martin hadn't turned up tonight; both fearing and, at the same time, hoping he would come through the door. Dicing with danger.

'Any idea where you're going?' Roger asked, leaning across Pauline.

'I'm not quite sure, probably Italy.' Anxious not to give too much away, by not mentioning Florence, Sasha looked at her watch. 'Anyway, this is not the end. I'll see you next week and at the exhibition.'

As she gathered her things Caroline also got up. 'I'll come with you,' she said and followed Sasha to the door.

'I've got my car,' Sasha said when they got outside.

'I know. I just feel very upset that you didn't manage to tell me before the others. It came as a shock. I thought we had a special friendship.'

'Oh, we have, Caroline.' Sasha turned to her with consternation. 'Of course we have, but it only happened the other day. I didn't get the chance.'

'You must have been thinking about it. It wouldn't be on the spur of the moment.'

Caroline was obviously deeply upset and Sasha put a hand on her shoulder.

'Please don't be upset. It has been in my mind, but no decisions.'

'To get away from Martin?'

'Only partly that. I'm tired, Caroline. It has been a difficult year. I'm also stale. I badly need a break. I couldn't make any sort of announcement until I'd talked to Trevor, my boss, and he's not terribly pleased because it is such short notice, but I think it will be OK. If it hadn't been the class today you would have been the first one to know, but Pauline and Roger's announcement kind of brought it on. A time for goodbyes. I really will miss you, but we'll keep in touch. We have become friends, real friends.'

'And if, or rather when, Greg goes to Afghanistan again?'

'You will be OK. You will be stronger and all the other women will support you and you'll get your strength from supporting them. I know it.'

She kissed her lightly on the cheek and then hurried across to her car, not realizing how emotional she felt about the tributes from this little group who had, in fact, become so important to her and to whom she had become too important – like Caroline. No man is an island, indeed.

Moira and Alice were unusually silent until they were halfway home.

'I am very upset about Sasha,' Alice said at last.

'But she's right. She would not have been our tutor anyway.'

'Somehow she's an anchor. Remember Martin said he didn't want to go to the advanced class?'

'But I think he had another reason for that, don't you?'

'You think there was a relationship?'

'I don't know what there was, but Sasha is always different when he's around.' Moira stopped the car outside Alice's door.

'Come in for another coffee?' Alice said.

'It is a bit late. Would you mind if I didn't?'

'Not at all.' Alice paused, as if choosing her words carefully. 'Only I did want to say, Moira, that although I am deeply touched and grateful for your invitation, I have decided not to come with you in the summer.'

'Oh, but why?'

'I just don't feel ready for it. I can't exactly explain, but perhaps another time?'

'You're sure you won't think about it?'

'I have thought about it and that's the decision I've made. I am truly, deeply touched, but it does seem a big step and one I'm not yet ready for. Please understand.'

Alice leaned over to kiss her and started to get out of the car. 'And thank Vanessa. See you soon.'

She turned towards her door and left Moira feeling puzzled and rather sad. The truth was she would genuinely have enjoyed her company.

When she got up to her flat Alice stood by the window, looking out, but Moira had already driven off. She hoped she hadn't been too brusque, maybe offended her. The fact was she felt she relied too much on Moira and her family to the extent that she somehow felt patronized by them, as though they thought they had a duty to look after her. They were the only real friends she had made. In the course of a long life she had found that large families were like that, which is why she had reconciled herself to a rather solitary existence, something she accepted and even valued, especially after the death of Sybil had left her virtually alone in the world. She felt she had inner reserves which she had frequently to call on. This was one of those times.

Feeling restless, she went into her bedroom, changed into her nightclothes and then made herself a cup of hot chocolate and took it to bed. She lay there drinking, slowly luxuriating in the warmth of her own home and bed and gradually relaxed.

But the truth was she was still torn and couldn't help wondering if she'd made the right decision. It would be nice to go to the south of France and be cosseted and looked after. She and Sybil used to travel a lot together during the holidays. She was always in charge of the arrangements and she kept a diary of their travels.

However, having said 'no' so firmly it would be unlike her to change her mind and she had thought about it a lot. She didn't want to be a hanger-on. It was a question of dignity, of independence. She wanted Moira and her family to know she had her own life, and she couldn't help feeling that they would think the better of her, and perhaps even respect and value her more.

Vanessa had not been to the swimming pool since Ian's accident. It had been a deliberate decision and her mother always took the children to their classes. Now the classes were over and Vanessa had decided to take the children swimming and to go swimming with them. She realized quite well that, at the back of her mind, was the strong desire to see Tim again and let him have sight of her in her bikini, which was rather disgraceful and leading to temptation which she knew she was in fact courting. She had that familiar, restless feeling again.

Vanessa was at the point in her life where, once again, she didn't know what she wanted. She had thought that Ian's accident was a kind of turning point and she would never be the same person again. All the introspection she had done as she sat day after day by his bed willing him to recover. All the good resolutions she had made. What had happened to them? Marion had happened, that's what, the knowledge that her upright, hardworking husband had been having an affair, and apparently quite a serious one, when she had thought him a pillar of rectitude and fidelity. It was the humiliation of knowing that she, with all her supposed good looks, had been incapable of keeping him. Why?

Nowadays it was as though Ian had never been away except that they saw a lot more of him. Life had settled down into the sort of humdrum routine that it had been before the trauma that affected their lives, and the fact was that Vanessa didn't like routine.

She wasn't made for routine. She saw herself as a young, healthy, wealthy woman with too much time on her hands looking for ways to occupy herself – good works, anything, even affairs to relieve the tedium and boredom of everyday life, of a husband with a steady job and a nine-to-five routine.

As the children splashed around she stood at the water's edge looking round. The pool was quite full and there were several guards on duty, but none of them was Tim. It didn't have to be. It was speculative that he would be there anyway. It could be his day off.

She supervised the children in the children's pool, sitting on the side dangling her feet in the water, and then she saw one of the guards she knew who came over to greet her.

'Hello, Mrs Fleming,' he said.

'Oh, hi there,' she replied.

'I haven't seen you for a long time.'

'No, my husband had a serious accident and my mother has been taking the kids for their lessons. By the way,' she said, trying to sound casual, 'is Tim around?'

'Tim? Oh, Tim has left us, some weeks ago. Is there anything I can do to help?'

Difficult to control that empty, sinking feeling in her heart. 'Oh, no thanks, the children have finished their classes. I just wanted to thank him. Is he still around in Redbury?'

'I don't know where he's gone, except that he doesn't work here any more.'

And from the funny, rather cheeky look he gave her as he walked away, she was sure that he knew, her humiliation made so much worse by the suspicion that Tim had perhaps boasted about his conquest of a bored and randy married woman. And how many more had there been?

When she arrived home her mother's car was in the drive and she looked as though she was just about to pull out.

'Hi Mum,' she called out. 'Don't go. Have you been here long?'

'About ten minutes. I just thought I'd pop in.'

Vanessa left her car behind her mother's, unbuckled the children from the back seat and gathered all the swimming things from the car boot.

'Been swimming, darling?'

'Yes. I felt like it after I picked them up from school.'

They walked towards the house, the children running ahead.

'Tim has left,' she said, turning to her mother.

'I know.'

'You knew and you didn't tell me?'

'Well . . .' Moira paused. 'No, I didn't tell you. I can't make any excuse, but I decided not to. Does it matter?' She looked curiously, anxiously at her daughter.

'No, of course it doesn't.'

Vanessa deposited the wet clothes in the utility room and joined her mother in the kitchen.

'Of course it doesn't matter,' she said again. 'All that's past, Mum.'

'Good. I'm glad.' Moira busied herself making tea. 'By the way, Alice doesn't want to come to France with us.'

'Why not?'

'I don't know. She says she's not ready for it.'

'Oh well, at least we asked her. Can't do more than that, can we?'

'I suppose not. Still, I'm sorry. I think she would have enjoyed it and I would have enjoyed having her.'

'Maybe we can talk her into it if that's what you want.'

'No, I don't want to talk her into it. If she doesn't want to come that's it. When is Ian due home?'

Vanessa glanced at the kitchen clock. 'Any time.'

'Things OK?'

'Mum.' Vanessa's expression was one of irritation. 'I wish you'd stop asking that. I wish I'd never confided in you. Things are *fine*. Back to normal.' Then she paused and gazed thoughtfully out of the window. 'The thing is, Mum . . . Well, I'm bored. I am terribly bored. I'm thinking of returning to air hostessing.'

'You're *what*?'

'Don't look so outraged.'

'I am rather outraged. Have you discussed it with Ian?'

'Not yet. I'm trying it out on you first. I can see it's not favourable.'

'Is that why you went to see if Tim was around? You needed something to do?'

Vanessa turned angrily on her mother. 'No it's not. Not at all. It's been in my mind for some time.'

'Then who is going to look after your husband, who has still not fully recovered, and the children?'

'I thought we'd get a housekeeper. We can afford it. I'll try to go for short-haul flights. Perhaps part-time. I don't know. I'll have to look into it, but the airline did say I could always come back and I thought I'd put out feelers. Of course with the recession and problems with airlines it may be out of the question, but even the thought of it has given me a lift.'

'I think you should talk to your husband first.'

'No. I'll first put out feelers and even if they are keen it won't happen tomorrow. It may not until next year and Ian will be well on the way to recovery then. Mum, I don't want to be a bored, unhappy woman for the rest of my life. That's what started the affair with Tim in the first pace. I need to be busy.'

'What about all your good works?'

Vanessa pulled a face. 'They kind of lapsed with looking after Ian. Also they pall too. They are hardly exciting or taxing, hardly a challenge. Mum, I'm not yet thirty. If I live as long as Alice I have another fifty years in front of me. Fifty years of stultifying boredom.' She glanced quickly at the clock again. 'Anyway I must get on now. I've got to get the kids' tea and the evening meal. Would you like to stay for supper?'

'No, I have a bridge evening.' Moira looked sadly at the daughter she loved so much and yet feared for. 'I never had a problem living a fulfilled life, Vanessa. Always lots to do even after Daddy died.'

'Then you were very lucky.'

'Yes I am. We belonged, I'm afraid, to a different generation. We didn't expect too much.'

Vanessa went to move her car so that Moira could get out of the drive and, after a fond farewell, stood watching her as she drove off, resolving in the future not to take her so much into her confidence. It was true they belonged to a very different generation, almost another world.

★   ★   ★

'Good day, darling?' Ian asked, as they faced each other across the supper table, both having helped put the children to bed. This was always a happy time and, yes, it was good to have him about more and the children loved it. There was a lot really to be grateful for and be happy about, but still that little lingering doubt that she was missing out on life persisted.

'Yes, I took the kids swimming. Mum popped in, about normal really. And you?'

'Mine was fine. There is talk about promotion now that I am based at home.' He gazed at her for a moment. 'Did you go swimming too?'

'Yes.'

'You haven't been for a long time, have you?'

'No. I was busy looking after you.'

'Is that bloke you asked here for Christmas still there?'

'No, he's left.'

'Do you miss him?'

'Why on earth should I?'

'I don't know, I thought you seemed close. Asking him for Christmas seemed to me distinctly odd.'

'I don't know what you're getting at, Ian.'

'Don't you?' She noticed how solemn, how knowing his expression was. 'Well, that's alright then.'

It was as if a chill had swept through the room and she shivered uncontrollably even though it was quite a warm night.

'We'll miss the news,' Ian said, getting up and limping over towards the TV, turning it on while Vanessa stacked the dishes and started to clear away.

The chill, the feeling of frost in the air, continued all evening and was almost palpable as they lay in bed side by side. They were a couple who had always had difficulty communicating, lived very much on the surface of things, rarely discussing issues and eventually Ian put down his book and looked at Vanessa who was half asleep.

'You OK?'

'Yes.' Eyes wide open, she looked at him. 'Why shouldn't I be? You're very mysterious tonight, Ian. Do you have something on your mind?'

'I suspect you were having an affair with Tim.'

She lay for a long time staring at the ceiling. Her breath seemed to have gone out of her, but strangely enough she felt quite calm. Now it was out.

'Why didn't you say anything before?'

'I didn't know how to. I didn't want to lose you, and when I had the accident I no longer wanted to because I felt you cared a lot about me.'

'I did and do. So why bring it up now?'

'Because I've been torturing myself thinking about it, wondering where you were and if you were with him. The rapport between you was quite striking and other people noticed it too. More than just friends, which was strange with a young man who was your children's swimming instructor. Even your brother talked about it jokingly. Hearing that you had gone swimming today brought it surging back. I can't bear it, frankly.'

'I haven't seen him since your accident. I felt terribly guilty and hated, even despised myself.' She fell silent for a moment and then went on quietly, 'But then I found out about Marion, so I felt a bit better.' She looked across at him. 'She left a lot of loving messages on your mobile.'

His expression was one of utter bemusement and he eventually stammered, 'But it was lost in the crash.'

'No, it wasn't. I found it in your briefcase where Marion had apparently put it and, afterwards, I destroyed it.'

'I see.'

'I talked to her about it when she was here. We had it all out while you were talking to Arnie upstairs. She was concerned and distressed that I knew and asked me not to tell her husband. Of course I would never have dreamt of such a thing.'

'And you never said anything to me.'

'Like you, I found it difficult to talk about. Besides I had my secret too and thought that, as we were quits, I'd leave it alone. You see, I don't want our marriage to break up. We have lovely kids, a lovely home and a lot going for us. Besides,' her voice broke, 'I do love you, Ian. It was just a fling. It meant nothing.'

'Marion was just a fling too. Unimportant. Temptation in a far-off place away from you, a bit of excitement. Besides, she was terribly in love with Arnie, and . . . I adored you, Vanessa, and always have.'

Impulsively she turned to him and whispered in his ear, 'Then shall we leave it at that? Never to keep secrets from each other?'

'Never. Never to have any.'

Eventually they went to sleep in each other's arms, like babes in the wood.

Fourteen

July

Packing up, tidying up was a hard as well as, sometimes, a sad and thankless business. Her emotions this time were mixed. Sasha had now received permission for her sabbatical. It had made matters a lot simpler and quicker in that Michael Stokes had agreed to stay on and probably also take her watercolour class, so there was no need to advertise her job. She was not sad to leave Redbury, at least for a time — the prospect of a year in Italy was too exciting — but she felt more sentimental about her group, especially the ones she had grown close to, who gathered round her in the canteen for coffee after class. She knew she would probably keep in touch with Caroline, but doubted whether she would with the others.

She was going down to St Ives to break the news to her parents and spend time with them. She would probably have no difficulty letting her house to a student who would be glad of the studio — Trevor would look after all that — and then she would be off. Freedom beckoned.

But first there was the exhibition and she had put packing time aside while she made a final selection and preparations for that. The Institute had limited space, and not only was there artwork from her group, but also from the advanced watercolour class, the oil painting, acrylic, life, drawing, and portrait classes. They all had to be accommodated, so the choice was quite difficult and she had brooded long and hard over it.

Of all the submissions Martin's was clearly the best, and considering that he had attended so few classes, some of his work was outstanding, including the beach scenes he had recently done. He must have stayed long after they left, or returned to complete them. Martin had a natural talent and it would have been a lot of fun spending a year in Italy in his company. But that was a thought which she very quickly banished from her mind as she had made her choice earlier that day.

Two from Martin had to be included and next was Caroline,
so two of hers were in as well. All in all sixteen were represented
from her class and she returned home tired but well satisfied at
the display which she was sure would earn her, as well as her
students, plaudits from those who attended the exhibition.

Sasha got home mid-afternoon and had resumed her packing.
Many things had to be cleared away and stored. She spent a lot
of time tidying the studio, deciding what to take with her – she
was going by car – and what to leave at the college where Trevor
had promised to find storage space for them. Not an easy task;
some stuff she would have to take to her parents. There were still
a number of canvases belonging to Ben stacked away in a corner
and she had a moment of nostalgia, tinged at times with sadness,
as she looked through them remembering the past they had
shared, so much that was good as well as much that was bad, and
thinking that these would have to go to Trevor for safe keeping
too. She was nearing exhaustion when the doorbell rang and
she hurried downstairs thinking it might be Trevor to discuss the
letting of the house. So she flung the door open in welcome only
to find Ben standing on the threshold looking, with some justification, like a person unsure of his reception.

'Ben,' she gasped, staring at him as though she'd seen a ghost.
'Funny, I was thinking of you.'

Now it was Ben's turn to look surprised. 'Oh? May I come in?'

'Of course.'

She stepped aside and watched him as he entered, rather hesitantly, looking around as though to refamiliarize himself with the
place where he had lived for the best part of ten years, which
he had once called home.

Sasha closed the door and walked slowly after him. He looked
older, different, better dressed, not quite the man she remembered.
Perhaps being away from her had done him good.

'I was just about to make a cup of tea.' Her voice was meas-
ured, controlled. She found it hard to smile at him.

'That would be great.' He turned and looked at her rather
apologetically. 'Sorry to spring this on you, but I remembered
I had left some paintings here and I'm thinking of having an
exhibition.'

'Really? That's why I was thinking of you; not my normal

activity I assure you. You see I'm moving and having a clear out. I've been doing the studio and found some of your paintings stacked there.'

He followed her into the kitchen again, looking around, watching her as she filled the kettle and got out mugs and plates.

'Take a pew,' she said, indicating a chair, and he sat down awkwardly, clearly nervous.

'I wondered how you would receive me, Sasha. That's why I didn't let you know I was coming.'

'Oh, I suppose you thought I wouldn't let you in.' Sasha gave a brief, rather mirthless laugh and poured boiling water on the tea bags in the mugs. 'I'm not so childish, Ben.'

'Don't harbour any ill feelings?' he asked hopefully.

Sasha sat down and pushed a tin of biscuits towards him. 'Not after all this time. That doesn't mean that I didn't consider what you did despicable.'

'It was despicable,' Ben agreed, putting his cup to his lips and drinking deeply as though the hot brew would give him courage. 'It was cowardly and I was, and am, deeply ashamed of it.'

'Well that's good to know. I know we weren't hitting it off too well, but I thought after all the years we'd spent together we might at least have discussed it, or was it that frightening?'

'I was convinced you didn't love me any more. There was some-thing about you. I found it hard to talk to you. You'd become . . .' Ben paused. 'Formidable. I'd begun to feel inferior, that I'd made a mess of my life and you despised me. You did keep me. I was a kept man and I began to resent it because I had had so little commer-cial success. I felt I had to get away, but it didn't excuse the way I did it.'

He looked at her as though he was waiting for words of forgiveness, but they were not forthcoming as Sasha continued to look a him intently, studying the way his changes of expres-sion reflected his moods: rebellion, contrition, and did she also detect longing, a certain wistfulness? Sometimes the schoolboy, sometimes the grown man.

'How have you been, Sasha?' His expression again reflected anxiety, insecurity.

'Actually I've been alright. Very busy. You didn't destroy my life, if that's what's worrying you. You just made it, for a time, very difficult for me.' She looked at him defiantly, not wanting to tell him how much in retrospect she had blamed herself, because she didn't think he deserved it.

'I know. As I told you, I'm not proud of myself. But otherwise how are things?'

'Things are OK.'

'Have you found anyone else?'

'No. Have you?'

'No.' Ben looked as though he was going to say something and then changed his mind.

'Where are you moving to?'

'Italy.'

'Italy!' Ben gasped.

'Only for a year. I'm taking a sabbatical.'

'That sounds great.'

'Where are you having your exhibition?'

'London. I'm moving too, sharing a house and studio with Frank Watkins. I don't know if you remember him?'

'Vaguely.'

'He's doing very well and offered to share an exhibition with me. Some place in Clerkenwell.'

'So you've been with your parents all year?'

'Yes. But I've also been working hard, produced a lot of new stuff. It was Frank who suggested I exhibited with him. I think my work has changed, improved. I'm not quite sure I'd show the ones I left here.'

'Well, come and see.' Sasha got up from the table, put their mugs in the sink and led the way upstairs, past the bedroom they used to share and into the studio. She saw him looking around with an air of nostalgia as though it brought back happy memories, pause outside the bedroom door. His canvases were stacked in a corner much as he'd left them and, with Sasha looking on, he raised them one by one studying them. 'What do you think?'

'It depends how much progress you've made. I think these are quite good, but then I always did. I always thought highly of you as an artist, Ben, but not so much as a man after you walked out on me.'

Ben stared at his canvases. 'Is it OK if I pick these up later?

I'm staying with Trevor. He says there is an exhibition tomorrow at your Institute and I'd really like to go. Is that OK?'

'That's fine,' Sasha said, with an air of relief that there hadn't been any question of him staying overnight. Some tension went out of the air. They had got beyond that, and she felt that with a new understanding there might even be the possibility they would remain friends.

'Didn't Trevor mention I was going away?' Sasha asked as they walked down the stairs and to the door.

'He said you were busy. Didn't say why.' Ben stood at the door facing her. 'I am really glad I saw you, Sasha, and we had this talk.' He paused and searched her face as if looking for something, a spark maybe, a flicker of interest. He moved closer to her. 'Maybe we can begin again?'

'I don't quite know what you mean, Ben.'

'Well, if there is no one else . . .' He trailed off awkwardly.

'If you mean resume our former relationship then the answer is firmly no. But if you mean staying friends, then we can try. After all we have a lot in common and we both love art.' She flung the door wide open. 'See you tomorrow,' she said, on a note of finality.

Sasha watched him walk away thinking how strongly attracted to him she had once been, and realized it was no more. What a long time she'd wasted pining for him after his desertion. She was glad now that he had come back to lay this ghost. She waited until he was out of sight and then shut the door firmly after him, on their past.

In that dreary summer it was a rare day of spasmodic sunshine when Moira picked up Alice to take her to the exhibition.

'I've something very exciting to tell you,' she said, almost before Alice settled in her seat.

'Oh?'

'Vanessa may be pregnant. It's early, but she thinks she is.'

'Is she pleased?'

'Oh, I think very. She couldn't wait to tell me. She has only missed one period, but she is usually very regular. However it's a secret, you know, until she is sure.'

'Of course. That is perfectly lovely news. You must be pleased too.'

'I am absolutely delighted and Ian is thrilled.'

'Is that young man still around?' Alice said, after a pause and immediately regretted her question when she saw the disapproving look Moira gave her.

'You mean Tim? Oh no, he no longer works at the swimming pool. Besides all that finished a long time ago. Vanessa was so distressed about Ian. She spent weeks with him at the hospital sitting by his bedside, never leaving him. She said Tim was a folly, an aberration that she bitterly regretted. I feel relieved because now that Ian is so much better Vanessa has said she feels restless and has been talking rather ominously of starting work with the airline again. If she has a baby hopefully that will put an end to all that nonsense once and for all!'

'For a time,' Alice thought to herself, but said nothing, feeling she had offended Moira by so much as mentioning Tim. Instead she changed the subject.

'I'm quite nervous about seeing my work on display.'

'You've no need to worry. Sasha always singled you out as one of the best. I even wonder if she'll select any of mine.'

'Don't be so modest,' Alice chided her. 'You know you're very good. Still, I do dread next year and no Sasha.'

'We must move on,' Moira said, pulling up in the car park. 'And it will probably be very good for her. Think of that. Look, there are already a lot of people here.'

The exhibition rooms were in fact packed, but as a desultory sun continued to shine some people had drifted into the garden where a marquee had wisely been set up.

Both Moira and Alice were pleased to see even a limited display of their work. There were some sea scenes by Alice and a still-life and one of her garden by Moira.

'I'm glad you've got your holly tree in.' Alice turned to Moira. 'It meant a lot to me.'

'And me too.' Moira squeezed her hand.

Alice returned the pressure and arm in arm they continued their tour of the exhibition, which showed what a variety of talent there was in the adult education classes. At first Sasha was nowhere to be seen and then she came in sight with a man on either side. She stopped when she saw Alice and Moira.

'Pleased with the exhibition?'

'Oh very,' Moira said. 'Altogether most impressive. We haven't seen it all.'

'This is my boss, Trevor Judge.' Sasha introduced the older man. 'He is head of the department at the college.'

Alice and Moira shook hands.

'And this is Ben Shipley. He is an artist who I was at college with.'

They shook hands with Ben, noting the rather sharp look he gave Sasha.

'Ben is a very gifted artist,' Sasha added. 'He is about to have an exhibition in London.' Something or someone behind Moira caught her attention and her expression changed.

'Hello Martin,' she said.

'Hi,' Martin replied, nodding at Moira and Alice who, after returning his greeting, moved away to inspect the rest of the exhibits.

'This is my boss, Trevor.'

The men shook hands.

'And this is Ben.'

'Oh, *Ben*.' Martin said his name with such strong emphasis, while looking at him with such obvious interest, that Ben returned his stare.

'Does my name mean something to you?'

'In a way, but I won't detain you.' Martin smiled at Sasha, murmured something non-committal and continued his inspection, leaving an awkward silence behind him.

'Who *is* that guy?' Ben asked, turning to Sasha.

'One of my students.'

'I didn't like the way he said my name.'

'I'm sorry about that.'

'He obviously knew who I was.'

Sasha remained silent and looked rather helplessly at Trevor who stood by observing the scene.

'Is he your boyfriend?' Ben continued, aggressively.

'No. Anyway it's no business of yours if he was.'

'You said you didn't have one . . .' Ben began, but Trevor put a hand firmly on his arm.

'Look, Ben, don't get excited. As Sasha says—'

'I don't care what Sasha says,' Ben interrupted him, roughly pushing his arm off and walking away.

'Oh my God.' Sasha looked after him. 'Surely he isn't going to cause any trouble?'

Trevor smiled at her. 'I told you that you had an effect on the men. Forget it.'

She looked up to see Roger and Pauline facing her, hand in hand.

'Oh good, you came!' she cried with pleasure. 'This is . . .' She turned to introduce Trevor, but he had moved off to talk to someone he knew.

'We just wanted to thank you again for being so patient and wanted to ask you to the wedding reception,' Pauline said.

'But that's wonderful. So soon? When is it?'

'Well we're not sure. Quite soon. We're having a register office wedding, just family, and then a reception for friends.'

'It's unlikely I'll be here. I leave for Italy in a few weeks. I'm driving down and taking my time. Firstly I'm going to my parents' next week for an extended stay, so I don't think it will be possible; but thanks for thinking of me.' She glanced down at Pauline's hand.

'My goodness,' she said. 'What a huge and very lovely ring. You are a lucky girl.'

Pauline rather shyly held up for inspection a large diamond the size of which obviously impressed Sasha as much as it had surprised Pauline when Roger insisted she have it. Apart from anything else, he assured her that in a time of recession it would be a good investment.

Now Caroline had emerged from the crowd and was looking at it too.

'A very lucky girl,' she said, glancing at the tall man by her side. 'I didn't even get one.'

'You got me, wasn't that enough?' Greg extended his hand. 'Sasha, it's very good to meet you. I've heard a lot about you.'

'And I've heard a lot about you.' Sasha paused to wave at Roger and Pauline who were melting away into the crowd. 'Caroline is very proud of you.'

'I want to thank you for helping her so much. She told me all about it.'

'That's what friends are for – and we *are* friends. Caroline is also a very good friend to me.'

'She will miss you when you go to Italy.'

'Don't worry. I'll be back. It's not forever.'

Caroline lowered her voice. 'I saw Martin was here.'

'Yes and Ben too; they had a bit of an encounter.' Sasha felt a nudge. 'Oh look, Moira wants to talk to me. I'll tell you all about it later.'

'Come and have a drink with us before you leave.'

'That will be great.' Sasha kissed Caroline on the cheek, whispering in her ear, 'You didn't tell me he was so good looking.'

'You just keep your hands off him,' Caroline joked, 'and find someone nice and more deserving of you in Italy.'

Beside Moira stood a stunningly good-looking woman, by her side a man leaning on a stick and a small boy and girl looking shy and rather lost.

'Sasha, I wanted to introduce you to my daughter, Vanessa, her husband, Ian, and children, Freddie and Helena.'

'We've come to look at Mum's paintings,' Vanessa said as they all shook hands, 'and to meet you and thank you. She says you've made a great difference to her life. She was lost after Dad's death.'

'That's an exaggeration,' Sasha said modestly. 'She is naturally very good. She could have done quite well without me. But I'm very pleased to meet you. We were very shocked to hear about your husband's accident.' She turned to Ian. 'I'm glad to see you have apparently recovered so well.'

'Thanks to my marvellous wife.' Ian took Vanessa's hand. 'I don't know where I'd be without her.'

Moira stood by beaming approvingly.

'We must be getting back. Ian gets very tired and the children are a bit restless.'

'Lovely kids,' Sasha said, as they began to move away. 'You must be very proud of your beautiful family.'

'I am.' Moira looked at her searchingly. 'And, Sasha, I do hope you will be happy too and have a wonderful time in Italy. You deserve it. Thanks again.'

'I will – and look after Alice, won't you?' She glanced past her at Alice who remained in the background.

'We will. Of course we will. We all love her. She is almost part of our family.'

Sasha began to feel quite emotional about this profusion of goodwill emanating from all sorts of people, even the relations of her students. When it came to the point goodbyes were always hard. She gazed after Moira's family thinking what an attractive couple they looked: happy, handsome, with lovely kids, rather enviable, as if emphasizing her own sterile, barren, and altogether unsatisfactory personal life.

She sighed and began to wander through the exhibition greeting people she knew, pausing to chat, looking at the different exhibits, proud that her group compared favourably with the rest, if a little regretful that Martin was so much better than anyone else. After her encounter with Moira's glamorous family she was aware of a sense of restlessness mixed with nostalgia, sadness, almost a feeling of panic that she might have done the wrong thing. After all was she was running away, but towards what? Was she expecting too much from Italy?

She paused by the window to look out at the garden to see if it had started to rain, but no, the sun still shone and people were emerging from the marquee, cups and plates in their hands, to find a seat at one of the tables scattered around.

Suddenly she stiffened and it was with a sense of incredulity that she made out the figures of two men engaged in what looked like a heated argument by the side of the marquee, confronting each other face to face as if they were on the verge of coming to blows: Martin and Ben. With a muttered exclamation she hurried down the stairs and out into the garden, standing in front of them just as Ben made a grab for Martin's arm.

'What the hell do you think you are doing?' she hissed, seizing Ben's arm, arresting it in mid air. 'Do you realize that everyone is beginning to look at you? You are making complete fools of yourselves, and me, incidentally.'

Both stared at her, moving back from each other. It was Ben who seemed the most out of control and, his face contorted with anger, glared at her.

'He said you did have an affair with him. You were lying to me.'

'I said I didn't think it was any of your business and I still don't,' she retorted. 'And I think you're making a perfect ass of yourself. You too,' she said to Martin. 'How did all this start anyway?'

'Don't look at me,' Martin said, with an air of injured dignity. 'I was just trying to have a peaceful cup of tea when this bloke comes up to me and starts shouting, asking questions. Well, I had to tell him the truth, didn't I?' He gave her a sly look and for a moment she thought Ben was going to lunge at him again when, to Sasha's relief, Trevor appeared by her side.

'What's going on?' he demanded.

'Look, I've had enough of this comedy.' Martin took advantage of the interruption and walked disdainfully away, leaving his cup on one of the tables and making his way towards the car park.

'These idiots were arguing over me, apparently.' Sasha was watching Martin disappear with confused emotions. He had deliberately tried to deceive and humiliate Ben. After all theirs had hardly been an affair.

Ben was still clearly out of control, breathing hard, face distorted. 'He, this jerk, told me that he and Sasha were having an affair after she'd told me they weren't.'

'I said it was no business of his,' Sasha corrected him, trying to recover her composure, 'and it isn't.'

'After all,' Trevor told him, 'you walked out on Sasha.'

'And bitterly regretted it.' Ben now looked almost on the verge of tears. 'Regretted it ever since. I made a mistake.'

Sasha began to feel that the situation was too much for her. 'Go away,' she said flapping her hands despairingly at Ben. 'I can't have people making fools of themselves, and me, in a place where I'm a teacher. It is deeply upsetting and I'm ashamed of you, Ben.'

'And *him*,' Ben shouted, looking in Martin's direction as though he would like to run after him. 'Be ashamed of *him*, the arsehole . . .' Trevor put a restraining hand on his arm. 'Come on, boy. That's quite enough for today.'

Sasha found she was still shaking as she watched them go towards the car park, hoping that by this time Martin had gone, aware of faces turned towards her, people gawping at her with interest.

'Everything alright?' Caroline asked, solicitously appearing as if by magic at Sasha's side.

'Well yes, now it is. Did you see them?'

'I did and I thought they were going to come to blows.' She looked at her husband. 'Greg was all prepared to do the heroic thing and intervene.'

Greg seemed to find the whole business amusing and had a smile on his face.

'Quite something to have two blokes fighting over you,' he said. 'You should be proud.'

'Well I'm not. I feel angry and humiliated.'

'Everyone is looking for you to say goodbye,' Caroline said, nudging her husband. 'They're all standing in the hall.'

'Oh dear, I hope they didn't see all that. I feel I'd just like to slink away.'

Caroline took her by the arm. 'You're shaking.'

'It was ghastly. I find the whole thing unforgivable. Thank heaven Trevor came up to get rid of Ben. I hope I never set eyes on either of them again.'

By the time she got to the hall Sasha had calmed down a little and it was true that almost the whole class had assembled. She went round, shaking hands, exchanging embraces, listening to their praise, thanks and regrets. Alice clung to her as though she couldn't bear to let her go.

'I'll write,' she promised. 'I'll be back and I shall expect to see some very good work when I do. We'll have a wonderful reunion.'

Eventually, still trailed by a small group of well wishers, she got into her car and drove slowly away. As she reached the gate she glanced back and saw that the disconsolate little group were still watching her.

At that moment her rage evaporated and gratitude took its place, gratitude and a sense of awe tinged with sadness as it came home to her just how much they would miss her, and how she would miss them, her faithful little band of students in the water-colour class.

H